MW00974958

CHARLESTON DAWN

JOHN DILLARD

PublishAmerica
Baltimore

ISBN: 1-4137-9992-2
PUBLISHED BY PUBLISHAMERICA, LLLP
www.publishamerica.com
Baltimore

Printed in the United States of America

Dedication

This book is dedicated to three people in my life, the first and foremost being to my wife and helpmate, Tami. You are indeed a gift from God. For over nine years I braved through divorce and then dating to find that God was busy readying you to love me just as God made me. Little did I realize at the time that God was readying me to see the beauty that you bestow to my life each and every day. Since the day that we met, I knew that God was up to something special. You continually move me ever so much with your heart, your compassion, and most of all your support when I have deserved it the least. You have always been there to pick me up and dust me off and to help me regain my way. I know God allows me to accomplish for the kingdom so much more together with you than I ever could have on my own. Indeed, not all of the times we have shared have been easy, and many have been doubly hard, but each time we have endured and grown close to God and to each other.

Tami, my bride, I am so deeply blessed to have someone who loves so much while expecting so little in return. I am thankful that you can read my writing most of the time and I thank you for the tireless hours that you spent typing and editing this publication during all the endless writes and rewrites. Your enthusiasm for life is amazing. You are constantly inclined towards me and despite me sharing all of my deepest fears and seen my worst faults, you continue to hold me up in prayer. I believe that our Bible is the very living word of God. I have searched His words and believe that I have in you one of the great marriages of the ages. Tami, you inspire me, I both adore and love you deeply. I am so deeply honored to be your husband and yes, I would do it all over again!

Madison, my eldest and now a teenager, when God created the idea and form of you, He gave to you a spirit of love and peace that

I know can only come from Him. I have watched you from birth and have watched you as you have traveled through life to date. Though you are yet so young as the world sees, you are yet so wise as you place God right in the center of that incredible gifted heart that you have. You are one of the elite few I have ever known who have the ability to make everyone that they see feel better about themselves and their life. You light up a room with your presence and your grace and wit. Always remember those words, "Dillards never give up," and constantly go back to our God Most High to gain His insight and wisdom. I am not sure why I was afforded the gift of a child as unique as you but I thank God daily for the joy and laughter that you have brought me. I continually pray that God will use you and your life to do great things in His name.

Andrew, now ten and already having been on a mission trip, God placed in you a heart and a willingness to hear. Just as God said in the New Testament, "He who has ears, let him hear," so you too have opened your heart and your mind to things never seen or shared before. You possess an innate ability to do great things in God's name. I watched you closely on our mission trip as you opened up your heart to God, to fellow servers on the trip, and to the people of Jamaica. I pray that you seek God in all that you do and know that He will honor your effort and greatly bless your life. In you I see a chance to hand down a heritage of the Godly men and women that are our ancestors. Be purposeful and intentional in all that you do always seeking His will for your life. Excel in everything, do everything, no matter how low or how high it might be, as if you are doing it for God Himself. I revel in the exhilaration of our talks and how you danced as I exhorted you to press on and to live all of your life, as God would have you to do.

I want to thank my many close friends and family, my mother and my father, who always lifted me up, David and Harriet Dillard, Donna and Gary Brooks, David Farmer, Hans Schuon, and all of my incredible nieces and nephews who brought me such great joy as we traverse through this life. I greatly thank my ancestors, most specifically Grace Dillard, my grandmother, who passed just three years ago at the age of one hundred and five, and to Grandpa John, who moved into heaven now twenty years ago. I plan to spend the first 10,000 years in your presence so, Madison, you will know where to find me. You each brought me closer to Christ through your lives, words, and your example. Though life has had many surprises I have learned that all we have here on earth are our fellow members of the body of Christ to help us along. Each and every one of you are so deeply loved and cherished. There is no way that I could ever adequately acknowledge enough what you each have meant to me. I deeply love you all so very much.

Most of all I pray that only God and His will were honored in the writing of this book and that to Him all the glory is due. I pray that I used only His words and that I brought edification to the perfect love that He has for you forever and ever. Amen.

Chapter 1

IT WAS A SULTRY humid day, the kind of day that makes it difficult to breathe, fearing to be out in the heat. The kind of day that oppresses your desire to be active, yet Joseph knew he had a job to do. Joseph King had moved to Charleston, South Carolina, several years ago hoping the coastal town with its grand vistas, expansive waterways and marsh areas, would give him a fresh start and a new lease on life. He loved the carriages and the cobblestone roads that captured the history of the city and served to enhance the exquisitely elegant homes that adorned the area. He loved the cuisine specific to that area, such as shrimp and grits. He loved gathering with friends for late afternoon shrimp boils that ran late into the evening. These wonderful gatherings were usually hosted by one friend or another and took place on one of the beautiful porches that overlooked the glorious homes and swirled iron gates that decorated the city. He had hoped for the freshness of a new beginning, one that would invigorate his soul and refresh his spirit. He longed to live the way he had been brought up, fresh and alive amidst the Word of God.

Joseph's wife, Debbie, had deceased ten years prior and left him alone with their daughter, Sara, who was now twelve. Debbie had fought valiantly but in the end, she had not been able to overcome the relentless and aggressive cancer that had spread throughout her lungs. It had started as a routine physical because she was experiencing some shortness of breath. The doctor had nearly missed diagnosing the disease, and only through a routine blood test had the illness been detected. At first, the doctors had hoped that the disease might be operable and the cancer removed, leaving the chemotherapy to clean up the rest and to ensure her continued improvement. However, during a routine procedure, they discovered the cancer cells had infiltrated her left lung. Because of their concern, they felt it necessary to remove the lung during the surgery to hopefully rid her body of the blight that had inflicted it. Initially the doctors had believed their results to prove successful, but upon follow-up two weeks later, they learned the operation had not stopped the disease and that it had continued to grow and spread to other parts of her body and her right lung as well. Upon hearing this prognosis, Joseph was devastated and dismayed. He wondered how this could have happened. He thought that this was something that only happened to other people. The doctors gave Debbie only a few months to live, five at the most. Joseph stayed by her bedside throughout the whole ordeal and was there as she took her last breath. It was hard on Joseph as he watched her slowly pass before his eyes. Although he knew God was in control and that He would work everything for good, Joseph wondered aloud how this could be good for anyone, but especially for his daughter Sara.

Joseph had originally met Debbie while he was an up and comer in the Navy. He had been stationed in the Chesapeake Bay Area of Virginia. They had originally met at a cadet's party through some mutual friends. They immediately began dating and then courted for a little over a year until they married and bought a home. They bought a very modest two-level, four-bedroom home. Debbie spent hours setting it up and decorating it to perfection. Within a few months of their marriage, Debbie and Joseph conceived a child. They were not planning on children at the time, but life does have its little surprises. Preferring to wait, they decided not to learn the baby's gender until the actual birth. Sara was quite a surprise indeed. Joseph remembered vividly Sara's entrance into the world. He first counted slowly her fingers and toes, marveling at each and every one. The second Joseph first laid eyes on Sara, he felt God's hand gently holding his, guiding his thoughts and actions. He thought of the miracle of the parting of the Red Sea as the Israelites fled Egypt and he remembered thinking that the mere moving of water in the Red Sea was dramatically short of the miracle he had just seen with the birth of his new daughter.

Sara, in that single moment, had transformed Joseph and made him reflect on the joy that he had been blessed with. Immediately, all the things Joseph had felt were priorities in his life did not seem quite so important. Joseph focused on making sure Sara was safe, properly cared for and brought up in the admonition and the love of the Lord. Sara was born just seven months before the doctors had discovered Debbie's cancer. Joseph remembered thinking about what would be next and how would he raise a child alone and on his own. He knew that he would never forsake her but he knew that he could never provide the nurturing that a woman could. Sara was just eleven months old when her mother passed. Although the doctors had hoped Debbie might live five months, she barely made it past four. The cancer rapidly spread and completed its deadly work.

When Joseph and Sara moved to the Charleston area, they opted to live in Mt. Pleasant, just three miles north of Charleston over the Cooper River. The home site was a little over an acre and was adrift in tall hundred-year-old oaks, from which moss hung heavy adorning their limbs. The trees grew closely to the house, almost as in a picture frame, and sat so majestically on the property that it looked as if the ground had ordered it there and the beautiful limbs were embracing it. Joseph and Sara had a good life and were content, but Joseph always knew and felt that something was missing. He had a good job, believed in God, but knew that God was calling him deeper and to live closer to Him.

Joseph, as a fifteen-year Navy officer, had studied and focused his military career on learning the ins and outs of captaining the big cargo ships. He loved the responsibility of guiding the ships along their sea routes and leading and teaching the crews as they fulfilled their duties. During his Navy career, Joseph worked his way up the chain of command to the rank of captain, responsible for an 85,000-ton frigate whose task it was to be ready within twenty-four hours for departure to ferry equipment, men and supplies wherever they were needed throughout the world. Because of the world's continuing changes and crises he was often placed in the thick of things. During wars and policing actions his unit was in high demand. That demand placed him and his unit in harm's way when conflicts occurred.

Joseph's first exposure to military conflict occurred during the first Gulf War when his ship was ordered to anchor itself just off the shores of Saudi Arabia to deliver men and supplies. The U.S. armed forces had been called in to drive the Iraqi insurgents out of Kuwait

9

and back across the border and into their own country. He remembers the first night they arrived, watching as the Tomahawk cruise missiles left from other ships in his convoy screeching at Mach 1 plus speeds to their ultimate targets deep in the heart of Iraq. He could not help wondering what the specific target of each missile would be and if they would reach their intended target. The trail of white smoke as it left the flame of the back of the missile fascinated him as it sped with incredible speed and accuracy towards its specific target. Cruise missiles were relatively new tools in the Navy's arsenal, and their accuracy was unparalleled as they sped along at treetop level and very seldom went astray from the path that had been pre-programmed.

Although Joseph was far from the hand-to-hand fighting, the memories and the long nights during the bombing crusades and the 100-hour ground war had left him puzzling and wondering. He wondered about where God was during a war and why wars like this and others had to occur. There always seemed to be so much pain and death in any armed conflict that Joseph had problems seeing through to God's purpose in such an event. Joseph was thankful that the superiority of the U.S. forces resulted in an overwhelming victory, but he knew thousands had lost their lives and were critically wounded in the conflict.

During this time of his life, Joseph had always accepted God's presence and authority and had even accepted Christ but he had yet to turn the whole of his life truly over to the one true living God. Joseph often felt God's presence and His nudging but Joseph resisted God's call. Joseph believed God's word in that God said that He would always take care of him and his needs but something always held him back from truly letting go. Perhaps it was some inward fear that God truly did not know what was best for Joseph. It was almost as if Joseph thought that God would miss it and not do what he wanted in his life for himself. Joseph knew this was naive and that his thinking was senseless but he just had a hard time turning it all over to Him. Joseph knew that He was the Alpha and the Omega and also the Great I AM, but somehow, when it came to his own life, he just had trouble letting go. Joseph read the Bible and knew of man's struggle to turn it all over and how each time that man did so, God met them in a powerful and meaningful way but yet he held tightly to the reins that controlled his life.

Joseph was raised in a small rural town of thirty thousand people deep in Alabama. His mom and dad, as most parents of their time, worked hard to eke out a living in the rural southernmost parts of Alabama. His father chose civil service as a career and worked for the post office for forty-five years until his retirement. It was not a great job, as he had little, if any, upward mobility, but it always provided an adequate income for him and his family. Joseph's father had died just three years after his retirement but had left the meager and older family residence almost totally debt free. Joseph's mother worked as a full-time clerk at the local grocery so that they would have enough money to make ends meet and sometimes to get something a little extra. Growing up, Joseph dreamed of what life would be like on the outside of his hometown, and when he had the opportunity to join the Naval Academy on his eighteenth birthday, he jumped at the chance. His parents were not thrilled about him leaving home so early, but they believed it would be a positive learning and growth experience, as well as to provide a skill and hopefully help him in starting a meaningful career.

Life at the academy suited Joseph well as its structure and rules gave him specific guidelines to follow. Joseph did well in the academy and he prided himself on his ability to easily outdistance his classmates both physically and academically. Superior results did not come easy for Joseph, though, and he had to really push himself to excel. But in doing so, he found that the self-satisfaction of his efforts and his achievements, awards and special acknowledgments, gave him great confidence. It was during this time that Joseph drifted from being close to God and pursued a more worldly life than he would have cared to admit.

Often during tours of duty, Joseph would venture into the local port town seeking an evening out with the boys. This most often seemed to include some late night drinking and partying with the local girls. He never really did anything wrong but he knew that he often drank a little more than he cared to admit. Although Joseph thought he really enjoyed this life, he often felt lonely during those times and often prayed and asked God to bring him home and closer to Him, just as he had done for the prodigal son. Joseph knew the prodigal son was eagerly accepted back by his father, and his return was instantly and deeply celebrated, but he knew that he wanted to be drawn back closer to God and a life that was closer to and more like Him.

Joseph met his wife, Debbie, just three months after the first Gulf War's end. Throughout his marriage he thought he loved her enough but something always seemed not to be complete. Although they talked often and at length, they were never able to really open up and be truly vulnerable to each other, so that they might help each other along life's way. Almost every time they were about to make a big breakthrough in drawing really close, something would happen to set them back even further. Over time, this lack of communication caused them many stumbling blocks and hard months and years in their relationship and caused them to seek counseling on several different occasions. Although these sessions helped them survive the crisis for the immediate time, the counseling was never penetrating enough to change their patterns, and the sessions and the growth were too inconsistent to really deepen their relationship, bond and marriage. This left both of them often feeling deflated and feeling they did not have enough energy to go another step forward. They often found themselves retreating to opposite ends of the house to spend their evenings alone doing their own thing. Debbie would often sit up for hours listening to song after song, almost as if she was rehearsing to be as melancholy as possible for a new day. Joseph often tried to reach out to her during these times, but with his own focus being inwards rather than towards her, he did not have the skills or the ability to reach out to touch her where she most needed it, in her heart.

Joseph prayed during this time to be a better husband and to be a better man for Debbie, but everything that he tried to do failed. At one point, he even took her on an elaborate vacation and everything seemed to improve for a few weeks, especially while on the trip, but invariably things would eventually return to the poor standard where they had always been. Each of them, over the years, grew more and more resentful of this pattern but neither of them seemed willing enough or even able to break it. Although Joseph felt he would be willing to give his own life for Debbie, he found that he was both unwilling and unable to live daily for her. He knew the biblical standard of loving his wife was to love her as Christ loved the church, but he was just not able to sacrifice daily, his needs, for her like he should have been able to. Joseph was a good provider and a faithful husband but as a couple, they were never able to reach the oneness that they both so greatly wanted and desired. Though this was directly opposed to how he wanted to feel, Joseph found that he could not help feeling that way.

Joseph still felt guilt about his part of having such a poor marriage to Debbie and that he was never able to make things right before her passing. This feeling of failure had haunted Joseph over the last ten years and he constantly prayed to God to lift the burden from him that he felt. In reality, God had freed him of this years ago, but Joseph remained trapped within his own fears and his own inability to forgive himself. He was afraid to feel and in his fear, was always waiting for something to go wrong, almost a self-fulfilling and defeating philosophy. Joseph knew he had to daily start over and pick up his yoke and his cross, but his fears kept him from moving on. In essence, he had created a self-actualized prophecy of failure.

About eight years after Debbie's passing, Joseph began praying a new prayer he had never had before. He prayed that God would bring a woman into his life that was dramatically different than the people he had known and dated before. Joseph was finally willing to look outside the "mold" that he had always looked for in a mate and to be open to God's leading. In the past, Joseph had always looked at the outside first and then the inside, but now he determined and set out to see who she actually was in Christ first. With his new leanings and the insight that God had given him, he began to see all women differently and he finally saw them the way God did, as a loving creation of the Master himself. Joseph remembered that when God chose David as King, God picked him because of who he was inside and not based on his outward appearance. Joseph wanted a woman who always viewed life from a positive perspective and focused on how to make things better rather than all the negative women he had known in his past. Past women in his life just refused to see God in all things and to constantly look to and strive for the best that God had to offer. Accordingly, Joseph was always struggling to keep things on an even keel for even ordinary day-to-day activities. Thus, when big things occurred in their lives, often he had no emotional energy at all to share to overcome any of these obstacles. Joseph believed that the right woman was out there, and he was determined to set out to wait on God to bring her to him.

———

Joseph's daughter, Sara, was a very precious and loving child. Joseph's wife, Debbie, had died when Sara was only a few months old, Joseph had raised her these past twelve years as best he could, bringing her up in the spirit and admonition of the Word. Joseph was often amazed at the simplicity Sara saw the world from, free of predispositions and suppositions about anything other than what just is. Her joyous heart often radiated and warmed a room with her infectious joy and laughter. Joseph often thought that this is the way God and he both wanted him to live. He prayed that one day he might have the peace to do so and unbind the chains that held him.

Sara remembered very little of her mother, as she had died when she was so young. Most of the memories she had were really created from having had picture books to look at over the years. For a while, Joseph had even left pictures of Debbie throughout the house, but one evening about a year after her passing, he felt it was time to let go of the past and to start moving forward, so he took down all the pictures except for the one in Sara's room, and from then on focused on a new beginning. Somehow, although he wanted to go on, he felt an emptiness and a longing that never seemed to be quenched. Joseph could not quench it because more often than not, he had focused on putting his faith on worldly things and not the living water of Jesus Christ. He prayed intently for the Lord to help him feel His presence but yet the longing and loneliness persisted. During many sleepless nights, Joseph cried out to Jesus to give him peace and a true and centered direction for his life, but yet, no answer came. He often wondered if the answer was always right there in front of him but he was just unable to grasp it.

It was summer now and Sara would soon be entering seventh grade. She had a very good year in sixth grade academically, as well as beginning to grow into a fine young lady. She had always been an above-average student and like most kids her age, talked too much and occasionally missed homework assignments. As a single parent,

Joseph did his best, which was much better than most, but he knew there was always something missing, something that he could not give. He was not able to reach his daughter's inner being the way he knew only a woman with a heart of God could.

Sara liked to try new things and constantly experimented with activities ranging from karate to softball to cheerleading. Her lack of fear and her zeal made her more than adept at anything she tried. Joseph, due to his demanding work schedule, often had to be away at work so he was forced to hire Yana, a nanny, to help tutor and care for Sara and to be there when she arrived home from school. Sara liked Yana and the two of them seemed to get along and do well together. Yana was an exchange student from Romania and was to start her senior year of college. She had been with Joseph and Sara for over a year now and soon she would be going home to finish school. Yana had come over in order to earn enough money to finish school.

Although Joseph had found Yana to be more than an adequate caretaker for Sara, he was leery of what success he might have in locating another. It was too hard to find both the time and energy to locate the right person to care for his daughter. As Sara would soon be entering her teens, Joseph knew it was a critical time in her life and development. Joseph was a good father and took his daughter to church almost every Sunday. Sara loved to hear the Bible stories at church and through nightly reading of Bible stories, had gained a good grasp of the Bible's characters and stories. Often, Sara would ask Joseph to read just one more story before bed and he always acquiesced. He was happy that she had a thirst for knowledge and yearned to know more.

Sara had started middle school last year and quickly learned that the barbs and impoliteness of the middle school children were much harsher than that of elementary school. Sara was hoping her second year of middle school would be easier and her summer would be one of fun and relaxation. Joseph and Sara had planned to go out west and explore the vastness of what America had to offer. Sara, like most children, longed for lots of playtime with Dad as well as her friends. Her favorite things included the trips they had taken together and the endless hours they would spend just being together. It was often difficult for Sara when Dad dated; she wondered who would be the new woman in Dad's life and often her taste disagreed with that of Joseph.

When Joseph looked at Sara, he knew that only God can truly and perfectly lead, guide and direct a child, but he knew that in order to do it right, he could not do it alone. One of Sara's favorite things to do was to sit and swing under the canopy of oak trees and moss that draped the lawn. They talked incessantly while marveling at all that God had done while knowing there was yet more to learn, more to discover, and more to do.

Sara had gotten very involved with the local YMCA and enjoyed the friends and activities to do there. She would often go for hours and enjoy spending many of her after-school hours there. Joseph, being a past Navy man, liked being and living near the water. He had purchased a twenty-six-foot fishing and powerboat, and when seas were calm, they would venture out more than ten miles from shore. Joseph enjoyed the pleasure of being alone with Sara at sea and he looked forward to the time he was able to spend maintaining his boat and carefully tracking his instruments and navigation system as he cruised out and into the open seas. He often marveled how the seafarers of old accurately navigated thousands of miles across the sea with only a sextant and the stars to guide them. Now with only a handheld GPS (Global Positioning System) he could determine his specific whereabouts in nanoseconds and within just a few feet.

Sara lived each day as it came, every moment as it occurred and was totally present each and every moment of her life. Unlike her father, who might dwell on past concerns, Sara, as only a child can, looked at each moment as it occurred rather than getting stuck thinking about what it all meant; who said it and why, and its context. Children lived in the moment just as we were all made to live and to be free to only focus on events and things in life as they occurred. Sara had a good life with her father, but deep inside her there was a feeling that even she could not describe. Like other girls her age, she was seeking to determine her own identity and place in the world. As one would imagine, this caused her to struggle between being the little child she had previously been and the woman God yet wanted her to be. Joseph tried to be both a father and mother to Sara, but he was never able to fulfill the void left by the absence of a godly wife and mother, try though he might.

Mary McCarey was most always a positive and driven woman. She was in her mid-thirties and had been born in Charleston proper and she had lived there all her life. Her family owned an historical home that had been in the family for three generations, and it was located just a few blocks from the Battery, which was an elevated walkway across from an array of beautifully grand homes that adorned the roadway facing out towards the Atlantic Ocean. The homes were just in the middle of where the Ashley, Cooper and Wando rivers met and formed the harbor of Charleston. Mary loved her childhood and the long walks she used to take with her dad at dusk after dinner and the long talks they would have on the rocking chairs on the side porch. These memories often filled her heart with joy as they permeated her inner being.

Mary's mother was involved in the Charleston Historical and Preservation Society and through this she developed a fondness for real estate and its restoration and had decided upon leaving college to become a residential real estate agent. She liked her job and enjoyed the satisfaction that she got from helping people find the home that they wanted and one that fit their lifestyle and their particular family's needs. Mary was always one of the top agents at the agency and she was well liked and respected by her peers.

Mary had been divorced now for several years. She lived in a small cottage home with her son, who was now nine. Her home was well decorated and exemplified the touches of her southern heritage. Her well-placed furniture and adornments made her home seem almost surreal. The home beckoned you in, invited you to stay and enjoy the ambiance that it provided. Guests would often stay and visit for hours as Mary served them tea and finger cakes, as had been done in the South for over a century. She loved her life and the simplicity of it all. Mary loved Charleston most for its heritage and the deep history that the city had.

Since the early days of America's colonization, to the beginnings of the Civil War, South Carolina had been a leader in the South and in the whole of the United States in both commerce and politics. Also, South Carolina had been the first state to secede from the Union and the first shots of the war were fired at the Union-held Fort Sumter as the southern troops tried to free the harbor of their presence and the blockade of its port. Mary often got goose bumps as she strolled along the Battery thinking of the courage and strife that had occurred there as people fought for what they believed in and were willing to die for. She often wondered if the purpose of the Civil War was to bring about a spiritual revolution to our country. She marveled that the generals on both sides of the war prayed to God to give them victory and believed that God was on their side. She marveled that perhaps all the earlier teaching of the war's cause might have been in error and that it was not about slavery and states' rights after all and that it was about God wanting to bring a country closer to Him. She marveled about the ways of God and about the mysteries of His actions and ways. Mary believed that His plan was foolproof and that His ways could not be thwarted, but yet she wanted to understand her Master more and to see His guiding hand in her life in a way that she could readily understand.

Mary's real estate business allowed her the flexibility to work around her son's school and summer schedule. A lot of her clientele were from out of state looking to either buy a second home or a place to ultimately retire in the charm and history of Charleston. She welcomed meeting the various people she encountered and felt that the diversity these newcomers brought to the area, to be a positive. Most of her clientele were upper middle class and well educated. Mary had learned to get to know her clientele well and intuitively to visualize the home that a particular family might desire. In doing so, she had proven to be very adept at satisfying her clients' needs and wishes and was widely recognized as one of the best the city of Charleston had to offer.

Mary's son, David, was very well liked and exemplified, at a very early age, the southern way that he grew up, lived and abided in. David had been taught to always appreciate and acknowledge even the simplest of gifts and favors he received. David would often spend hours fishing along the Battery when he would stay at his grandparents' home either for the evening or overnight. Grandpa Billy would spend hours with David explaining the ways of God and the way in which a man should go and how he should live. The countless time they spent together fishing built a bond between them that would never be broken. David deeply admired his grandpa and often would spend time at their home, especially if Mary had to work or had a social engagement. Often, clients would come in from out of town and Mary would spend the weekend showing them the city and helping them find that perfect home.

Due to her love of the city and its history, Mary involved herself in the Charleston Historical and Preservation Society, which prided itself on protecting Charleston's rich history and heritage. Often in the name of progress, one of the older homes would be threatened and the committee would have to quickly meet and discuss its next step. Frequently these meetings would result in deciding to have a fund-raiser to heighten awareness of the project and to raise funds for its execution. The local paper, *The Charleston Sentinel*, provided favorable articles for these events and as such, they were accordingly well attended.

One of the homes that had come to the attention of the Charleston Historical and Preservation Society was that of the local Presbyterian minister, Thomas Adams, who had printed the first paper ever produced in the area. He had died in 1828 and although the home had remained in the family since, it had suffered neglect the last several decades and now its once-proud heritage was being threatened. Its clapboards and cracking plaster showed the effects of the beating sun and driving rain. Little by little, the structure had fallen into such disarray that there were leaks that threatened the whole of the structure. Mary was particularly excited about saving this home even though she was not entirely sure why. Mary was passionate about preserving the architecture of the city of Charleston and its history, though, and the society gave her the perfect opportunity to give back to the city that had given so much to her.

On the day of the fund-raiser, Mary readied herself as she began the day. Laying out the evening gown she planned to wear to the event, she smiled whimsically to herself. She had just purchased the dress and loved the way it belied her figure and the way the spaghetti straps fell across her shoulders. She hoped that she enjoyed wearing it that evening as much as she did buying it from one of the specialty boutiques earlier in the week. She and David would spend the day at her parents' with David and Grandpa Billy enjoying several hours of fishing while she spent several hours catching up with her mother, Mary Sue Loudermilk. Grandpa Billy and David did not catch many fish that day, but neither one of them seemed to care. David would wind up spending the evening at Grandpa Billy's while Mary helped host the event. The fund-raiser was always a favorite part of Mary's life and she looked forward to each and every one of them. Typically, most of the social elite attended the events along with a few of the newcomers to the area. Mary enjoyed interacting with all of the people that attended and often found herself surrounded by old friends and many of the local professionals and politicians. Often these fund-raisers resulted in large sums of money being raised for a project and Mary expected this evening to be no different.

The night of the fund-raiser, the news carried a story of a different sort. You see, Charleston was a very welcoming city and seldom did anything happen to disquiet her solace. However, it appeared as if the previous evening, a residential real estate agent of a competing agency had not been heard from since the time of her last appointment. Mary dismissed this from her mind as she listened listlessly and preferred to focus on the upcoming events of that evening's fund-raiser. As Mary readied herself she thought of how pretty the evening was and that a full moon was expected. She knew her son would be having the time of his life at Grandpa's and looked forward to a leisurely time herself.

Tonight's event, like most others of its type, was held at the Charleston Museum. It housed most of the significant artifacts and historical documents of the city and the surrounding areas. The museum had several years ago aligned itself as a staunch supporter of the Charleston Historical and Preservation Society and was one of its strongest alliances in preserving Charleston's past for future generations. Many times the two organizations had teamed up to support a special project and to help preserve a particular vestige of the city. The two organizations worked so well together that often, outsiders not intimately involved with the organizations could not tell where one group started and the other ended. They often shared resources on projects so as to most efficiently and expeditiously achieve their shared goals of furthering the integrity of Charleston proper to future generations.

As Mary drove to the fund-raiser, she remembered thinking of the Sunday yet ahead. She planned to pick up David before heading over to St. Ann's Lutheran Church. She enjoyed the sermons there and felt that David was really beginning to find himself comfortable with his new church friends. They usually attended the eleven o'clock service and then had dinner afterwards at one of the local restaurants, often with her parents, and then spent the early afternoon hours at their home.

As Mary pulled her car into the parking garage, she thought briefly of her past and all the possibilities that might have been. As she strode into the main atrium of the museum, she admired the splendor of the decorations that had been done, always simple, but elegant, just the way she preferred. As her eyes quickly scanned the room, she noticed many familiar faces as she contemplated whom to talk to first. She saw her childhood girlfriend Tracey Barnes, who had recently had her first child, a boy who was now two months old. They began talking about everything from how the baby was doing to how Tracey and her husband were getting along. Things between Tracey and her husband seemed to be going well and Mary was happy for her. Tracey and her husband had tried for a little over two years to have a baby and had all but given up when Tracey had learned she was pregnant. Mary always believed Tracey to be content and well centered and had really enjoyed their twenty-year plus friendship.

It was then and there that Mary first saw Joseph, who despite being in his mid-forties was a very handsome man. Although he appeared confident, he did not seem full of himself. Mary had met many men in her time that behaved as if they owned the whole world. She was not looking for that type of man; she wanted a man who wanted to be friends first and then who knows, maybe something more lately. Mary was looking for a man of substance and whose integrity and faith were steadfast, someone that would create a safe place to fall during all the events, both good and bad, that might occur in her life.

Joseph was talking amongst a group of several men and women. Mary could not help but notice his deep blue eyes, his dark complexion and his short well-cropped salt-and-pepper hair. Mary noticed that he seemed very amicable with the other guests. Although Joseph looked somewhat familiar, she knew that she had not seen him before. Mary could not help but think of what it might be like to meet him and to find out if perhaps he might be alone. Although she had not even met him yet, she caught herself several times during the evening even thinking whimsically about the possibility of meeting him.

The evening turned out as she had predicted with all the normal sequences of hellos, formal greetings and a speech about the home to be saved and its particular niche in the lore of Charleston's history. Mary caught herself becoming a little too content after sampling a few of the hors d'oeuvres, and perhaps even a little sleepy. She had noticed that the last speaker talked a bit longer than normal and she had even noticed a guest or two trying to politely stifle a yawn. Mary had all but forgotten about noticing Joseph earlier in the evening and had decided to have just one more beverage before she left. The bar was located on the other side of the atrium from where she had been standing so she had to make her way through the sea of guests. As Mary neared the area in front of the bar, she noticed Joseph standing there and he slowly turned to speak gingerly to her.

Joseph too, it seems, had noticed Mary earlier in the evening and how she seemed to know everyone there. He assumed that she must be a lady of status and substance as she spoke and moved easily amongst all the dignitaries present. He had noticed her form and figure and how her blonde straight hair flowed well beneath her shoulders. He caught himself several times during the evening stealing engaging looks in her direction. Joseph once even felt as if he had caught Mary's eyes from across the room but he quickly dismissed the idea, as she had to turn to greet someone else in the room. He could not help but dwell on how softly her bangs dangled over her eyes, almost as if dancing on air. Joseph always admired a pretty woman but he had never met one whose inner beauty matched that of her outside. He had wondered for years if God would ever bring the right woman to his life, someone who was a complement to him. Joseph knew that beauty was only skin deep but over the years, he often found himself matched up and caught up with the wrong type of woman. He wondered if the long flowing blonde hair belied her inner beauty.

Joseph had come this evening on an invitation from some of his friends who had been permanent residents of Charleston. Although Joseph was a relative newcomer to the area, he seemed to mix well with all of its attendees even though, at times, he had wondered why he had come. Even though he was enjoying himself, he wondered if he truly fit in with the elite of the city of Charleston. Tonight his daughter, Sara, was staying at home with Yana and he hoped that they were having a good time. Joseph had dated several women since his wife's death but none of them were able to fill the void that he had felt for most of his adult life. He had known and dated several women for an extended time period but none of them seemed to be in sync with who Joseph truly was. It seemed as if everyone he had known either wanted to change him or predominantly looked at him as a good provider and not for he himself. Joseph never really believed in love at first sight but he continually abided in the faith of God's providence. Joseph had not really met anyone at all in the Charleston area and he wondered if the fresh start he had sought when he moved to the area and to Mt. Pleasant would ever happen at all.

He often thought of his past life and how his wife, Debbie, had passed. Joseph and Debbie never had a great marriage as they often failed to truly communicate and sometimes even failed to really open up and talk at all. It always seemed as if they were two ships passing in the night, never really seeing who each really was. Their masks remained on throughout their marriage with each of them being truly afraid to open up and to be vulnerable. Joseph had always been faithful and was so till the very end. He consistently questioned God as to why she had to die; it just didn't make sense to him. It seemed at times as if he could only focus on what he had done to negatively impact his marriage and that it never seemed to be rich like those of his friends. Joseph longed for the day when perhaps God would lead some special someone into his life. Someone God had chosen and reared up just for him, who might truly be the right woman for him and his life.

Joseph tended to dwell on past things that he could not control and this seemed to leave him fearful when it came to relationships. Although he knew that he had not been pursuing the right type of woman for himself and for Sara, Joseph seemed to always wind up with the woman who would detract from and not add to the richness of his life. He had frequently prayed to God, especially over the past year, to bring into his life someone totally different from the others he had known in the past. He was often afraid of where God's leading might take him if he was truly open to it, but knew if he followed his own heart, like in the past, that he was doomed to failure. Joseph noticed Mary, as she seemed to almost glide across the room toward him and neared the bar. He felt his pulse quicken and he felt himself nervously swallow. It seemed as if time stood still as this woman, whom he had stolen glances of all night, entered into the immediate area where he was now standing. He contemplated what he might say and he wondered whether or not she would be receptive to his voice and overtures. He slowly turned to face her and…

The late night news was just coming on. Amid the normal everyday chatter that seemed to be on every night's broadcast was a shocking update on the residential real estate agent who had been missing since her appointment late yesterday afternoon. A man had been out kayaking around seven earlier in the evening and had happened across her body lying face down in the marsh. The body was found in a small tributary of the Wando River called Foster Creek. The creek is approximately five miles upstream from where the Wando River meets first the Cooper River and then joins the Ashley River to form the Charleston Harbor. Early reports indicated that she had been there for about eighteen hours and that she appeared to have been dead before her body was left there. The area where she had been found was remote and not a part of the marsh that was actively traveled. The kayaker who discovered her was taking a path that was so shallow that he only took it at the highest of tides. In fact, the kayaker who discovered the body normally limited his travels to the much deeper and more heavily traveled Shem Creek. This discovery and the grisly crime committed greatly concerned the populace of the area as their normal, peaceful community had been violated with a heinous act that always seemed to happen elsewhere. The police were already beginning to form a task force to investigate what they initially believed and were investigating as a homicide.

Charleston has always been recognized as being one of America's most hospitable cities and often rated number one in the United

States. The gentle nature of its people and the slow pace of its lifestyle were what attracted people to the area, and kept them coming there and often even relocating to enjoy its ambiance on a full-time basis. People often would visit the Charleston area just for a weekend jaunt only to find themselves several years later moving there and becoming permanent residents. Unbeknownst to Joseph and Mary at this time, something evil had occurred to upset the city's tranquility and as they would later learn, have a great and permanent impact on their lives. As the newscast droned on to other lesser issues, the fund-raiser continued unaware of the tragedy that had befallen the city. Little did they know that their lives, all their relationships, and their faith would soon be greatly challenged.

Mary was a very gentle and caring soul who led with her heart and her compassion for others. Often she would do for others rather than take care of herself and the needs of what she wanted at the moment. During her past marriage, she had done everything she could to please her ex-husband, Tim, but it seemed no matter what she did to try to please him, he was never satisfied. Mary often caught her losing herself while she tried to be what others wanted her to be and not what she was supposed to truly be. Intellectually she knew that these habits would never make a good and healthy long-term relationship but she seemed unable to break her old familiar patterns. It felt as if the pain of her past kept reuniting with the present all too often. Mary had met Tim while they were both in college, she was a junior and he was a senior. Tim, like her, was a born and bred Charlestonian, whose family had lived in the city for several generations. In fact, Tim's father had served on the city council for several terms, and had always been active in the city's governmental affairs.

When Mary and Tim married, it seemed as if the whole of Charleston's social elite turned out for the event, with over four hundred guests. The women were immaculately dressed with mostly black long evening formal wear. It often seemed as if the room was adorned with beautiful black sequins and flashing diamonds and jewelry as the women moved and sashayed across the room. The men all wore tuxedos of the finest tailor-made fabrics, mostly of Italian blends. The wedding was held where Mary and her family had attended church for over twenty years. The bridesmaids and groomsmen were delicately and precisely placed so as to accentuate the bridal couple as they said their marriage vows. Mary still remembers the reservations she felt about going through with the marriage and even during the days and the immediate moments preceding the ceremony, but she felt unable to change the course and the direction that had been set out for that day. Unfortunately over time, her instincts proved correct.

Tim was a good man, about to assume the helm of his father's business, which imported sugar cane from the West Indies. To most outsiders, Tim seemed like the catch of the century at first, but as the courtship wore on, Mary noticed that oftentimes, Tim seemed distant and reticent. Mary had decided that perhaps this was just part of his demeanor and that everything would work out between them and she believed that somehow she would be able to please Tim and make him happy. But there, even on her wedding day, she wondered if God had indeed blessed their marriage and this union. Mary wanted a God-centered marriage but it seemed as if Tim did not want or potentially even have an active relationship with God. She got caught up in the excitement of it all, as did the local paper and the whole of the society of Charleston. Charleston society described her impending marriage in almost fairytale fashion, but nothing could be further from the truth.

Although the marriage ceremony was, in itself, a huge success and was followed by a glorious three-week honeymoon in Europe, Mary could not stop wondering if Tim was the right man for her. The first week of the honeymoon seemed to be almost idyllic, but the later weeks and especially the last few days seemed to be less about them and more about him. During those final weeks of the trip, Mary lay awake several hours in the middle of the night praying that God would indeed make them one. She hoped and believed if somehow she could just try a little harder, do a little more to please him that everything would work out. She knew she would always be there for Tim, but she began to wonder if indeed he would be there for her.

Over the next several years, Mary's marriage to Tim seemed to be moving forward well enough, especially to those outside it. They seemed to be the perfect couple to all who saw them. Socially, they were seen at all the right places and events. However, as their marriage wore on, Tim became more and more reticent and distant.

During their fourth year of marriage, Mary and Tim conceived. Neither Mary nor Tim was actively planning on having a child, but in going in for a routine checkup, Mary learned that she was pregnant. Tim seemed to accept the idea of having a child but never really warmed to it. As the pregnancy entered its second trimester, Tim had begun to pull further and further back from her, leaving her feeling even more alone and afraid. Mary, ever more determined, put on a positive face, planned for the birth of her first child, and prepared for the prospect of motherhood alone.

By the time the baby was born, Tim had pretty much totally abandoned the marriage. His mood swings were now more severe and he was spending a little too much time at work and at the gym. When the new baby, David, reached two months, Tim announced that he was moving out of the house and that he would be seeking a divorce. Although Mary intellectually had been expecting the news, she still found herself stunned and devastated. At first she tried to talk Tim out of it, but she had learned from the past that all of her talking would be to no avail. So after a few days of earnest discussions, she resigned herself to the fact that her marriage was ending and she had to plan accordingly. She had always tried to look forward and to see the best and to be positive, now all she could see was a long, tough road ahead. She surrounded herself with her parents and friends and planned for the life that seemed to be her only path, that of being a single parent. After her divorce, she had opted, as a convenience, to continue to have the same last name as her son and to not change back to her maiden name. Life had dealt Mary a severe blow but she determined to set out to deal with the hand that she had been dealt.

Chapter 2

JOSEPH'S HEART raced and his pulse quickened as Mary approached. When Joseph's eyes first met hers, he felt peaceful and sensed an immediate urge to care for the woman that God had just placed in front of him. Mary's eyes met his gaze, both in intensity and intent. She sensed his warmth and sincerity. Mary did not know what God had in store for her at this moment and in this meeting, but the feelings of tranquility and excitement filled and emanated from every fiber of her being as they exchanged their initial greetings with each other. Joseph remarked as he deeply smiled, "Hello, I'm Joseph, I could not help but notice you earlier in the evening. I feel so lucky that our paths crossed this evening."

Mary almost gasped awash and basking in the attention of a man that seemed so…perfect. "I'm Mary, I'm honored to meet you and to make your acquaintance. I agree and do believe our meeting is most gratuitous."

Joseph was just blown away. Never before had his skin tingled so. Here she was, in his presence and seemingly enjoying him as much as he was her. Joseph noticed her beautiful smile and her almost angelic countenance as they talked. The way she tilted and moved her head and her form intrigued Joseph. As he studied the lines of her face and her sparkling eyes he knew that this woman was not like anyone he had ever known before. Joseph knew that God preordains everything that ever occurs even before time began and he believed that God alone had arranged their meeting. Joseph was just beginning to feel God more often in his life and more strongly than ever before. He felt God nudging him deeper and deeper into conversation, interest and intent with Mary and this beautiful woman that was before him.

Life has a way of sneaking up on people, especially when you are busy making plans. Joseph had dated very little during the preceding year, preferring for the first time in his life, to focus on who he was in God first. Joseph began to focus on who he was in Christ and in doing so, drew closer to the cross and to whom God really wanted him to be. He diligently prayed to be open to God's leading and to be obedient to who God wanted as the woman in his life and to not focus on what he wanted for himself. In the past he knew he had tended to focus on the outward beauty of a woman and not of her true inner self and in doing so, he learned over and over that these selection criteria allowed him to select predominantly women who loved themselves first and foremost. It seemed as if the only people they had room to love were themselves and that their hearts would always remain hardened. He wanted a Christ-centered relationship, one with which each of them could look to God first for their guidance and peace and then might radiate God's warmth and love back to each other. Joseph knew that this was God's wish for his life and now he was ready to seek God's best.

Though Joseph felt his prayer sincere, if he were to be honest, he feared God's best for him might result in a woman who might not be pretty nor attractive and maybe even one who did not take care of herself. But as he gazed deeply into Mary's eyes, he saw a sparkle there and he listened intently to each and every word, watching her mouth as she spoke. He was captivated by her mannerisms and her smile and he found her to be breathtakingly beautiful in his eyes. Her firm features, her womanly figure, her inner peace, her confidence and her engaging personality seemed to make the rest of the room disappear.

Mary drifted, imagining what it would be like to have his hand brush along her cheek, and his warmth was proving to be intoxicating to her. She felt herself, for the first time in years, feeling and coming totally alive. She noticed how he gingerly and delicately inclined towards her, making her feel very warm indeed and perhaps even a little faint. Mary learned of his past naval experiences and of his present position as a harbormaster for the Charleston Harbor. Mary was fascinated by Joseph and hung on every word he said. The minutes seemed as mere seconds as they learned more about each other and enjoyed the ambiance and pleasure of each other's presence.

29

As the fund-raiser neared its close, Joseph knew with great certainty, that he did not want the evening to end. They were but a few blocks from the Battery of Charleston's harbor where the Ashley, Cooper and Wando rivers meet. The Battery was an elevated seawall built decades ago to protect the elegant homes that adorned the harbor and the adjoining historic district of homes and shops. The seawall had an elevated walkway on top that made it ideal for an evening or afternoon stroll. The beauty on both sides of the walkway was intoxicating to locals and visitors alike. On one side you had the natural beauty of the harbor looking out towards the Atlantic Ocean and on the other side, all the history and the charm of Charleston's most elegant homes. The streets of Charleston were known for being safe and well attended from the early hours of the morning and until a little before midnight. Joseph nervously asked if perhaps Mary might enjoy a walk along the Battery to soak in the full moon and the cool evening air to continue their conversation. He wasn't sure of her answer, yet he knew he had to ask. Although Mary briefly hesitated, she readily accepted and knew that she would be safe as long as he was by her side.

A full moon was present that night and its light sparkled and danced across the waters and waves out across the harbor towards Fort Sumter and the open seas of the Atlantic. They walked gingerly, closely but not touching, along the grand homes of the Battery and the harbor. Joseph never had felt more alive than he did at that moment. He knew that something magical was happening and determined at that moment to see what was in store for him and Mary. Although he did not believe in love at first sight, he did believe in providence and the continuing guidance and omniscience of God's hand. As they strolled through the evening air, their conversations ranged from their children to their families to what they were looking for in their life. Neither one wanted to or seemed to pry, but neither would have cared if the other did. Mary felt like an open book to him and wanted to learn more of this man and who he might be or what part he might play in her life.

They walked the entire length of the Battery, and then they turned to walk back, stopping to admire the full moon that seemed even brighter than before. There was not a cloud in the sky and the air was crystal clear. The moon seemed to follow them as they had traversed the Battery and its beauty was intoxicating. If no one had known better, they would have felt that the couple's gentle gait and conversation were that of a couple who had known each other and been married for years. As they neared where they turned away from the Battery and towards the museum where the fund-raiser had been held, Joseph felt an evil presence in their midst, as if someone was watching and following them. As they turned and walked a block toward the museum, Joseph turned and looked behind him, noticing a man who appeared disheveled who stopped walking as soon as Joseph turned. Joseph, sensing danger and a desire to take care of Mary, placed a gentle hand in the small of Mary's back in an attempt to protect her and yet move her along a little quicker. After they had left the area where Joseph had felt the presence of the danger, he quickly dismissed his initial concern as he resumed to walk toward their cars at the museum parking lot. The closer they got to where their cars were parked, the gentleman who Joseph felt had been following them appeared to stop and hang back.

As they finished their stroll, it was almost 1:00 a.m. and they walked back to where Mary's car was parked. They made plans to see each other again, perhaps for dinner the following Wednesday. Joseph and Mary exchanged numbers and e-mail addresses and made plans to talk again soon. Joseph wanted to embrace Mary before she left but he felt it more appropriate to just warmly say goodbye. Joseph watched as Mary drove off, choosing to stand there for a moment taking in the enormity of the evening. Joseph slowly walked toward his car and began the slow trek home towards Mt. Pleasant. As he drove, he thanked God for just the chance to meet Mary and for feeling so alive. Joseph noticed again how radiant the brightness of the moon shone and grandly lit the way home and thought to himself how thankful he was for the opportunity to meet Mary and for her to be such a woman of fine inner and outer beauty.

Joseph's Monday started off pretty much the same as every week, complete with meetings that seemed to go on forever and the catch-up of items and events that had occurred over the weekend. The harbor was always its busiest the first of the week as the large cargo and regular merchant marine ships entered and left the Charleston Harbor for ports both near and far away. Often the loading and unloading of the larger ships could take in excess of two and sometimes even three days as every available square inch of space, both in the holds and on the ship's deck, was utilized. Joseph marveled how it always seemed that towards the end of the loading of a ship, as soon as he thought there was not room for one more container, it always seemed the logistics and loading experts found space for just one more to be loaded and stored on board.

Though Joseph had been at his job and position for over two years now, it still offered him what seemed to be hourly challenges. Many of the different ships and vessels, both commercial and residential, vied to have priority over each other as well as the other conflicting needs and other uses of the harbor. His task was to coordinate their movements from a few miles out into the Atlantic Ocean into the harbor and up the Cooper River where the commercial docks were located. The Cooper River and its docks were the only one of the three rivers navigable for the large cargo and commercial ships. The Wando and the Ashley rivers were both too shallow and its bridges too low for utilization by the bigger ships and vessels. The technological equipment Joseph had available as harbormaster was state of the art and he always had all that he needed and all current information that he could possibly ever want was at his fingertips. Joseph generally felt like he had some fairly good control of the general events of the day and in the harbor. However the only thing he felt he did not have any way to influence were the volumes of requests that seemed to permeate his day as the captains and ships and everyone else each sought their own special needs and interests. Also, almost always there was an event that occurred that needed his immediate attention and energy.

God was stirring in Joseph's heart particularly this week and he was reminded of Ephesians 5, verses 25 to 27;

"Husbands love your wives, just as Christ loved the church and gave himself up for her to make her holy, cleansing her by the washing with water through the Word and to present her to himself as a radiant church, without stain or wrinkle or any other blemish, but holy and blameless."

32

As Joseph contemplated these verses he was reminded of his meeting Mary and how angelic and special she seemed. He poured over and over these verses in his head and they became alive in the spirit. For the first time in his life, these words had deep and penetrating meaning to his soul and spirit. Although Joseph knew that he had only just met Mary, there was a great appreciation to God Himself for having met her and he thanked Him for allowing Joseph to be graced with Mary's presence. Often during the day, his mind wandered off to their initial meeting and that late night stroll along the battery, and he smiled to himself marveling about the joy that he felt and the mystery of it all. Joseph was learning to take life as it came and to not look beyond the moment and in all things to give thanks for the present.

Although Joseph had always wanted to, he had never had a true Christ-centered relationship in either his marriage or thereafter. Joseph knew that he was a believer but was never able to truly let go and let God be the true driver and at the helm of his life. Joseph longed to be able to pray and meditate with a godly helpmate and that they each could help the other along in whatever life might bring and they might encounter together growing and drawing closer to each other and to Him. Joseph wanted to call Mary but he hesitated, not wanting to appear too pushy or persistent.

On the way to work, Mary dropped off her son, David, at school. Mary enjoyed the flexibility of being a real estate agent as it allowed her the time she needed to take David to and from school most every day and to mostly be there for him when he returned. After David did his homework, they would usually spend several hours together playing and just hanging out before dinner. David was just starting to learn how to really enjoy riding his bike and they would spend hours together riding their bikes. On those rare days that she could not be there to pick David up, her father was happy to be there to pick up the slack. Often on those days, her father and David would do something special together for a few hours until Mary was able to finish up her work and come home.

As Mary left the school and headed towards her office, she dreamily thought of meeting Joseph and what it all might have meant. She had pretty much resigned herself to remaining single, at least until David went away to college, but she had recently prioritized herself to focus on following God, wherever that might lead. Mary had done a lot of introspection these past few years and the self-evaluation had really begun to help her see herself as He had made her and to come into her own as a child of God. Intellectually, Mary always knew God had a plan for her life and His best for her in mind, but she had resisted in the past, somehow believing she could decide for herself what to do.

Joseph's mind raced over and over back to his meeting with Mary. Late Monday afternoon, he decided to write her an e-mail. In his note, he wrote, "Mary, I had the best time I've ever had meeting you this past Saturday night. Our talk that evening and our walk along the harbor to the moon's glow just seemed so, so perfect! I'm really looking forward to our dinner Wednesday evening. Ever since we met, I can't stop thinking about you and the moments that we were able to share. There was something incredible going on that evening and I can't wait to see you again, to see where all this goes, and to see your beautiful smile. Very Fondly Yours, Joseph."

He thought his e-note was less forward than perhaps a phone call might be, but personal enough to let her know of his initial and continued excitement he felt about their meeting. He re-read it several times before he finally pushed the send message button on his computer. He smiled hoping that she would obtain as much joy from reading it as he did in its writing.

Mary happened to be in the office when her mailbox noted that she had a new message. As she often did, she immediately stopped what she was doing to see what it was. With some anticipation, Mary opened the note hoping that it might be from Joseph. A warm smile gushed over her face and her heart skipped a beat as she began to read slowly and to savor each and every word. Mary read each word, meditating over it, and then the note as a whole again several times, beaming as she intently and with great warmth read the message on her screen. She sensed something was happening inside her towards him and immediately began to type a reply. "Joseph, it was great to get your note, what a wonderful surprise! I have thought of our meeting many times since and I believe something might indeed be stirring in the air! I can't wait for our dinner on Wednesday and to see what might be in store for us. I'm thinking about you. Mary."

When Joseph received Mary's e-mail response, he had prayed and hoped that perhaps the way that he had felt about their meeting was mutual and that Mary was inclined to their getting to know each other much better. Of course, he had exchanged initial notes before with other women he had met over the years, but Mary seemed to be dramatically different somehow, different than anyone he had ever met before. Later that evening after Joseph had readied Sara for bed, he decided to go into his study and read some of his favorite Bible verses. Joseph's eyes were drawn to Psalms 27, verses 1-3.

"The Lord is my light and my salvation—who shall I fear?
The Lord is the stronghold of my life—of whom shall I be afraid?
When evil men advance against me to devour my flesh, when my enemies
and my foes attack me, they will stumble and fall.
Though an army besiege me, my heart will not fear.
Though war break out against me, even then will I be confident."

As he read God's words that were written carefully by King David over two thousand years ago, over and over again out loud and in his mind he thought of God now for the first time as being his only true Father and protector. Although Joseph was always raised in the church, he had somehow read all the words, heard all the sermons, but the Word had not permeated his true inner being and had somehow seemed to just not sink in. He drew deeper and deeper into prayer, asking God to forgive him for his past sins and thanking him for His death on the cross, thus allowing him to be saved and to live in heaven with Jesus forever. Joseph felt a heaviness in his heart being lifted as he began, for the first time ever, to totally let go of his past. The peace of Jesus seemed to radiate in the room and in his heart; Joseph abided deeply there with the Alpha and Omega of the universe. The excitement of the day, exchanging e-mails with Mary and his one-on-one talk with the one true God gave Joseph comfort as he drifted off to sleep.

Meanwhile, Mary's evening consisted of spending time with David doing homework for about an hour after school and then a short walk after dinner. She had a little bit of a brighter step this evening as they began their stroll along their normal course. After David had gone to bed, she retired to her room to read for a bit. Mary enjoyed reading an hour or so late in the evening and then watching a little television before falling off to sleep. After reading for a while, Mary happened to turn on the evening news only to find an update on the Saturday murder of the real estate agent. It seems as if just six months prior there were three murders of women who were real estate agents in the Wilmington, North Carolina, area that remained unsolved. Police believed that these three murders in Wilmington and the one now in Charleston, bringing the total to four, were all done by the same perpetrator. Police believed that the patterns of all four of the murders were similar and they were trying to develop an MO on the perpetrator so that they might share it with the public and that it might aid in his capture. Although the police would not release the specific details of their investigation, they shared that most of the patterns and events of all four murders were similarly matched and that all the populace should be on extra alert. Fortunately, Mary's life had always been sheltered from evildoers and mischief, and so she dismissed this as having nothing to do with her as she drifted quickly off to sleep.

Upon arriving at work early on Tuesday morning, her office was abuzz with the news of the murders and several of the women had not come in to work as their husbands, fearing for their safety, insisted that they stay at home. Slowly, the reality of it all began to hit her; there was a murderer loose in the city and his target was real estate agents. The Charleston police had teamed up with other cities within a 200-mile radius and had formed a task force to investigate and had hired the best detectives available to lead it. Police planned visits, to be held over the next few days, for informational meetings at real estate agencies to discuss safety precautions. Agents were teaming up with "safety buddies" to whom there were to be accountable to during the whole of the workday. Being a safety buddy required each of them to "check in" during the day and to constantly report their physical whereabouts. At least every hour they were to talk to ensure that they stayed connected during the day. Mary was fairly independent and did not like the idea of "reporting in" to anyone but she realized it probably was a pretty good idea.

Joseph, by now, had also heard the news and immediately placed a call to Mary. While Joseph was dialing the number a strange feeling came over him. He felt a need to care for Mary, to protect her physically and to safeguard her heart. Joseph wondered how it was that a single and such an unexpected meeting could have prompted such a response. Nonetheless, Joseph did desire to get to know Mary better and to look after her safety, her needs, and her desires. Although Joseph had only known Mary for a few days, he saw her as a delicate flower that needed to be cared for and watered by a special gardener, a gardener that would guide her mind, spirit and soul. Joseph had never felt this way before but he knew there was something uniquely special and warm about this woman God had placed immediately in his viewfinder. He was greatly relieved when she answered on the first ring. Mary told Joseph about the planned procedures and how the task force would be visiting there tomorrow at noon.

Wednesday morning came and went with nothing significant having occurred. Mary's parents called asking that she and David come and stay with them indefinitely until the murders were solved and the perpetrator caught and brought to justice. However, being true to her continuing independence, Mary acknowledged that there was nothing to worry about and that she would be fine staying at home. Mary always thought that her parents worried a little too much so she quickly dismissed their concerns as just more of their excessive worrying.

The police task force arrived as scheduled around lunchtime and described in great detail how the buddy system would work. Listing every available specific, the police task force personnel described some of the consistencies that they had detected in the four abductions and murders. The lead detective remarked, "We suspect and believe that perhaps the perpetrator is a man and that he had followed his victims and learned their patterns, traits and habits before making his move. All the victims appear to have been assaulted and then murdered and the body dumped far away from the hustle and bustle of people."

One of the victims was discovered so late in the decomposition process that her dental record was the only thing that was available to be used for identification. The task force further shared that three of the four victims had been single like Mary. This sent chills up her spine. The detective indicated that it was possible that this might not be a reliable and predictable pattern but felt that he would be remiss in not stating what they had found.

It seemed as if the quiet and safe city of Charleston that Mary had always known had now been rocked. Mary sensed that there was now a very deep and dark danger amiss in her fair city and she immediately began praying for a hedge of protection for both herself and her associates. She quizzed the task force about how this could go on for so long and still not be solved. The task force detectives tried to assure her as best they could that they were doing everything that could possibly be done to catch the perpetrator as soon as possible. Because the crimes now spanned two states, it was obtaining heavy regional news coverage on all the networks, and nationally the story received some coverage as well.

Mary, as a child, had always feared God. She knew God as the God of the Old Testament who would flood the waters of the earth, saving only Noah and his family. She knew the God that struck a man dead solely for trying to catch the Ark of the Covenant as it fell off its cart before it struck the ground. She had difficulty seeing the love of Jesus through her lens of the God that she had read about. Mary often contemplated some of the Bible's verses and carefully examined those against the way she had been brought up. The Bible was always there in her home as a child but it was never opened and read together as a family. Though Mary and her family were active in the church, it just always seemed as if it were something they did while they were there. The sermons and precepts they studied and listened to at church were never discussed once the family arrived back home. It was almost as if they had two separate sections of their lives, the church part and then the home. Mary had always and still believed her parents to be Christians, it's just that especially in looking back it always seemed odd to her that the Bible was never a topic of open family discussion. It almost seemed as if the two worlds never really connected.

Mary had always wanted a solid foundation for a marriage but never really knew how to create it. Often she would stop and read of the biblical standard for a godly marriage. In Ephesians 5, verses 22 & 24 she would read:

"Wives submit to your husband as to the Lord for the husband is the head of the wife as Christ is the head of the church, his body, of which he is the Savior. Now as the church submits to Christ, so also wives should submit to their husbands in everything."

These last verses especially caused Mary deep consternation. She would read them slowly over and over... "submit to their husbands in everything." Mary had always felt that a marriage was a partnership, a merger of two equals. Somehow this verse made her feel second class and she did not understand how this could be so. In her previous marriage to Tim, Mary did not submit to Tim in any way. She always felt just as important as Tim so she could not see how these verses could possibly be correct. Yet God kept calling Mary, His daughter, His child, to abide and be secure in the love of His truth. Mary, though reluctantly, was beginning on a very deep and meaningful basis to get in touch with God's Word, and the words of a sermon she had recently heard deeply moved her. The pastor explained the verses in a way that resonated deep into the inner recesses of her soul. The pastor talked about the meaning of headmanship and that it did not mean superiority and that submission did not mean inferiority. The pastor talked of how Christ, in being submissive to God's will, died an excruciating death on the cross. She believed that Jesus was indeed who he said he was, that of being God incarnate, in the flesh. Therefore, Mary was able to abide in and know that at any time God could have come down off that cross and saved himself. But in his being willingly subject to the will of God, the Father, he gave himself as a willing sacrifice for all. Tears poured down Mary's face as she thanked God for what He did and to imagine it was just for her. She knew His love was real and it made her heart fill to overflowing. As Mary prayed, she asked God to forgive her for not being willing to be submissive in her marriage. Tears of pain ran down her face as she acknowledged for the first time that she also had greatly contributed to the failure of her past marriage to Tim. Mary knew that Tim had left the marriage and that she could not do anything about that, yet, she knew that she had not been totally present and willing to love, as Christ would have her to do. As she continued praying, a torrential downpour pummeled her office and she could scarcely see anything at all out the front window. As tears rolled down Mary's cheeks, she knew she was free of the bonds that had tied up her heart for years. As each tear fell, she felt the pain of her past being washed away tear by tear. As it continued to rain, it seemed to fall in buckets as she was praying to God to pull her in and to fill her up with Him.

As Mary asked God to make her heart more like His, the rain stopped as suddenly as it appeared and God seemed to talk to her. Though the voice was not audible, He spoke to her, His words penetrating deep into her heart and soul, saying, "Come to me, my child, abide with me. I knew you before you were born, I know the numbers of hairs on your head. I made you to be with me. You are a sheep of my flock and in you I find great joy. Love me as I love the Father and I will never forsake you."

As she was hearing God's words, the sun broke and the most brilliant rainbow she had ever seen appeared. Its colors were majestic and dazzled against the still gray sky. In quiet humility and praise, Mary replied, "I am here, dear God, use me, fill me with who you are and who you want me to be."

Chapter 3

JOSEPH THOUGHT the day, more than most, seemed to be exceedingly long. It was the day he had waited for, it was finally Wednesday, the day he got to see Mary. Joseph wanted to pinch himself to make sure he was really there and that tonight with Mary would be as before. Due to all the activity in the news, and with a serial killer loose on the city of Charleston, Joseph made plans to pick Mary up from work so that he could ensure her safety. As he drove toward her office, he caught himself talking to God about Mary and praying for a hedge of protection around her. Joseph cared deeply about her safety and wanted to do everything he could to care for and protect her. As he pulled into her office parking lot, he caught himself getting even more excited to see her as he got out of the car and walked towards the front door of her office. The receptionist at the front desk said that Mary was presently on the phone and that she would be right out. Joseph nervously thumbed through an architectural magazine, choosing to stand while he waited. Joseph paced slowly back and forth in the waiting room as he anticipated Mary's arrival.

As Mary came around the corner, Joseph's eyes lifted toward her. He felt himself gasp as he drank in her beauty. Her hair, her eyes, her form, moved him. He noticed that her countenance was spirit filled. Joseph moved toward Mary...wanting to reach out but hesitating, saying, "It's great to see you."

Mary almost blushed in his presence, taken aback yet again by the intoxication she felt solely by him being there. There was something unique about Joseph. She felt like she wanted to nurture him, to grasp his hand, to feel his touch, and to feel the essence of who he was. Yet she determined in her heart to patiently await his leading. As they drove toward the restaurant, they talked about what the police had now unequivocally stated and acknowledged that there was a serial killer in their midst. Mary brought Joseph up to date about all the details of the meeting that the task force had conducted at her office. Mary noticed feeling safer than she had ever felt before with Joseph as they drove back across the Cooper River toward Mt. Pleasant. The sun was beginning to fall from its perch high in the sky and it was beginning to change hues as the light danced across the water and the scattered clouds. Mary noticed that the light danced on the tips of the waves in ever-bending and shimmering bits of light, making thousands of light reflections on the water's surface.

Joseph had always liked all the quaint little restaurants along Shem Creek in Mt. Pleasant and the ambiance that they provided. Shem Creek was a deep-water tidal creek that was navigable by both pleasure boaters and commercial shrimpers alike. Shem Creek fed into the Charleston Harbor just a little less than a mile east of Patriots Point. Joseph took Mary to his favorite restaurant, being sure to request his favorite table overlooking the water. He had called ahead to the manager to be sure that he knew Joseph would be there tonight and to make it a special evening to remember. Joseph could sit there, late in the afternoon for hours, mesmerized by the shrimp boats as they returned from a day's work, as they unloaded their day's catch and got the ships ready to head off early the next morning. Joseph often thought of their labor as a good honest day's work. He admired people that worked with their hands and the simple essence of their efforts and their lives. Joseph and Mary were seated at his favorite spot and the waiter brought them a menu. He noticed as they began talking that he was again awash in the joyous ambiance of her presence.

Soon their conversations turned toward their past relationships and what in life mattered most to them. Joseph, in his past, had always sought out women that he never seemed to be able to please. Although Mary seemed different, he still felt it important to be open and honest about his past experiences and who he truly was and yet hoped to be. Joseph openly and honestly talked about his faith, his hopes and his dreams and shared freely from the heart.

Mary deeply appreciated and admired Joseph's openness and his candor. She noted that Joseph was willing to talk about his fears as well as his hurts. As Joseph discussed his past marriage and how his wife had died, Mary noticed her own heart reaching out to Joseph as if she had always known him. At one point, Joseph even acknowledged candidly and honestly to her that he had learned over the years that he could not make a woman happy and that he had learned that only God could fill a thirsty spirit and the void that existed in the human heart. Mary thought of Jesus at the well with the woman from Samaria and how Jesus had told her that only He could offer living water from which man could drink and never again thirst. Mary found herself awash in this truth. Mary caught herself time and again listening both to Joseph and, in her mind, she heard God crying out to her, "You are my child, my bride, come to me."

Joseph listened to Mary intently as she described her work, her family and what had contributed to hers and Tim's divorce. As she talked about her marriage and how it had failed, he noticed that she talked predominantly of her contribution to its ending. Most people he had known seemed to always play the victim and talk solely of how they had been wronged and what had been done to them. Mary, however, was curiously frank about her failures. Joseph inclined toward Mary as she spoke, eager to hear all the words that she said, both spoken and unspoken. Just as he had walked with her late on Saturday night, Joseph noticed a most genteel presence, and tonight it seemed to radiate from her, as before, as she engaged him further.

As the evening progressed, Joseph mused that he hardly remembered ordering and had merely poked and prodded at his food, hardly tasting it at all. Joseph recalled that for the past year he had felt all but invisible to women and how women had hardly seemed to notice him at all. It was as if God himself was saving Joseph for just the right one. It seemed now, as if Mary was seeing him as no one else ever had, just as he was. This brought an immediate smile to his face. As he looked into Mary's eyes, he saw himself. He saw a wounded child of God, cognizant of her maker, and optimistic of her future. He felt himself praising God for their meeting and offered himself to God saying, "Use me as you will, I am but yours and willing to obey."

Joseph was shocked that his feelings were so deep, so penetrating at this moment. He felt the love of Jesus cascading over his soul and poured out love openly and freely to her. Though intellectually

Joseph knew he had just met Mary and that he did not believe in love at first sight, he felt himself caring deeply for her. He felt not as he had done with others in the past, but Mary, as a true sister in Christ and a joint heir to the Kingdom.

They talked for more than three hours and Joseph hoped it would never end. They were each so engrossed in the evening, they hardly noticed the sun as it set. Its golden and orange hues danced across Shem Creek and the marsh towards the sky and it seemed to stretch forever against the backdrop of wispy clouds. The restaurant, for a Wednesday, was a little less crowded than usual. As they were finishing up dessert, it was then that Mary sensed a presence. Often in the past, she had ignored these premonitions but had learned as of late to be more in tune to them and to pay attention. There was a heaviness that hung in the air that made her feel as if something was amiss. Joseph noticed her sudden unease and the change in her demeanor but dismissed it as first-date jitters. She looked about the restaurant and saw several patrons scattered about the bar as they finished up their after-dinner coffee, settled the check and prepared to go.

As they were leaving the restaurant, she remembered a small dinner party of about eight guests her parents were having at their home on Friday evening and she invited Joseph to attend. Mary was surprised she felt as comfortable as she did asking him so early to meet her parents, almost too comfortable. Joseph eagerly accepted the invitation while inquiring about what might be appropriate attire. Joseph mused at how the evening seemed as incredible as their first meeting. Although he had not expected it, the budding of the ambiance of a potential relationship with Mary pleased him greatly. Joseph drove her back to her office where she got out and into her car to drive home. In order to ensure her safety, Joseph followed her home. She pulled her vehicle in the driveway as he stopped and walked up to say good-bye. Getting out of the car to meet her, Mary approached Joseph. Gingerly he touched her left arm with his right, "I can't speak for the two of us, but I feel so very drawn to you in a way that I cannot put into words."

Meeting the intensity of his gaze with that of her own, Mary looked deeply into his eyes as Joseph spoke. Then, reaching slowly with her left arm, she reached and held his right and when Joseph stopped speaking she looked even deeper into his eyes and feeling the warmth and sincerity there, replied, "Joseph, I feel it too!"

Those words were angelic to him and he knew that he had found a safe place to fall; a place where his heart could rest and his soul might find true peace. The ambiance of Mary's presence was, well, in a word, intoxicating. Lifting his right hand to Mary's shoulder, and then to the nape of her neck, Joseph ever so gently drew Mary closer to him, almost as if pulling a cloud or a dream until he no sooner felt her full embrace returning his. They held each other there in the headlights of her driveway. They had felt something special, something unique and unbeknownst to them, and yet, they were a thousand miles away from enjoying the beauty of it all.

As Mary turned to go inside, she lightly brushed Joseph's cheek with her lips and spoke softly, "I am so very glad to have met you, and can't wait to see you again, Joseph."

Joseph replied, "Yes, tonight like before was magical. I too believe that good things are in store for us and I can't wait to see where this taking us." He waited until she was safely in the garage and then left for home.

As Joseph headed back across the Cooper River Bridge toward home, he thought of how much God had done for him. For the first time in his life, he had to admit that there was a call he felt God had placed on his life and what it all meant. He remembered a verse in Romans 6:13, "Give yourselves to God...Surrender your whole being to him to be used for righteous purposes."

Joseph contemplated the verse as he drove in his driveway. He stopped to look in on Sara only to find her sleeping soundly. He thanked God for every good and perfect gift he had ever received. Lying in bed, he soon fell fast asleep resting in the peace of Jesus and the memory of Mary and the beauty and the majesty of their time together.

Charleston was still abuzz about the killer on the loose. The task force was working twenty-four hours a day, seven days a week, to come up with any potential leads. So far absolutely nothing they had researched and investigated had turned up anything at all of any consequence. The task force was working diligently to come up with a profile of the killer that they could begin to use. The best experts available were analyzing anything from evidence to analyzing and detailing grit behind the victims' fingernails, to any similarities of any type at all between the victims. The task force and the police were appropriately tight-lipped about the details of their investigation, but those in the know were aware that they were not making much progress.

The rest of the week, albeit just two days, seemed to fly by for Mary. She had several appointments with two potential buyers and one listing appointment. Although Mary felt doubtful about the success of it, she had been faithful in checking in her physical whereabouts with her safety buddy. Joseph and Mary talked for half an hour or so on Thursday evening and it was agreed that Joseph would pick Mary up at her home on Friday evening and that they would ride over to her parents' together.

Mary began readying herself about an hour before he was to pick her up. She showered slowly, enjoying the water as it traced her face. Mary felt revitalized as she exited the shower and began to plan what she would wear for the evening. After several attempts, she decided on a figure-fitting, simple, mid-length dress. The black satin fabric fell over her shoulders into a v-cut back and front that appropriately accentuated her slim figure in a classy and elegant way. The black sandals she chose to wear with the dress added to the elegance of the dress and further accentuated her tanned legs. She chose a simple black shawl to wear over her shoulders in case the evening air grew cooler. She carefully clasped her favorite, gold and diamond cross necklace around her neck and decided to wear her usual diamond earrings. She combed her hair into an elegant twist and pinned it up off her neck with only a few long strands hanging down to add a softer look. After adding a little makeup she was ready and shortly thereafter, she heard Joseph's car drive up and she headed toward the door to meet him. He had scarcely reached the outside porch when she opened the door and invited him in.

Joseph admired the way she had decorated her home. It seemed elegant but most important to him, it seemed warm and full of love. Mary gave him a tour of the house, pointing out family heirlooms that had been handed down through the generations. Joseph noticed how simply, yet tastefully she had placed each and every item throughout her home. Although Joseph felt greatly at home there, they yet had a dinner to attend to.

As Mary's parents, Billy and Mary Sue Loudermilk, lived just a few blocks away from her home, they decided to walk and enjoy the beautiful summer air, the gentle breeze and the smell of the open sea. They strolled hand in hand a little slower than either of them normally would have walked as to enjoy the solitude of being alone side by side taking it all in step by step. As their homes were in close proximity, they arrived there shortly and entered Mary's parents' home.

Joseph really enjoyed meeting Mary's parents. Billy and Mary Sue Loudermilk had been married for forty-two years and had lived in one of the majestic homes overlooking the Battery for the last twenty-two years. Most of the family money had been accumulated through miscellaneous land holdings that had dramatically grown in value over the past several decades. Two generations back, the Loudermilks had been simple and relatively poor farmers raising cotton and corn. As the Charleston area grew, the land that the Loudermilks' granddad had bought a hundred years ago, several hundred acres for dollars an acre, was now worth $100,000 to $200,000 an acre depending on the land's location, suitability for building, and zoning. The Loudermilks were very cognizant and appreciative of how much they had been financially blessed and they did everything they could to give back to the community from which they had gained so much and to help those in need. Joseph felt at home immediately and really enjoyed how hospitable Mary's parents were and that they were so down to earth. It was so refreshing to Joseph that a family so deep in the city's history, so wealthy, were yet so humble. He learned of the history of the home and how it had been handed down from generations past.

The home and its grounds were absolutely incredible with its three stories overlooking the natural beauty of the harbor. The home's sides were carefully poised to embrace the wind from the sea. There was a mild and gentle breeze blowing in that evening which cooled them as they toured the garden. It was obvious that the garden had been carefully planned and immaculately maintained in order to maximize the beauty of every inch. Once back inside, Joseph admired the ten-foot ceilings, the incredibly carved moldings and the beautifully restored hardwood floors. He deeply admired the hundreds of detailed features that added to the magnificence of the home.

Dinner that evening was simple and yet elegant and was then followed by an after-meal tea. Joseph almost felt as if he were dreaming as he watched Mary converse with both her parents and their other guests. Though a newcomer to such social elite and to her, he could think of no place he'd rather be.

On Sunday, Mary and her son, David, drove out to Mt. Pleasant to join Joseph and Sara for church. Mary noticed as Joseph walked into the church that he seemed to be even more alive than before, almost as if he had an aura while he was there. The topic of the service was the Song of Solomon, chapter 8:6-7;

"Place me like a seal over your heart, like a seal on your arm; for love is as strong as death, its jealousy as unyielding as the grave. It burns like a blazing fire, like a mighty flame. Many waters cannot quench love; rivers cannot wash it away. If one were to give all the wealth of his house for love, it would be utterly scorned."

Joseph placed his arm around Mary as the pastor said these words. He knew that God had something special in store for him and he desired greatly to learn of His intent. As Mary felt his arm around her, she felt aglow as the pastor read on from Song of Solomon 4:7, 9-10;

"All beautiful you are my darling; There is no flaw in you...You have stolen my heart, my sister, my bride, you have stolen my heart with one glance of your eyes, with one jewel of your necklace. How delightful is your love, my sister, my bride! How much more pleasing is your love than wine, and the fragrance of your perfume than any spice!"

Mary knew that the Song of Solomon was a love story and sonnet but never before had the words had more impact or meaning. She placed her left hand gently on his knee, feeling almost as if to acknowledge how safe and protected she felt. After the service, the four of them went out to a restaurant for dinner.

— ◆ —

Over the next several weeks, Joseph and Mary spent every day they could together. They often included the kids and for several evenings they went over to the beach for a picnic at Mt. Pleasant until late in the afternoon and to watch the sunset. Joseph and Mary continued to share their faith openly and what God was doing in each of their lives. Joseph had never understood what a truly godly helpmate might be before but he was beginning to understand. No matter what the subject, whether easy or difficult, Mary was there to talk to Joseph, to be his confidante and his encourager. As Mary encouraged Joseph, he felt more and more able to not only be the man God wanted him to be, but Joseph learned he was able to help guide Mary as well. Joseph felt empowered when he was with Mary and he tried to focus on being sensitive to her needs and to meet Mary just as she was.

All seemed right in Joseph and Mary's lives; they had met and they were growing together and closer, while all the while submitting to the authority of God. With God as the true center of their relationship, they were able to deal with old pains and hurts and to indeed find a safe place and to help comfort and invigorate each other. They indeed seemed to truly care and to be willing and able to help each other down the path of life.

Though everything was going well in Mary and Joseph's lives, the evil that lurked the city was still out there. Mary continued keeping tabs on and reporting to her safety buddy, and the fear that had gripped the city somehow seemed to be subsiding. Everyone hoped that the evil that had been in their city was gone and things might be returning to normal. However, the task force continued its around-the-clock investigation, cautioning the public that the killer had not yet been caught. Updates continued daily on the news but the police continued to remain tight-lipped about most of the details of the investigation. Over the years, the task force had learned only to release certain bits of information about the specific details of an investigation and had found that releasing too many of the details of an investigation actually hampered rather than furthering its resolution.

The mayor of Charleston, James White, was a respected businessman both before and after he was elected. Mayor White was able to use his contacts to assist him and to call all the cards he had due when he had decided to run for election. Charleston was a very close-knit community and when any significant events happened in the city that impacted them all, from the most influential and powerful to the average working man. Mayor White, like Mayor Giuliani in New York City during 9/11, personally spoke to the patrons of the city advising them to stay alert and to be on constant vigil. Mayor White's words assured the populace that everything that could be done was being done and that indeed ultimately they would prevail. As a general rule, the populace of the city was comforted by his words, but he knew deep in his heart that there was yet a hard road to go and a murderer to be caught.

Detective Teri Stone, a twenty-two-year veteran of the police force, who had spent the last twelve years working his way up to his present position that he had now held for three years, headed the task force. His organization, drive and intuitiveness had garnished him a reputation that extended well beyond his geographical area of responsibility. Detective Stone consistently saw what others did not see, which allowed him to direct others who worked with him, thus dramatically increasing the efficiency of his department and to carry out a more accurate investigation. Detective Stone always acted in a professional manner and never seemed to let circumstances or events get him ruffled. Just recently, his ability to intuitively study a crime scene had allowed him to assist the local DEA (Drug Enforcement Agency) break a cocaine ring that had operated in the city. By being able to trace money as it went through the system, he was able to determine the existence of a money-laundering scheme inside of what everyone had previously thought of as a busy profitable local business. Through his team's efforts and under his tutelage and guidance, they were able to trace the deposited monies that originally had been thought of to be revenue, back to their originator, who had been depositing illegal drug profits into the business account. The head of the scheme had been dealing his wares on the streets for years and no one had previously even suspected him of any wrongdoing at all. It was only by Detective Stone's intuitive and thorough work that he was able to see through what appeared to be an above-board business to ultimately seeing justice done. Detective Stone loved his work and the challenge that it offered. His zeal and his enthusiasm had drawn him even a little national acclaim for his excellent police work. Detective Stone worked well with many local city officials at all levels and even played golf occasionally with Mayor James White.

Detective Stone had taken the science of forensics and elevated it to almost an art form. He had studied forensics while in college, even taking advanced courses, and had continued on in his pursuit, even writing several articles that were published on the subject. Detective Stone knew that in order to best solve a crime you had to first understand the crime scene. He had learned that you could not allow anything to be missed, because you never knew what might have significant value later on in the investigation. Detective Stone became so adept at being able to document his crime scene so well that colleagues were able to pick up and run with the trail steps and documentation that he provided from the initial crime scene investigation.

By carefully approaching a crime scene and being careful not to destroy any evidence, Detective Stone was able to record and pick up the tell-tale traces that others did not see, tiny bits of evidence the perpetrators left behind. Detective Stone never assumed anything when at a crime scene, as even the simplest minute detail might provide the difference between capturing a perpetrator and bringing someone to face justice and having an unsolved crime. Detective Stone also worked closely with the medical examiner's office, whose forensic studies of their own coupled with medical histories, finger printing, blood samples, dental records, and by studying the body of the victim, made them able to determine the cause of death. This detailed and thorough analysis gave investigators clues as to how the victim died and if they were murdered at the original crime scene or somewhere else. Often he discovered perpetrators would commit a crime in one location and then try to hide the victim, and therefore the evidence, in another location. Often through detailed analysis of a crime scene and conversations with the medical examiner, covering everything from bruises, drag marks and blood flow, he was even able to determine how a body might have been transported and when.

DNA testing was also a huge breakthrough for forensics and their related investigations. By studying an individual's region of the country and their specific profile data, you can determine a DNA fingerprint, which has the ability to assure that the likelihood of a positive match was well above the court's standard of proving a case beyond a reasonable doubt. Also, available to Detective Stone was the National DNA Databank. This databank stores data that can be used to help develop additional investigative leads from which might be added to analysis and capture of biological evidence at the crime scene to more thoroughly develop a profile and to fine tune their investigative efforts.

Already Detective Stone, through analysis of all four murders, was beginning to put together a profile by which police would be able to use the physical traits, characteristics, and personal traits of a perpetrator. Absent a direct positive lead to a specific person or an event that might lead to same, Detective Stone had learned that this narrowing of the probable characteristics of a perpetrator could dramatically help narrowly focus their investigative efforts and squarely put them well down the proper path to solving a crime as quickly and efficiently as possible.

Detective Stone's innate ability to combine all of his technical skill, his ability to never assume anything unless he was able to determine something with absolute certainty, and his intuition consistently helped to bring him and his team to task on even the hardest cases. Before he had taken over the investigation, which was now deemed to certainly be to find a serial killer, there did not seem to be any correlation between the victims, but now he had a hunch that still needed some analysis and exploration to finely determine its direction.

Chapter 4

JOSEPH WAS HAVING a rather trying day at the office. As Charleston's harbormaster he managed the waters just outside the harbor in the Atlantic Ocean, the harbor itself, and the three rivers that combined together to form the harbor. Often having to prioritize and coordinate the key activities of the harbor, including commercial, recreational, and military, resulted in a very trying and tedious day. Often these competing needs had diametrically opposed results and impacts and it was his job to optimize the use of the harbor as harmoniously as possible to the advantage of all. The whole of his domain included managing fresh- and salt-water resources, tributaries, tidal creeks, dunes and estuaries; it was more than enough for any one man to manage.

Today's work in particular seemed even a little more challenging for Joseph than others. It seems as if a small twenty-five-foot pleasure craft was taking water and its engine had stalled. Normally this would not have been that great an issue, but this particular pleasure craft had stalled in the only true deep channel in the harbor that was used by the large cargo commercial ships. As of yet, the stalled craft had not been able to be towed out of the channel so as to free the operation zone that the larger ships used within the harbor. It often seemed to Joseph that others on his staff could have handled things like this, but invariably the responsibility—and therefore, usually, the frustration—fell to him. Joseph found just enough time and stopped long enough to pray and ask God to give him the strength to do all that he should and could do and to do it in a way that edifies Him. This seemed unusually hard today as the captains of the large commercial vessels seemed to be unnecessarily impatient and became even more so as the day unfolded.

Today reminded Joseph of an incident that occurred some six months ago that resulted in a ship's grounding. Often in the rivers, changing currents caused silt shifts and they were made even worse from natural runoff and from real estate development. This was especially a problem where the three rivers converged, met and formed the inner part of the harbor, which results in the need to have to continually dredge the channel to keep it open. It seemed as if that day the ship had grounded as a result of the moving silt causing an otherwise passable area to become impassable. Joseph remembered that this impacted traffic in the harbor for two full days as dredging and towing had to be coordinated to free the grounded ship. Joseph felt that he almost lost his wits those two days as he tried to return the harbor to a normal traffic flow when everything seemed to conspire against him.

As he tried to respond as best he could to the problems of the day, he caught himself thinking of Mary and how she might be doing. Joseph finally got a little breathing room from the pressure of the day and was able to allow himself the luxury of slowing down a bit and picked up the phone to call her. He had learned that Mary was seldom in her office so he called her on her cell phone.

Mary was out on the road and in the field that day showing property to a prospective client who was in from out of town. She had a pleasant day although it had proved to not be entirely productive. She had spent the better part of a day with a couple whose husband was being transferred with his work, to Charleston. As Mary contemplated the events of the day, the couple seemed unable to gain any common ground in what type of house or lot they were looking for. Mary imagined the couple was going to have to do a lot of talking that evening about what exactly they might be looking for. To date, Mary had focused her business around gaining and selling listings and was not a captive agent to any one subdivision. She enjoyed the diversity this offered but she had always wanted to work exclusively in one subdivision and had recently received a very enticing offer to do so. The developer that managed the property offered her the position because she had heard of her reputation for excellence and had sought her out to be the lead agent at the property managing a staff of six. The new subdivision was a very exclusive property and backed up along the marsh on the ocean side of Mt. Pleasant. The subdivision was to have more than six hundred homes and, of course, very tight architectural controls. Mary liked that she would be able to be instrumental with how the property would be finished out and that she would be able to leave her mark of the ultimate detailing and overall look of the community. She was contemplating the offer in her mind, as she was driving back to her office to finish up some loose ends.

When Mary's phone rang, she immediately saw on her caller ID that it was Joseph's office and she picked up the call on the first ring. Joseph asked about her day and brought her up to speed on his. He always enjoyed the moments that they were able to touch base during the day and to catch up with each other a bit. Although Mary was a little down about the day, Joseph was always able to sense that she was excited about receiving his call and he enjoyed her mostly positive and upbeat demeanor. The little calls to Mary during the day gave Joseph comfort that she was safe and that all was well.

Mary caught herself getting lost in the conversation, so much so that she missed her normal turnoff and had to circle back around to go down Meeting Street toward her office. Mary generally had a keen sense of what was going on around her but today, apparently lost in her conversation with Joseph, she failed to notice that for the last three to four miles, another vehicle had been trailing her. Through all the missed turns and corrections, Mary was being shadowed. As she turned off into her office parking lot and was winding her call up with Joseph, the vehicle that had been following her drove on by and kept going undetected. As Joseph and Mary hung up from their call and said their normal good-byes, she walked into her office to finish up the day.

As Joseph placed the phone back into its cradle, he smiled. He felt himself being drawn deeper if they were to...

Just then, Joseph's radio squawked again and one of the commercial ships' captain was seeking clearance on entering the harbor. Though his mind never wandered far from thinking about Mary, he was once again deeply immersed in the work of the day.

Detective Stone was just starting his day when he got a call from the sergeant down at police headquarters. Another real estate agent had turned up missing. Detective Stone's heart immediately sank. It was not his nature to get emotionally involved, but there was something about the loss of a life, and how many women had already been killed weighed heavily on him. Detective Stone intellectually knew he was not to blame, but he took the disappearance of this new agent personally. He had always prided himself on his work and even excelled at it, but that was no consolation to him upon hearing the news that another life was at stake. More than any other case he had been involved in, none had moved nor motivated him like this one had. Knowing that all of these women had many of their best years ahead of them and then all of that stopped cold because of a serial killer on the loose.

Detective Stone drove immediately to the agency where the missing agent had worked to find the office in emotional turmoil. Although he had expected it, seeing all those people so upset who obviously knew and cared for the missing agent so much, grieved Detective Stone deeply. He always had a way with calming people down, especially if he were able to talk to them one on one, but in a group setting he had always found it difficult to calm everyone down. Detective Stone had learned through experience that when people were more calm than not that generally people gave better, more focused, and more detailed information than when they were emotionally charged. The missing agent was Vicki Green and she was thirty-two years old and had not been seen or heard from since two o'clock yesterday afternoon. Detective Stone learned that she was married and had two children. He thought of what her children and husband might be dealing with at this very moment. He prayed that the missing agent, Ms. Green, would show up alive somewhere and that all would not be as he grimly feared. Detective Stone had never personally lost someone who was near and dear to him, unlike so many people that he had to talk to.

When Mary heard the news, she quickly called Joseph and asked if he had heard about the new missing agent. Joseph, as always, was glad to get her call but when she shared what she had heard he found the news very disturbing indeed. Mary shared that the missing agent was not from her agency but that of a competitor. Mary knew several people that worked at the agency and had previously even met the missing agent and her husband, Bill.

Joseph suggested that they pray together so he led, "Dear Lord, We know that your ways are not our ways and that we are not supposed to know the meanings of all the events that occur in our lives. God, our hearts are open and crying out, help us, Lord, to know the will that you have for our lives. If it be your will, please bring Vicki back to her husband, Bill, and their two children. We are afraid for her safety and we know that you know where she is and whether she is okay. God, please place a hedge of protection around Vicki and protect her family. Please take care of my loved ones and know that we are entrusting you for their care. In Jesus' name, we pray. Amen."

Mary felt better after their prayers together but she could still fell her heart racing and the rapidness of her pulse. She paused and tried to breathe deeply several times in order to try and calm herself down. For the first time since the first disappearance and murder, she was afraid, not only for the missing agent, Vicki, and her family, but for herself. Joseph could sense her anxiety and said he'd be over that night for dinner so that they could spend the evening together. Although they wound up having a pleasant enough evening together, there was an air of tension because of the anxiety and fear that hung in the air.

Joseph stayed until the late evening news aired. There were no further updates on the whereabouts of the missing agent. The task force and the police force interrogated everyone they could find or think of that might have any clues at all. The task force had also added additional manpower to intensify the search effort and to hopefully further the investigation. County, city, and state police were now working along with federal agencies to pool together all their resources and information in an effort to solve the crimes and to thereby quell the fear that filled the city. Mary and Joseph watched in silence, as they feared the worst while silently praying that the madness might soon end.

Detective Stone was still down at headquarters at 12:00 a.m. and planned to work on until much later into the evening. Although many avenues were being explored, none appeared to bring any conclusive direction for the task force to really sink its teeth into. He knew that often, hundreds and even thousands of ideas and leads had to be "worked through" in order to solve a case, but it offered him no solace, especially not with so much at stake. Detective Stone intellectually knew that he was doing everything he could, but he could not help but hope that the next thing they looked at might prove to be the piece of the puzzle that helped them solve the case. Search teams throughout a twenty-mile radius were doing door-to-door canvassing and the missing agent's picture was being splashed nonstop on the news in an ever-widening search to locate her. Roadblocks were also being formed on several of the key thoroughfares in an effort to help find her as soon as possible. Detective Stone had learned through experience that every hour that went by it became more probable that she would never be discovered alive. He was doing everything he could and more in an effort to safely conclude the successful search for Vicki Green, but he knew time was against him. He worked on until 3:00 a.m. and then drove home for three hours of sleep and was back in the office the next morning by 7:00 a.m. Worn, tired and frazzled, Detective Stone diligently set about anew to look for that missing piece of information that might help him get that one strategic lead and to allow him to put it all together and get this case solved.

Mary spoke to Joseph that evening and she felt a little more relaxed but there was still a tension in her heart that she just could not calm. Joseph tried to assure her that he would be there in a moment's notice but nothing seemed to take the fright away from her. Her parents had called earlier in the evening and again asked if she and David might come and stay with them for a while. Mary replied that she felt like it would be better for David if they stayed at their home so as to keep things as routine as possible. David had overheard the news and Mary did the best she could to comfort him and assuage his fears. After a few extra stories at bedtime, David finally drifted off to sleep.

Mary went to bed a little later and lay there for what seemed forever wide awake. After watching a little television, the late news came on and there was no new information on the missing agent. Mary quickly turned off the set and turned on the bedside lamp. She sat there in silence thinking about the events of the day. She had a tough time concentrating all evening. Although she tried to help David with his homework and focus on spending some quality time with him, she just was not able to keep her mind from worrying about the missing agent, Vicki Green, and her family. She hoped against hope that she would be found unscathed but she feared greatly that she would not be found alive.

As she lay there, she began to pray, "Dear Lord, I know that you teach us not to worry about tomorrow and that tomorrow will worry about itself, but you know that I am afraid. I am scared for my life, my son, and my new relationship with Joseph. God, please keep my loved ones safe, hold them in your hand and let them feel your love. God, I know that there is no hiding from your truth and that you see into the deepest part of my heart. There is no turning nor hiding from your truth. Search me, oh Lord, please forgive me for all my sins and forgive all my transgressions. Give me the strength to live for you and to be the salt and light that you would have me be in this world. Please guide my hand and still my heart. In Jesus' name, I pray, Amen."

Mary felt more relieved after her prayer but still was unable to drift off. As she lay there, she thought about all the events in her life, meeting Joseph, and how proud she was of David. She could not sleep for what seemed like an eternity. Midnight passed and then she heard the clock strike 1:00 and then later, 2:00 a.m. Just after she heard the clock strike two, she said a brief prayer and drifted off to sleep.

Joseph's night was not much better. Although it was nice to have Yana, his nanny, to help with Sara, it never seemed to be of much comfort. Although he felt that Yana helped out a lot, especially with all those girl things that Sara seemed to be getting into, it never seemed to fulfill the thing that was missing in both his and Sara's life. Sara was beginning to become quite a young lady and he never seemed to be able to address all the womanly issues that she was beginning to have. Yana was as helpful as anyone could be and was really a good caregiver for Sara, but she was not someone to whom Sara could count on to be there through thick and thin. Sara knew that Yana would be going home soon, and this, as expected, had caused her to be a little more uncertain than normal.

Sara was really starting to bond with both Mary and David. Joseph felt that their relationship was God-ordained, but he did not want to move too fast nor put any undue pressure on the relationship, especially now with a serial killer on the loose. Joseph was worried for Mary's safety and he knew that Mary was afraid for her own self as well. Joseph wanted to be there to care for Mary twenty-four hours a day, but he knew that at this time that was just not possible. Joseph agreed with Mary's parents, who thought it best for Mary and David to come and to stay with them, but Mary would not have anything to do with it. Joseph did everything he could to get her to go, but she insisted on staying at home and keeping things as normal as possible. But with a killer on the loose, things were anything but routine.

Joseph thought of the trying events that had occurred at work that day and that his day would be more of the same tomorrow. But he could not take his mind off Mary. There were so many things that he adored about her. He felt that her personality was just so cute, her charm, her wit, her smile, and her belief in God moved him. Joseph had never felt this way about his deceased wife and had come to believe, until now, that it was not possible to both love someone so completely and to be so completely loved in return. Joseph had begun to think of what he and Mary would be like if they were to unite as one in marriage. He felt that it would be a marriage of biblical proportions and that they would be stronger as one for the Kingdom than they would ever be separately. Joseph had not told Mary that he loved her, as he wanted to be absolutely sure that these feelings were God-ordained and true. Joseph had never believed that marriage should be based on love as its primary foothold as love was a feeling and because he knew that feelings come and go. Joseph relied heavily on the true covenant belief of marriage; as being the true one thing that held relationships fast. Joseph knew that one's word and then their true marital covenant with God were the only way that a marriage might truly work. Joseph knew that failure could not be an option for him if he were to marry again and that he wanted God's best for his life.

That night Joseph cried out to God, "Father, Abba, the Alpha and Omega, show me the way that I should go. Put Mary in your protective care and let her know how deeply she is cared for by you and by me. Please order and guide her steps and keep her safe in your love. You know the past, the present, and the future. Guide us in the way that we should go and order my steps so that they honor you."

Joseph slept restlessly that night, never really sleeping for more than an hour or so. Each time he awoke, he prayed to God for Mary's care, for Him to love and protect her and that God would bring them closer to each other and closer together with Him.

The next two days rain fell in buckets. It seemed as if the rain would never stop. The marsh area and some of the lowlands became so saturated that the water almost seemed to rise up from the ground. Local tidal creeks, ponds and low areas became standing pools of water. Joseph had never remembered it raining this hard before. Visibility in the harbor was so limited that ships had to rely exclusively on their radars, sonars and depth-finding equipment in order to navigate. Without the advantage of eyesight, ships and traffic in the harbor slowed almost to a crawl. Joseph settled in for what he knew was going to be a long day at the office. It seemed to him as if all week he had gone from one crisis to another, mainly because he had. He had always responded well to this type of intense pressure and that had greatly contributed to his success in the Navy and present position. However, the extra pressure worrying about Mary's safety weighed heavily on him and was beginning to take its emotional toll. Things at work were tough enough but his main concern and focus were the safety and well-being of Mary and David.

With the pressures of the missing agent continuing to mount, Detective Stone was diligently working on the case. The continued driving rain greatly limited their ability to function well outdoors and had slowed down their investigation and search efforts dramatically. It seemed as if everything was going against him and as if he were making no progress at all. He knew that with every unsuccessful effort, he was excluding one more thing, thus narrowing the parameters of his search even further, and thereby bringing him one step closer to success. Although intellectually he knew this to be true, Vicki Green had still not been found. Detective Stone knew better but he felt that he was almost going backwards rather than forwards in the investigation. He was beginning to feel like the task force team was unraveling a bit and he was feeling pressure from Mayor White and the press. Neither the papers nor Mayor White were actually directing any of the anxiety and angst on him, and each of them were actually doing everything they could to assist him in his efforts. However, because of his strong desire to excel and his own personal pain from not having solved the crime yet, he was indeed starting to feel the heat of the investigation. Having a killer on the loose and an agent missing did nothing but further his own personal frustration. He had always been his own worst critic and now with so much at stake, he felt the pressure building.

Because of the driving rain, every effort that the task force tried to undertake was unduly slowed. Outside forensic analysis and investigation of any type were not only hampered but also virtually stopped as the pounding rain destroyed any traces of outside evidence. All of the task force cars were accordingly having trouble with visibility, street flooding, and of course, just getting in and out of the car was miserable. Detective Stone hoped that the rain would soon stop so he could resume perhaps some portion of normalcy in the investigation.

Mary's days continued to wear on but they did not seem to be getting any better. Over the two days of rain she had two separate people in from out of town looking at property. One of the customers was desirous of moving to Charleston, as they were approaching retirement, while the other couple was looking for a vacation home, preferably a town home so as to keep their maintenance requirements to a minimum. Although the people Mary was working with were pleasant enough, the consistency and volume of the rain made it difficult not only to focus but also to enjoy any part of her day. Also, with what was now believed to be a confirmed serial killer on the loose, the prospective newcomers to the area were concerned about their own safety, if indeed they were to move there.

Mary tried to placate their concerns albeit weakly, as she indeed herself was scared. Though she knew God was in control, she felt an uneasiness deep down in the pit of her stomach. Try though she might, she was afraid, almost to the point of being debilitated.

Joseph called Mary several times during the day in order to check on her, how her day was going and to ensure that she was safe. Although Joseph knew Mary had a safety buddy there at work, he felt compelled to check in on her as well. Their talking comforted each of them for a brief moment but it seemed as if the angst Joseph felt for Mary's safety originally, returned almost as soon as they ended their call. Mary, as well, was briefly comforted but her fears arose and returned when they completed their call.

The news continued to blanket the airwaves with both a physical description and a picture of the missing agent, Vicki Green, and her last known whereabouts. The normally docile city of Charleston was still being rocketed and was buzzing about there being a killer in their midst and as to when he might be caught. The story was beginning to pick up consistent national exposure, which was soon to negatively impact the local economy, as tourism was one of the leading industries that brought millions upon millions into the area. Hotels, rental cars, air travel, and general tourist spots were already experiencing a downturn as people either cancelled their reservations completely or turned to now more serene and safe locations to visit.

While Mayor White was sensitive to this issue, his main concern was the populace that lived in Charleston proper. He was now in his third term of office and most everyone generally loved him as he truly cared about the people that he served and worked for. Mayor White was not afraid to make tough choices that everyone else seemed to shy away from, but he did it with such class and sensitivity that everyone involved thought Mayor White had their best interests at heart and in mind. During the investigation's tenure, Mayor White consistently called the task force, asking Detective Stone if he might offer any help of any type that he might be able to provide. He often stopped by personally at the task force's office to show that he was one hundred percent behind their efforts and to personally lend any assistance that he might be able to give. Even the people that worked directly for Mayor White respected and admired both his tenacity and fairness. He was a man's man, yet with a very open and giving heart.

After two days of hard rain, it stopped just as suddenly as it had started, the skies parted and the sun shone brightly. It was late Friday afternoon and some of the townspeople and citizenry were already beginning to go home from work for the day to start their weekend. Toward dusk the sun set with a beautiful array of oranges and reds and a few white willowy clouds. It seemed as if the whole town stopped for a moment to enjoy God's show, but as soon as the sun went down, it seemed that most of Charleston's citizenry went in for the evening for protection. Also because of reduced tourism, the normally busy restaurants and tourist spots were much less crowded than usual.

Joseph and Mary opted for a quiet evening spent at Mary's having dinner with the kids. Joseph picked up a few things on the way over from the grocery and Mary prepared something simple for dinner. Especially with the kids around, Joseph and Mary talked little, if any, of the recent news and updates of the murders and the missing agent, but each of them knew that it was there and it was hanging heavy on their minds.

Life, it seemed, was both the best that it could be and yet the worst it might be. Although Joseph and Mary felt it was God leading them down the path to be together as one, both felt disappointment about how they had failed others and themselves in their past and they had never let go of the demons and doubts in their lives that continued to haunt them. They each desired to be free and to live in the love of Jesus, but the chains of their past hung heavy on their hearts. They knew God had a plan for each of their lives and that He was ultimately in total control, but they each had never truly enjoyed the freedom that comes in living totally free and in the love of Christ. Joseph and Mary, each in their own way, prayed to God that evening of the fears and anxieties that hung heavy on their heart, asking that He become the true center of their lives and to separate themselves from the fears within and to live solely in the peace and joy of Jesus.

Chapter 5

Tides in the harbor and tidal creeks were unusually high due to the full moon and the heavy rains. Detective Stone's task force was back in full swing looking at the highways and byways for the missing real estate agent, Vicki Green. As of yet nothing had turned up, not a clue. Detective Stone was at his wits' end but he knew to stay true to task and to keep following his instincts and doing the things that he knew always worked. He was following every available lead and working diligently to pursue locating the missing agent and to bring her safely home before it was too late. As the last agent had been found in the marsh, he had personally contacted the Coast Guard and the Charleston harbormaster, Joseph King, to be on the lookout. This put Joseph a little more at ease because he knew Detective Stone was doing everything that possibly could be done, but also it brought Joseph's fears even closer to home, as it served to remind him how real all of this was. Joseph had never met Detective Stone but through his recent efforts and the news coverage, he was sure that the best man was on the job and that everything that could be done was being done.

After discussing the investigation with Detective Stone, Joseph set about to see what steps he might be able to implement to educate his people how they could help. Joseph arranged for extra patrols of the harbor and the Ashley, Cooper and Wands rivers in an ever-widening search. He felt better knowing that he was now actively contributing to helping stop the fear that gripped the city and perhaps somehow contribute to the ultimate solution of the crime. Joseph intellectually knew that his contribution would probably be ever so slight and that no one piece of evidence would catch the killer, but he hoped that somehow something he did would make a difference.

Mary was trying to go about her day, but her mind was never far from her fears that now seemed to grip her most every moment. She still wanted to stay at home and had so far resisted her parents' wishes for her and David to come and stay with them. She received a call late in the day from the Charleston Historical and Preservation Society about a new home that had come into their purview as a potential home that they might be able to assist in its preservation and restoration. It was exciting to her to think of arranging and assisting in having another fund-raiser and taking all the necessary steps and procedures to see if the proposed home might qualify. Mary hoped that this would be a diversion from what else was going on in her world and to help alleviate the anxiety that she now constantly felt.

The fund-raisers themselves initially garnished thirty to forty percent of the total monies needed for a restoration project. Most of the other funds were raised through private funding and endowments as the project was underway. All of the monies were raised to finance almost all of a project in the initial fund-raiser, leaving the rest to be paid out of the Historical and Preservation Society's general fund. The actual owner of the residence furnished upfront or had available all of the monies to cover the hard cost such as the brick, mortar, and lumber, with the fund-raising monies being used for all of the soft costs and planning. Usually these soft costs could be approximately thirty to forty-five percent of the hard costs of a project, which required the committee to raise tens of thousands of dollars for each project alone.

Tim Tuttle was a member of the Preservation and Historical Committee, and it was he that discovered the home that needed restoration. He learned of it by examining the interesting past of a residence along Meeting Street while looking through the historical archives at City Hall. The home was a few blocks away from the Market area in the Old Historic District of Charleston. The Market area of Charleston is where local artist merchants and craftsmen exhibited their wares. The area where the residence was located was dotted with restaurants, specialty stores and professional offices, which made the find a little more unusual than normal, if for no other reason than solely its location.

It was determined that the home itself was inside the inner city walls, which were a brick wall surrounding what used to be the old city of Charleston in the late 1800s. As the population grew, miscellaneous debris and fill was utilized to convert the otherwise unusable space into areas that could be used to adequately lay a foundation on which a home or a building might be set. It was in this way that the old city of Charleston grew into the area as it is known today. The present historic district was now several blocks to over a half mile beyond the city's original walls. In fact, the whole of the market area of old used to be a tidal creek that ebbed and flowed with the tide. Over the years, fill and debris piled over and over again, such that it became filled and therefore, suitable for building.

From preliminary examination of historical records and data, it appeared as if the residence that was now under consideration for restoration was built before the Civil War and was used by both the North and South as a headquarters while each of the respective armies were quartered there. Tim Tuttle was an active student of the Civil War, and he went on to read about the actual battles and troop movements that had occurred there. He was fascinated as he read and thought that the home might be an ideal candidate for the Historical and Preservation Society to take on as a project. It was indeed he that first contacted the Historical and Preservation Society about the home, and then he had made the call to Mary to discuss its restoration.

Tim, over the years, had become quite fascinated with lighthouses and their history. As such, he had learned to really appreciate lighthouses' contribution to the history of this country and what part they had played in its development. Although most of the lighthouses that have been preserved to the current day were not in operation, Tim knew that in the past lighthouses had played a significant historical and strategic role in both commerce and in military issues. Lighthouses were mainly used as guides for direction and distance and to warn ships of navigational hazards. Most of the structures were built over a hundred years ago and were useful both in peace and wartime. During the Civil War, the lighthouses were used to aid the Southern blockade runners whose goal it was to keep the shipping lanes open, and therefore, the war supplies and food to the South so that they might continue their war effort.

Tim took his love of history of lighthouses and began to expand it to have a growing fondness with all types of restoration and the furtherance of history and the ecology for future generations. It was in this zeal that be became a member of the Charleston Historical and Preservation Society, and through some incidental research he was doing, he had discovered the house that might be a candidate for the society's consideration and restoration.

Tim was widowed and had two children in college. In prior years, he had worked full-time at the college as a history professor. He loved his job and often encouraged others so much that they became as zealous about history and his passions as he was. Although Tim knew progress was certain, he believed that the price that he had to pay for such should never be at the expense of destroying the environment. Tim loved history and all that it had taught him and he did his best to preserve it for future generations. Although he had been widowed for approximately eight years, he still wore his wedding ring and frequently talked fondly of his wife. She had passed away slowly before his eyes, withering away as leukemia ate at her from the inside out. He was always by her side, especially in those last weeks. Although the doctors did everything they could to save her, in the end, there was nothing that could be done, save making her comfortable.

Tim still greatly missed his wife and believed and waited for that one day they would be reunited. He longed for the day that he might see her again. Tim came from a family of means and as a result did not even have to work. He chose to work and enjoyed having a career and the interaction that he had as a professor with his students prior to his wife's death, but since, he just could not make sense out of working anymore. Tim's world had all seemed to cave in on him the last eight years and his saving grace appeared to be the time he personally spent studying history.

The *Charleston Sentinel* ran front-page articles with Vicki Green's picture along with a complete physical description. Every lead that came in was closely evaluated and investigated in an effort to locate her alive and as soon as possible. Detective Stone was ensuring the task force be staffed around the clock in an effort to bring the case to a swift, positive and resolute closure. He no longer left the office even for a few hours to go home to rest but now dozed only a few hours each evening on a couch that was in his office. He and his staff were all exhausted but they continued to press on. Detective Stone and his team were the best at what they did and they refused to let the nonstop work or long hours deter them from succeeding. He believed that in order to unravel a mystery or solve a case that you had to work exponentially harder than those who perpetrated the crime in order to solve it, and he was determined to do so. Detective Stone knew each and every case usually hinged on just a small and what often seemed trivial shred of evidence that everyone else had either overlooked or considered unimportant. He was determined to find that little missing piece he almost always, in all his prior cases, found in order to restore tranquility to the fine city of Charleston that he knew and respected so well.

Detective Stone knew that if he stayed on course and on task that eventually almost every criminal was or would be caught. There was almost always one slipup, albeit ever so slight, that helped nab even the most professional criminal. Sometimes it boiled down to a tiny shred of material, a hair follicle, a piece of chipped paint, a reticent witness, or perhaps something even more insignificant. Science as well as the technology of today was able to help solve cases by assisting in moving a case beyond a reasonable doubt that before might only be hypothetical. DNA and fiber testing were very reliable and could be used to build such evidence that was almost insurmountable to a defendant. Detective Stone loved his work but it was times such as these that made him age beyond his true physical years.

Forensics had recently discovered a fiber not belonging to the last victim that was on her person when the body was discovered. It had taken some time to determine that it was a certain fiber type and color that wasn't as common as others. Although this initially excited Detective Stone, he was soon to learn that ten thousand shirts using this fabric had been sold in the Southeast alone. Though this wound up being ultimately a disappointment, he determined to work even harder on the details and specifics in order to solve the case.

Joseph and Mary decided to spend most of the weekend together and make it as quiet a weekend as possible. They spent Saturday out on Joseph's boat with the kids. They left late Saturday morning from the local marina where Joseph kept his boat stored and spent the day out at sea with the kids. They drove out to catch the Gulf Stream and did some bottom fishing, catching several good-sized fish that they were going to clean and have for dinner. Seas were mild to moderate that day with the skies being partly cloudy. It was late in the summer now and the days were starting to get shorter. They came home tired about six that evening and grilled the fish at Joseph's home. They talked and played with the kids until late that evening and then Joseph and Sara drove Mary and David home. While on the way home, they made plans to meet for church on Sunday.

At church that Sunday the sermon was on serving on short-term mission trips. Joseph had always wanted to go on one but had always wanted to go with someone special to make the experience even more deepening both between the person he went with and their relationship with God. After the service, they went by the sign-up board and talked to the leaders who were there to discuss each trip and specifically what their goals were. Joseph and Mary were excited about the prospect of going and each agreed to pray about it. The more they talked and prayed about it, the more excited each of them became. The mission trip they selected was to be an excursion to Jamaica and was a family trip with the children going to serve together with the adults. Although the trip was many months away, they both believed they would be a family themselves at some point soon and they eagerly signed up agreeing to Sara and David. For Joseph, he mused to himself this was just one more example of what he certainly felt was to be a permanent relationship and marriage.

Several weeks passed and no breakthroughs were made in the case, but still Vicki Green had not been found. Her family, as well as the task force, feared the worst but pressed on hoping their worst fears were to be unfounded. Try as they might, Vicki's family tried to hold fast to the notion that she was alive. But as every day passed, their fears became more and more real and they felt that they might not ever see her again. Vicki's children especially were having a tough time and each night cried themselves to sleep. Vicki's husband tried to put on a good front mainly for the children, but as day after day lapsed, he struggled more and more. On several occasions, he had himself gone out to search but each time, it had been to no avail.

Mary began trying to focus her mind and her efforts on the fundraiser for the new home Tim Tuttle had located. The Historical and Preservation Society formally voted and unanimously decided and agreed to approve going forward with the process of restoring the Meeting Street residence. Efforts were now starting and would soon be in full swing to solicit support and funds for the project. Mary had learned that if she focused on bringing the key political, business and press support to a project, that the funding would follow suit and would almost take care of itself. As a project would near its zenith, Mary would find herself almost totally immersed in it. She had learned that during those times, her own business briefly suffered but she knew that she would more than make up for it with the additional clients and new business relationships she would obtain from all the new contacts she would make during a project's implementation and completion.

One of the things that had made Charleston such a Mecca for history was first and foremost, the history that occurred there. Secondly, it was the Charleston Historical and Preservation Society's attention to detail, preserving its history for future generations. For each project the society embraced as their own, they were very careful and meticulous to assure that all the history about a home or building that could be discovered was also authenticated. The information was studied and assimilated so as to present the most accurate picture of the history of a home. To do this, the society studied county, city and state archives, newspaper articles and stories, letters from that era that had been preserved over the years. Although technology had made it possible to search faster than ever before, it had not made the work any less tedious or difficult to ensure that a property's true history was correctly recorded and its detail documented. During this time of the study, Mary often felt like a detective herself in studying the puzzle that was initially presented her when the society first learned of a home. Although she did not do most of the fact gathering, she was responsible for pulling it all together and then telling the story in a way that flowed and captured the true essence of the history and the folklore of a structure. Over the years, the historical accounts of different residences and business alike had been intricately woven into the fabric of what the Charleston community had been and still was and contributed and what many considered established the primary framework of the city's lore. Charleston's prominence in the development of the United States was widely known and well respected because of her attention to documenting and preserving and telling the history of her story well.

During this fact-finding time, Mary would greatly interact with the detailed researchers to strive to piece together and to make sense out of what sometimes appeared to be random facts about a property. Though most times Mary was able to offer some initial insight to more directly attune researchers' efforts, periodically she was herself baffled about how the events of a particular property unfolded. During the investigative period, she periodically would travel to the property to personally inspect and document certain findings. These trips were also very useful in order to determine, as specifically as possible, the way the home was constructed initially. Often these trips would involve consultations with the present as well as past homeowners in order to truly understand all the changes a property had gone through. These conversations alone were often key research points to helping determine events and histories of a property that to date had previously not yet been known. Once she had personally discovered about an owner who had owned a property for twenty years in the mid-1800s, who was a key member of the South Carolina legislature when it seceded from the Union right after Abraham Lincoln's election and just before the start of the Civil War. In fact, its owner had even been present when the initial shots of the war were fired by the Confederate forces firing cannons on the Union Army that was then holding and occupying Fort Sumter.

Also during these trips to a property Mary would learn details about a structure by visiting it and studying the physical structure of a property itself. By chipping away very minute chips of paint layers, it was often possible to determine a home's original colors and building materials so that these could be utilized again when the property was restored to its original luster. Often as well, the original flooring and woodworking could be salvaged and restored by careful review and analysis. Often the substructure and foundations for the structures dry rotted, usually due to age. By providing and reconstructing a solid foundation, the original materials could then be placed in their original position and their original fit, finish, and charm restored.

Usually a residence of this age would have layers upon layers of roofing laid one on top of the other. During the restoration process, these would all be removed so that a home's original roofing could be discovered and then the process could begin of reinforcing, as needed, the actual roof structure itself and then subsequently utilizing the original roofing. The ultimate goal of the restoration process was to create essentially a brand-new home which was an exact match of the original structure and hence essentially a historical reproduction. The society had learned that by utilizing the original materials, supplies, and colors the majestic feel of the original home came to life. The deep hues and the woodwork of these restored homes recreated the magic that created the elegance of the Charleston mystique. Mary loved her work and the society and how her efforts directly impacted the charm of the city. Mary's work made her feel like a Michelangelo, so to speak, as she reformed these homes to their original majesty.

Joseph's work continued to wear heavily on him. No matter what issue came up, there seemed to be another one right behind it, ready to take its place. Joseph had just gotten things back to what seemed to be more normal workflow when one of the medium-sized oil tankers had a loading accident. Although this was a relatively small oil spill, especially when compared to accidents like those of the super oil tankers when they grounded themselves, it was no less serious in the need to contain it and to clean up any damages that might have been caused.

The Environmental Protection Agency immediately scrambled and had a cleanup crew on site within twenty-four hours. Oil, being lighter than water, floated on top of the water, making it easier to locate, fortunately for the cleanup crews and unfortunately for every other form of aquatic and natural wildlife. When the ship was offloading commercial-grade oil, one of the flow valves had blown spilling almost one hundred thousand gallons in the Cooper River before they could even get the preventor activated. The spill quickly floated out toward the whole Charleston Harbor. With the flow of the Cooper River into the Charleston Harbor and with the downstream merging of the Ashley and the Wando rivers, the oil had dispersed over a widespread area within a very short amount of time. Also, the rising and the falling of the tide assisted in making the problem even worse, causing the deep black oil to cover the shoreline.

Priority was given to all cleanup efforts and once again the Charleston Harbor maritime traffic was slowed almost to a standstill. Intensive cleanup efforts of the oil, of what could be easily siphoned off the top of the water, were done for several days while the beach and riverside cleanup would be much more tedious and would go on for several weeks.

Of course, there was all the negative press that came with any such spill, none of which directly affected Joseph but all of which did nothing to clean the oil from Charleston's waters any faster. The news coverage of the spill along with the past coverage of the serial killings had an immediate negative impact on tourism. Thousands of people who had already planned vacations to the area called and cancelled their reservations and trips to Charleston proper. Many of these tourists were predominantly coming just for the sun and the beach but a large majority of the tourists were also coming just to visit the historical aspects of the city were also cancelling their trips. The one-two punch of the double negatives of the killings and the spill greatly impaired hotel occupancy rates, and patrons at normally heavily attended restaurants were almost non-existent.

The Environmental Protection Agency's cleanup rapid response team was making good progress in even cleaning up the spill in the first forty-eight hours. By utilizing computer modeling, they were able to determine the locations to place their skimmers in order that they might be the most efficient. The skimmers were being run twenty-four hours a day in order to try to contain and then clean up the oil spill as soon as possible. The skimmers were simply run back and forth over the area of the oil slick and the oil was simply skimmed from the surface. Especially in a relatively well-defined spill, skimming was the most widely utilized and most effective process of removing the oil from a spill area. Cleanup of the shore and beach areas, however, were much more tedious and time and labor intensive since these areas often had to be hand scrubbed as cleaning machinery, especially in rockier areas, could not be utilized.

Joseph knew that the last several weeks' work incidents were totally unrelated events, but they dramatically highlighted the continuous pressure he had been under. The latest oil spill would result in many additional overtime hours as both he and his team worked in unison with the EPA to strive to return the harbor to as normal harbor schedule and as soon as possible. Joseph longed for the day when his work might be a little more normal both at work and at home. His constant fear and worrying about Mary's well-being and safety kept him constantly on edge. Although he, like in his Navy days, was handling the pressure well and was continuing to meet the daily duties that came his way, however, the toll of the day-to-day grind of all the extraneous pressures was beginning to wear him down. Joseph was having trouble sleeping at night, which of course, only seemed to exasperate the problem. Joseph knew he really needed a break from all the stress but that was not to come anytime soon.

During what everyone hoped was the last few days of the cleanup of the spill, the skimmers were busy working, as they had been around the clock. The skimming vessel named the *Skimmy Dipper*, was working on the far side of the harbor just a few hundred yards past Fort Sumter. It was about 2:00 a.m. and the crew was covering a two-square-mile grid that all of the crew felt like they had covered already before many, many times. The skies were partly cloudy with the quarter moon being hidden for the better part of the evening. The vessel was far enough from the more heavily populated portions of the harbor that when the clouds blocked out all of the moon they were left to rely solely on their own vessel's lights and their instrumentation. Although these lights were functional, they did not brighten any more of the seas that the immediate area just around the ship. The seas in the harbor that evening were moderate so there was not much for the crew to do except to continually check their gauges to monitor the oil collected. By continually verifying their exact position, by using the ship's GPS, the crew was able to ensure that the slick was eliminated as systematically and efficiently as possible. Regularly checking their course and speed against the GPS, the ship's crew was able to ensure that they ran almost the exact course they plotted. Water currents, of course, continued in any cleanup operation and continually corrections had to be made in the cleanup and appropriate adjustments made. The skimmer's captain and his crew were seasoned professionals and they were approaching this with appropriate zeal and enthusiasm as well as a very business-like approach to getting the job done.

A little after 3:00 a.m., the crew was making what seemed to be another routine pass when the crew first noticed something peculiar in the water. At first, it appeared to be an oil-covered bird floating about and the crew slowly swung their searchlights around to investigate. The skimmers were manufactured to handle small amounts of floating debris or even smaller birds, but this appeared to be a pelican or perhaps even a large fish that predominantly are found bottom feeding on the harbor's floor.

The clouds were still blocking the moon's light, accordingly, the crew was prevented from being offered a clear visual because of their lack of extra heavy-duty spotlights and the oil that saturated the floating item. As the ship came within a few feet, they came up with the item floating just a few feet off the ship's aft. As they neared the form, everyone on the ship was quiet, collectively, and they all gasped as they neared what appeared to be oil-slicked hair. The crew watched in total silence as the captain stopped the engines and they drifted closer with the captain remarking, "Oh no, I think it's her!"

Mary and David had enjoyed having a quiet evening at home. David had worked on his book report that was due next week and also on his math homework. After schoolwork, they had enjoyed a quiet evening barbecuing chicken out on the grill, enjoying the evening air. Mary loved the little evenings like this that they spent together and the sense of peace and joy that they brought. After dinner, Mary's neighbors noticed them outside and came over after dinner to visit. The neighbors, Doug and Neddy Cook, had just returned from their vacation and they shared about their travels and pictures, while visiting for a little over an hour until it became time to get David ready for bed.

Shortly after the Cooks left, it was time to get David ready for bed. Mary and David read for a while, particularly enjoying David's Bible stories for children. David loved to hear over and over about David and Goliath and especially about King David and his many victories. David drifted quickly off to sleep but Mary, feeling a little restless, tried to watch a little television before turning in for the evening. Just after midnight, Mary finally drifted off to sleep only to awaken shortly thereafter and to lie awake for almost two hours before falling sound asleep.

Awoken suddenly, Mary instantly sat up on the edge of her bed. She thought she had heard a door slowly close and click as when it does when the latch slowly slips into place. Mary had been very groggy as she had fallen asleep just a few hours prior. She was in the middle of the deepest REM portion of her sleep and was resting soundly when she had been awakened. Her room was partially lit as Mary had left the hall light on for David when he had fallen asleep. Mary did not hear David stirring so she assumed that he was still very much sound asleep. Mary's pulse raced as she tried to awaken herself from her slumber. She could feel her heart beating faster and faster as though it were going to jump from her chest. Frozen by her fear, Mary lay there motionless with a thousand thoughts going through her mind. She thought of how she now wished she had purchased an alarm system several months ago and also regretted never buying and learning how to operate a handgun.

Mary was beginning to gain control of most of her senses and the paralyzing fear that she had been feeling was beginning to pass. She glanced over at the clock noticing that it was almost 4:00 a.m. Mary's motherly instincts took over and began to impact her decision-making as she grabbed the portable bedside phone next to her bed and quietly walked ever so slowly down the hall toward David's room. As Mary neared his room, she heard rustling downstairs. Hearing this, she quietly and quickly entered David's room, immediately locking the door behind her. Mary heard footsteps coming up the stairs, fearing for the worst grabbing David, pulling him close, and retreating to a corner of David's room behind the bed. Thumbing nervously on the phone she dialed 911 and then held it to her ear. There was an eerie silence and it was then that she noticed that the phone was dead. Mary huddled there in the dark with David barely awake but having no sense at all of what was going on. Mary prayed, "Father, into your hands I commit my spirit. Though I walk through the valley of the shadow of death, in you I will find my peace and in You alone I place my faith and love." Just as she was finishing her prayer, the door clicked.

The phone blared. Detective Teri Stone heard it on the first ring even though he was deep asleep; its ringing seemed to make the entire room reverberate. It took him until the third ring to become conscious enough to realize that his phone was ringing and until the fourth ring to stretch out and answer it. It was 4:00 a.m. and like the past several weeks, he was catching a few hours' sleep on the couch in his office. The only reason he went home now was to change clothes and shower. The voice on the other end of the line was that of the captain of the *Skimmy Dipper*, who was using a ship-to-shore phone to call him at his office. The captain notified him of their gruesome discovery and asked him what he should do next. Detective Stone asked his coordinates and call sign, scratching them out on a pad, so that he could get to him as soon as possible.

Detective Stone immediately went down to his car and while on the way to the docks, he called the sergeant at home, who handled and coordinated the activities of the Charleston Harbor Police. He awakened Sergeant Blanski as well, asking the sergeant to meet Detective Stone at the docks and to drive him out to where the body had been found. There was virtually no traffic on the streets due to the lateness of the hour and Detective Stone quickly arrived at the docks just a few minutes ahead of the sergeant.

As they boarded and untied the sergeant's harbor cruiser, Detective Stone updated the sergeant on the details of the phone call as well as the coordinates to which they were heading. Sergeant Blanski was a veteran on the force of more than twenty years and was someone Detective Stone knew he could trust completely and implicitly. The partial moon was still fading in and out from behind the clouds as they motored over to the site. Detective Stone had a knot deep in the pit of his stomach as he sensed his worst fears would soon be confirmed. He had felt a constant gnawing at him now for more than two weeks as the investigation trudged forward. Though the discovery of the body, if it was her, would be an important part of the case, he knew that its discovery would greatly intensify what already seemed to be incredible political and news coverage pressure to find the killer. As he neared the site where the *Skimmy Dipper* had anchored, he thought of how the oil and its cleanup from the body might impede and possibly eliminate the likelihood of forensics being able to gleam any evidence from the discovered body. Pulling alongside the ship, Detective Stone thought quickly and quietly of his next move. He placed a call to the coroner's office to alert them and to summon him to the scene just as they were finishing tying up.

Mary had heard the door click and then she had sat motionless without a sound for what seemed like hours. Although she could feel her heart pounding, she was careful not to make a sound. Mary breathed very shallow breaths so as to keep her very own breathing from giving her away. David lay in her arms asleep, barely moving while Mary held him close, listening intently in the dark. The soft glow from the light on the alarm clock emanated enough light so that she could barely make out forms and shapes in the room. As her eyes continued to adjust, she noticed outside that the window was open to the cool fall air. She noticed that there was little if any moonlight and that the wind was lightly blowing the curtains. Although she was on the second story of her home, she knew that the roofline for the front porch was right below the window, making it easily accessible for anyone who had scaled up the home from the first level. Mary thought about crying out for help hoping that one of her neighbors might hear, but she feared that this would only serve to help the intruder determine her exact whereabouts and location. Something inside her told her that the intruder unequivocally was the serial killer and that she and David were in grave danger. She had not heard any noises outside the door for what seemed like an eternity and then…

Joseph had just received a call from his office. One of the members of the task force, at Detective Stone's request, had called his office to notify him of the discovery of the body in the harbor. By now, they had been able to determine that the body was certainly a female victim matching the general physical description of the missing agent, Vicki Green. Joseph's first thoughts turned to her surviving husband and two small children, noting that immediately his heart hurt deeply for them. Joseph drove to the docks; he thought of what his role might be at the scene and that he was certain that he would see Detective Stone there. As he went over the Cooper River Bridge toward the docks, he looked off to the southeast of the harbor toward the direction he would be heading soon. Silently praying, as he drove, for God to stop the killings and to stop the murderer that reigned terror on his beloved home of Charleston and especially for Mary and her safety.

It was then that Mary heard a footstep. It was that unmistakable sound that the hardwoods made when they squeaked as someone walked on them. She had previously always enjoyed this nuance in her home but now the noise deeply frightened her beyond what she thought she could possibly bear. It was now almost 4:30 a.m. and Mary estimated she had been huddled there with David asleep in her arms for what seemed to be forever, but had actually been almost an hour, during which, she thought of both her terror and what maybe her life really might be. Mary found this almost to be ironic, that such a thought could cross her mind in the midst of her deepest fears. Mary wondered what this meant and then again, she heard the hardwoods outside David's bedroom door squeak.

The first mate of the vessel *Skimmy Dipper* turned the body over slowly while it was still in the water, the body gently rocking, moving with the slight to moderate seas that morning in the harbor. Detective Stone watched intently as the crew got into position to pull the lifeless body up to the ship's deck as it gently lay in the murky, oily water. As soon as the body was beginning to be hoisted aboard, the moon came out from behind the clouds, causing the oil, both in the water and on the body, to glimmer in the moonlight. The whole of the crew stood in silence as they witnessed the sickeningly eerie scene. As the body was slowly and gently eased aboard, Detective Stone recognized that the clothes she wore were those that matched the description of the ones Vicki Green was last seen wearing right before her disappearance. Though Detective Stone knew that finding her body was one more step in the process of solving the crime, his heart sank. Nothing that he had ever witnessed before had prepared him for the horrible sadness that he now felt and the life that was now lost.

Mary heard what she believed to be the paper deliveryman as his car had gone by and then she heard large rustling as the paper rushed through the bushes, followed by a soft thud. Mary had continually experienced problems with her paper delivery in the past as a result of his frequent throwing of the paper into the large bushes just to the left of her driveway, near her home. It was an area of her yard that the shrubbery was so thick that it was very difficult to see into, much less walk in to retrieve a paper. Mary had called and complained to the paper several times and finally complained enough to gain their attention. Luckily, today the deliveryman had once again thrown the paper and it had sailed over the driveway and deep into the bushes again. Accordingly, the driver had stopped, backed up his car to the edge of her driveway and gotten out in an effort to move the misplaced paper to her driveway where it belonged.

As soon as the door closed on the route driver's car door, she heard several steps down the hallway and toward her stairs and then the rushed clatter of feet of someone hurrying down the steps and out of the back door. Mary breathed a sigh of relief as she realized the intruder had been scared off. She yelled out, "Help, there's someone in the home. Call the police!"

Mary waited as she was before, huddled behind the bed in the corner of the room, until she saw the blue emergency lights of the patrol car as it turned down her street. It was only then that she awoke David, who had slept through the whole ordeal, and they both went downstairs to meet the police.

Chapter 6

DETECTIVE STONE was methodically examining the body while still aboard the skimmer when the coroner arrived. The coroner was very methodical in his examination of the condition of the deceased body as he strove to begin to understand how she had arrived there and how she might have died. As the coroner continued, he was very cautious to ensure that any evidence available might be retained, being sure to take over a hundred photographs so as to document any evidence that might potentially be gleaned. The oil was thick and caked to her body and it made it very difficult to study the grisly scene. It was determined that the cleanup and the rest of the examination would be best handled at the coroner's office. Neither of them was prepared to face the inhumanity of how Vicki Green had been laid to rest and her life taken from her. Detective Stone always followed his hunches but he was very diligent in ensuring that he did not jump to any conclusions. Approximately twenty rolls of film were used so as to explicitly document the scene. Each time the bulb flashed, Detective Stone's heart sank, as he knew that the initial outcome of his efforts to locate Vicki Green alive had failed. One of Detective Stone's qualities that made him so successful was that he used each and every failure and roadblock to both challenge himself and to make a new benchmark to meet so that he could always strive to be better. Detective Stone knew that this chapter of the investigation had now been written and it was undeniably a failure; gritting his teeth and clenching his jaw so tight that his muscles ached, he vowed to God to locate the killer and prayed to God asking for His guidance to do so.

Shortly after the coroner, Joseph arrived at the crime scene, driving one of the harbor boats. Any time he was on official business of the harbor, he used their boat rather than his own. It was a forty-foot vessel equipped with all the latest technology including radars, depth finders, and even some diving equipment in the event it was ever needed. The boat was large enough that it really needed three crewmen to properly run and manage the boat itself and to monitor all the equipment and their readings. This morning however, due to the earliness of the hour, Joseph left with only a crew of two and had opted to drive the boat himself. As he neared the skimmer, he slowed his craft to almost a crawl and then used the boat's thrusters to gently nudge the ship alongside the skimmer.

Due to his vast naval experience, Joseph seemed to almost artistically move his ships so that others who tied the boat up hardly had to do anything but step off the boat and slide the ties along. As Joseph walked up to where the body lay, his heart sank and almost in anguished prayer, he quietly cried out, "Dear God!" Joseph initially froze in his tracks, noting that the scene felt so surreal, but yet it was all too real.

Detective Stone approached him and remarked, "We believe it's her. I had thought you would want to know as soon as possible so I had my men call you."

Joseph was asking Detective Stone what he could do when Detective Stone's cell phone rang. He quickly answered and then pausing turned to Joseph. "It's Mary, she's okay, but someone broke into her home. I have one of my patrol cars there now and two more are on the way over. There's not much more I can do here now and the coroner can handle the rest. Let's go!"

Joseph suggested they take the harbor boat and the two of them jumped in, untied and sped off. Detective Stone had called ahead so that as soon as they arrived at the docks, they had a car waiting. Although it was only a mile to Mary's home, it seemed like a hundred miles to Joseph. As soon as they arrived at Mary's home, Joseph jumped out of the car as it was stopping and rushed to the living room, where he grabbed Mary and held her close. It felt so incredible to hold her and to know that she was safe. Almost instinctively he said, "I'm here. I'll always be here, and I'll not let anything happen to you."

Mary had not shed a tear but when Joseph held her and said those words, her heart just melted. No one had ever held her like that before nor spoken words so strong. Feeling immersed in his arms, she began to cry. Slowly at first, focusing on the raw fear that she had just felt but then she began crying from the innermost parts of her heart. Mary thought only of her son, David, and this man, Joseph, who God himself had brought into her life. In that moment, time just stopped and she talked to God, "Please forgive me for what I have not been. Please take and mold me to what you would have me be. Please help me decrease so that you might increase. Thank you, God, for Joseph, for whom you have made and for who he is to me. I pray that I always seek to edify him in your name and that I always bring him honor. In Jesus' name, I pray. Amen."

As tears continued to roll down her cheeks, Joseph held her even tighter, pulling her deeper toward him. She buried her head deeply into his arms, body and shoulders striving to be even closer still. After what seemed like several minutes, Mary slowly looked up and into Joseph's eyes. In them she saw herself, a loving human, at times alone and afraid, but yet with a spark and zeal to do what's right. She wanted to live with a man as husband and wife, complete with God as their true figurehead. In this moment of fear, there was also a feeling of safety and a yearning to be with him.

She wanted him and looked into his eyes deeply and Joseph spoke, "I love you, I need you and I want to be with you. That is how I feel when I am with you and did not previously think it possible to ever feel like this. I know that love is so much more than a feeling but I know that we belong together and that we should live as one."

Mary watched Joseph intently as he spoke. She focused on each and every word and believed and accepted his words as true. Mary had wanted to hear these words from Joseph almost since day one as she felt the same words as he spoke. Although she wanted to be eloquent, all she could say was "Joseph, I love you. Me too, me too!"

Detective Stone had decided to give Joseph and Mary a few moments together and he used the time to talk with the police who had originally responded to the call, being attentive to each and every detail. He listened intently for any clue or detail that he might glean that might lead him one step closer to solving the killer that roamed

Charleston's streets. As of yet, there was no evidence to link this break-in with the killings, but he unequivocally considered them to be linked. Detective Stone's task force immediately began documenting every detail and looking for fingerprints. Detective Stone knew he would be there for several hours and would then call the coroner's office to discuss any initial findings of his examination.

At this time, the break-in was solely termed just that, but the task force investigated the scene with all their might and resolve and researched it as part of their murder investigation. No detail was left undocumented and they searched for each and every piece of evidence that they could uncover and then all were recorded and documented. Investigators initially determined that the intruder had entered through the back door. Although there was a deadlock on the door, Mary had not been in the habit of locking it shut. The task force concluded that the intruder had probably utilized a credit card to slide between the lock and the door and then had simply opened the door. Due to the length of time the intruder was there, each and every room of her home was studied intently. Searching for footprints both inside and outside the home so that they might extrapolate the height and weight of the intruder. It was about an hour after sunrise now and the task force began canvassing door to door to determine what anyone might have seen or heard. Initially there were no discoveries forthcoming, but Detective Stone knew that most of those occurred only after carefully and methodically examining every piece of the puzzle. Detective Stone resolved to redouble his efforts and that of his task force. He knew that would mean going to Mayor James White to ask for additional resources and more sleepless nights, but he knew he had to do whatever it took to take this killer off the streets.

Mayor White planned a press conference for two that afternoon. In it he announced, "As of today, I am granting additional resources immediately to catch the killer that has terrorized our citizenry. Ten additional detectives are being assigned immediately to the investigation and to Detective Stone and his task force. I will personally do whatever is necessary to aid in applying needed manpower and any financial resources, in order to speed the swift resolution of the case; I stand ready to defend and commit to the betterment of the city and her people."

Mayor White went on that the case was wearing heavily on him and his staff. He acknowledged that he was going to ask the FBI, as well, for additional manpower and resources. Mayor White's office had always had a good relationship with the personnel at the offices of the federal government and he leaned on them heavily when appropriate. The national databases and resources should be able to provide much-needed additional information and resources to the task. The FBI databases alone were often invaluable in solving cases as in them they contained fingerprints and bios and histories of any past convicted felons. Also, the FBI's powers had been recently expanded with the recent laws to protect the United States from terrorism giving the FBI even wider discretion of powers that could be drawn on to help solve cases and gain needed information.

Joseph stayed at Mary's home all day and into the night. Mary and Joseph decided that it would be best for David to stay home from school. Though David had slept through the whole of the break-in, the inundation of the police and the, what seemed to be, thousands of questions was unsettling to both David and Mary. Joseph and Mary had decided to call out for pizza for dinner and Mary caught herself unduly startled when the deliveryman rang the doorbell. Mary had experienced a very trying night and had stayed on edge all day. Joseph's presence did much to help assuage her fears and to be a calming influence all day. Joseph's affection and concern for her safety were always on his mind since he had met Mary, but somehow this event drove home to him how much he truly cared for her. Joseph wanted to talk to Mary about their future but he knew today just wasn't the time.

Joseph and Mary decided it would be best for all if David went to school tomorrow morning and for the two of them to get back to normal as much as possible. Mary decided that she now had to go stay with her parents for both her own safety and David's. As David loved being with Grandpa Billy, this did much to take his mind off the early morning events. Joseph was pleased that Mary had finally acquiesced to stay with her parents, as he knew they would be much safer there. Joseph helped Mary and David pack and stayed there until they got settled before leaving for home about eleven-thirty. The drive home was only eight miles or so but tonight it seemed unusually long. Mary's safety hung heavy on his heart but he felt a great release now that he had told her how deep his affection ran for her. After checking in on Sara, and finding her resting soundly, Joseph crawled into bed a little after twelve. After an hour or so of sleeplessness, he decided to take a couple of sleeping tablets to help him doze off. About forty-five minutes later, he finally fell deep asleep.

Joseph arrived at work about seven in the morning. On his way to the office, he called Mary at her parents' home to check in on her and David. Mary had said they both felt fine and had a fair night's sleep especially given the circumstances. David was busy getting ready for school, and Grandpa Billy was going to drive him there and pick him up afterwards to go fishing. Mary said David was in good spirits and that he was looking forward to spending time with Grandpa Billy after school. Mary was planning on staying at her parents' all day and potentially going into the office sometime tomorrow. This news put Joseph at ease even if for just a day, as he knew that neither Mary nor David would be alone during the next twenty-four hours either day or night.

Once at the office, Joseph resumed right where he had left off the day before, right in the middle of an oil spill cleanup and trying to coordinate what was an unusually busy harbor. Despite containment efforts, portions of the oil spill made its way out into the Atlantic and soon drifted out into the Gulf Stream. The Gulf Stream was usually one to ten miles off the entire Atlantic Coast driving the cooler waters of the north into the warmer seas of the south. The cooler waters brought nutrients and provided food for the plethora of fish that thrived in it. Normally, everyone saw the Gulf Stream as a positive, but all it did in this instance was to spread the spill. The Gulf Stream helped spread the oil all the way from just south of the Charleston Harbor at Folly Beach to Beaufort, South Carolina, and then on to just south of Savannah, Georgia. Although most of the oil had been contained, the Gulf Stream and its current helped send black patches of oil which, when they hit the beach, formed black dots along the beach for hundreds of miles. Joseph's involvement in the cleanup stopped just on the south side of Folly Beach, but there still remained remnants of oil within the harbor of which the cleanup would continue for several more weeks. Most of the oil in the harbor had now been skimmed from the water's surface but the shore was dotted with large batches of oil. The cleanup efforts along the shore had been initially focused from south of the Cooper River Bridge to just south of the Ashley River Bridge, where the tourist traffic was the highest. The homes along the battery were always one of the primary draws of tourists as they visited the area and it was here that the oil cleanup was initially started and then spanned out from there. Things at work for Joseph over the next several days would return to normal but his mind and thoughts always drifted back to Mary and her safety.

Mary stayed all day as planned at her parents' home, never even straying as far as the mailbox. From her parents' porch, she could see the continuing cleanup efforts of the oil spill, especially those in front of her parents' home and all along the Battery. Mary opted to sit out on the front porch most of the morning enjoying the cool ocean breeze, her morning coffee, and her mother's company. They talked for hours, which helped Mary relax and to regroup from the pressures of the day before. Toward late afternoon, Mary decided to call in to her office and to see if she had any voice mail. For times when Mary was out of the office, she would have her voice mail forwarded to her cell phone so she could stay in constant contact with her clientele and her office. She went to her purse to look for her cell phone and did not find it there. She assumed that in her haste she had failed to pack it. Using her mother's phone, she was able to call in and retrieve and return any calls that she felt could not wait. Mary felt that she would be safe to return to work the following day but planned to have her and David continue to stay the nights with her parents. Mary vowed to not let fear rule her life and to trust that God was large and in charge and that He would make everything turn out okay.

Detective Stone immediately began utilizing the new personnel and detectives that were assigned to him by Mayor White and began working even more closely with the FBI and the plethora of new information and databases that were now at his fingertips. The task force spent the last two days at Mary's home examining it over and over again for any trace of evidence that might be gleaned from the scene. The task force examined the area around Mary's home inch by inch and then the area inside her home just as meticulously. Lots of fingerprints were found but they were apparently those of Mary, David, Joseph, Sara and Mary's parents and friends. Detective Stone knew that whoever had been in her home had taken great care not to leave any fingerprints of any type. Detective Stone believed that the intruder probably wore gloves as he was in the home for too long a period to have "wiped down" all the possible areas of contact. Detective Stone had already concluded that the person he was seeking was extremely intelligent and the lack of evidence at the scene did nothing to dispel this thought. Detective Stone knew he had his hands full and he prayed that he had the strength and ability to be up to the task.

Chapter 7

MARY WENT BACK to work the second day following the break-in but was unable to focus her attention for more than a few seconds on the needs of her real estate business and clientele. It seemed as if all anyone wanted to talk about in the office was the murders and if that wasn't bad enough, it was pretty much all she could think about herself. Mary briefly talked to several potential customers and it seemed as if all they could talk about was the murders and if she feared for her own safety. The out-of-towners especially were questioning the prognosis of the solving of the crimes and for their own safety if they were to visit. After a brief lunch, Mary decided that she had had enough stress for one day and began to focus her thoughts and efforts on other things.

Mary began to think about the new fund-raiser that was coming up next month. Although each and every event had always proved successful in raising the needed funds, she always felt apprehension about the size of the monies to be raised, and this event was to be no different. Many of Charleston's more affluent citizenry attended these events as well as many of its more successful business owners. She had come to learn, over the years, who would contribute and approximately how much each and every time asked. Mary had learned that most of the regular individual members gave anywhere from $3,000 to $10,000 per project and that the corporate sponsors' contributions historically ranged from $5,000 to $20,000 each. Regardless of what was going on in the economy, either regionally or nationally, the funds raised on each and every project remained relatively constant. Several years ago the local economy had taken a much larger than normal downturn and yet the contributions

90

continued to roll in relatively unchanged. Mary assumed that this was due to the fact that most of the society's members' families had been here for generations and that they had accumulated lots of "old money" or at least enough to pull themselves and their chosen charities through any downturn in the economy.

The Charleston Historical and Preservation Society was now entering its fiftieth year and boasted more than four hundred members. The society was formed after several townspeople had gotten together to protect several homes in the area from being demolished. By helping preserve a few select homes initially, five of the original members decided to formalize what they believed to also be their calling of preserving the city of Charleston, and thus the Charleston Historical and Preservation Society was born. The society had continually grown over the years of its existence in both membership and influence and was now pretty much the standard and authority on all historical renovations and new construction as well. The society had participated in helping to preserve and restore the nationally renowned Rainbow Row, which was a row of what are now private residences. When they were initially built, these homes were used primarily as stores and commercial shops where townspeople could both buy and sale needed wares and services. The shops were originally painted different colors so that townspeople who were illiterate, and therefore could not read the shops' signs, could identify a certain store by its color. Almost all of the homes were built as three-level structures and still remain that way. The owners of the shops often used the main level for their business and then the upper two levels as that of their principal residence.

The society was also heavily involved in the reconstruction needed to all the homes that were damaged by Hurricane Hugo. Hugo had been a direct hit on the city of Charleston and caused severe physical damage from the sustained high winds and flooding, especially that which was caused by the tidal surge. The tidal surge was especially bad during Hurricane Hugo as the ground was heavily saturated from the hard rains and already boasted several inches to a foot of standing water in most places. The excessively high and sustained winds served together caused a series of waves approximately eight to twelve feet higher than the previously high waves that already existed. The rush of the force of the waves created a storm surge that caused substantial damage, especially to those homes along the coast and the Battery. Almost all these homes had heavy damage as almost all the residences along and near the water needed substantive repairs, reconstruction and renovation. The society was able to utilize their collective research and historical data to assist the homeowners in restoring the finely crafted homes to their original splendor. It was during this time that, like prior catastrophes such as the Civil War, the townspeople pulled together to overcome adversity. Although the storm itself and its initial cleanups were extremely hard on the townspeople, the end result of the cleanup and rebuilding was that the people of Charleston were more close-knit than ever and the city never shone more brightly.

Mary remembered Hurricane Hugo well. She and David, along with her parents, opted to stay at home and ride out the storm. The wind howling through the windows, the flying debris and the shattering glass convinced Mary that the next hurricane would result in their evacuation and riding out the storm several hundred miles inland. The interior of Mary's home suffered relatively minor damage but the structure from the foundation to the roof suffered extensive damage. Immediately after the storm, contractors clamored into the area from all over the country and were in such high demand that it took Mary several months to have her home scheduled for repair to get the needed work done. Eventually Mary's home and hundreds more like it were painstakingly restored to their original luster.

The society had also played a large part in the preservation of Charleston's few remaining cobblestone streets. Local developers had tried to pave over these streets in order, in their opinion, to improve its passability. In fact, the developers had been able to obtain a permit for the roads paving when at the last second, actually the day the construction was to occur, Mary helped spearhead an effort for the society to obtain a temporary restraining order to halt the paving. Mary worked through the society and then with the developers to assist them in seeing the advantage of preserving Charleston's cobblestone streets and therefore part of its heritage and legacy. Indeed the society, through its efforts, helped form the city itself and was an integral part of what the city was yet and is to become. Mary enjoyed that she was contributing to the history and preservation of

Charleston through her involvement in the society and eagerly performed her tasks there.

Mary was wrapping up the day and getting ready to leave work to pick up David from school on the way home. She had intently looked over her office several times from end to end in an effort to find her cell phone but to no avail. Mary tried to call it hoping that its ringing might give away its location but still no luck. She resigned herself to looking throughout her home and her car once again before finally giving up on its whereabouts. Her cell phone was an integral part of her business tools and there was no way she could run her business without it. Mary thought to herself as she neared David's school that she'd have to buy another one soon if she could not locate her old one. David bounced into the car talking non-stop about the activities and lessons he had performed that day at school. David was just in the midst of finishing up a science project and could not wait to get to Grandpa Billy's to work on it. Mary knew they would need to stop by her house to pick up the partially finished project and perhaps look for the phone if she had time and then head over to her parents' for the evening. This morning, before they both had left, Grandma had promised pot roast for dinner this evening, their favorite. David and Mary were looking forward to a quiet evening at home visiting with her parents.

When Mary got to her home, she had forgotten to anticipate what she might find there. During the morning after the break-in, she had made available to Detective Stone a key to the home should he or members of the task force need to go back to resolve any miscellaneous questions. Mary then remembered giving Detective Stone her cell phone number if he needed to reach her for any reason. Detective Stone had tried to reach her for several hours but upon receiving no return word, opted to drive on over and let himself in. Mary mentioned to Detective Stone that she had misplaced her cell phone and asked him to keep an eye open if they were to see it. Detective Stone was there along with three other detectives searching for any clues that they might have initially overlooked. He asked Mary a few brief questions to clarify some points of concern that seemed nondescript to Mary, and then David and she picked up the science project and headed to her parents' for dinner.

Due to the lack of prints or discernible evidence at any of the crime scenes, Detective Stone had concluded that the murderer was either well learned or perhaps had a very high IQ. Due to the age of the victims, all in their early thirties to early forties, he had hypothesized that the perpetrator was perhaps between forty to fifty years of age. He also believed that he was looking for a man who was at least five feet eight inches tall at least 170 pounds and in fairly good shape. He supposed this to be the case because of the age ranges of the victims and their size and weight. The victims all ranged in size from five feet two to five feet six inches and weighted from 115 to 135 pounds. He believed that the murderer had to be approximately the size he estimated because of what appeared to be the relative ease in which the victims seemed to have been initially captured or entrapped. All of the victims displayed little, if any, signs of a struggle, which also suggested that either they were surprised when assaulted or perhaps they were made to feel comfortable by him and then assaulted.

Detective Stone believed that the victims perhaps even willingly were led to where they were taken hostage and then taken elsewhere and killed. All of the victims' cars, except for the last, had been discovered in locations that ranged in distance from five to fifteen miles from their last known whereabouts, and they were discovered in locations where they normally would not have traveled, such as parking lots of old abandoned warehouses.

The investigation was starting to wear deeply, both physically and emotionally, on Detective Stone and he looked as if he had not slept for weeks. His working relationship with the mayor and the city council was still excellent but the local news was starting to step up the heat and had begun second-guessing what should be done next. Detective Stone was used to this and had even anticipated it, but many of the detectives and staff on the task force were not so able to handle the extra pressure that was now being applied. Detective Stone's leadership was not in doubt or being called into question, but there was starting to be grumbling among his staff. He diligently worked to address each of these rumors or challenges that the proper amount of damage control would often help stop a story from spinning into items and events far greater than their original true value and would even often start to have a life of their own.

Detective Stone knew he did not have an unlimited amount of time to solve the murders and that to date, all he had was a very few hard facts and way too much of conjecture. He knew that to solve a crime you had to think outside the box and that hypothesizing was necessary in order to determine how a crime might have occurred, but he knew that pretty soon he needed to have some concrete evidence or a break in the case. Detective Stone knew he needed that one big break that would help him head in the right direction and might greatly accelerate its resolution. Often a task force would spend days and weeks to prove or disprove a theory, but he knew it would be a major coup if the case were to become more focused and less scattered. He knew that most every case hinged on a single piece of evidence, and he determined to be even more resolute and to not rest until the case was solved.

———

Joseph began his day early with a meeting with the Environmental Protection Agency. The EPA had been involved since day one of the oil spill and had steadfastly monitored its cleanup. The cleanup efforts had removed the larger portions of the spill both in the water and along the shore and the spill was no longer a visual nuisance. Most of the efforts now would shift to monitoring of the toxicity levels of the water and as to when plant and fish life might return to normal. At this point, the normal ebb and flow of the tides and the normal current of the rivers into the harbors and then to the ocean had a cleansing effect of its own, as Mother Nature has always tended to work things out in the end. The meeting took over two hours and had three representatives from the EPA present as well as a host of representatives from other regulatory agencies. It seemed to Joseph that often during the conversations each representative was more concerned about their special interest and protecting themselves and their agencies rather than focusing on the issue of the cleanup itself.

It had been two weeks since the last real estate agent's body was found in the oil-soaked harbor. Joseph had not slept well for several weeks now and was always worrying and even fretting over Mary and her safety. Joseph knew that in Matthew 6:34, Jesus said, "Therefore do not worry about tomorrow, for tomorrow will worry about itself. Each day has enough trouble of its own." Joseph really identified with the second part of the verse, as he saw trouble each day, but living in the present was always so hard. Joseph knew people who he felt were able to deal only with the issues of the current day but he deeply struggled with even the concept much less its application to his daily life and thinking.

Today as Joseph drove from home to his office, just before lunch, he prayed, "Dear God, I know you are there. I know that only You are in control. I know that I can trust you and that you will always look after me and those that I love. Dear Lord, I am afraid, not for me, but for those that I love. I put Mary, as she has always been, in your protective care. Please protect her. Please place your shield around her and keep her safe. In Jesus' name, I pray. Amen!"

Mary's day started off much the same as Joseph's, immersed in a staff meeting complete with the broker of her office and all of the staff and agents. The topic was the financial structure under which contracts could be processed and commissions were to be paid, and it seemed to Mary as if her commission plan were being cut yet again. Mary sat there thinking why this and why now. Sometimes she mused, there seemed to be more rules and regulations and effort required to produce what seemed to be an ever-dwindling profit. After the meeting, Mary opted to go out to lunch with some of her fellow agents, while trying to relax and focus on just being and not worrying so much for her safety and that of David. Mary and her fellow office members were still practicing the buddy system at work, checking in and making sure they knew where each other were twenty-four hours a day now. Just a week ago they were only checking in during regular work hours, but with the latest agent's murder, the buddy system had been upgraded to around-the-clock accountability.

After lunch, Mary went back to the office briefly, only to confirm that she really did not feel able to focus on work at all. It was such a pretty day outside with a nice gentle breeze blowing in, so Mary decided that she needed to take the rest of the day off. Mary decided to spend the rest of the day on the beach on the Isle of Palms, which is just five mile east of Mt. Pleasant and just over the intercoastal waterway. Mary drove over to her parents' to pick up a bathing suit and a book to read at the beach. While at her parents', Mary made arrangements for her dad to pick up David after school so she could lounge about and not have to hurry back. As Mary drove over the connector towards the beach, she noticed the white wispy clouds and felt herself relax for even just a little bit, for the first time in weeks. Mary accelerated slightly as she slowly smiled, opened the sunroof and turned up the music, excited about kicking back and relaxing on the beach. She arrived at the beach about three in the afternoon, pulling out her book after setting up with her chair facing out towards the ocean. The gentle sound of the waves soothed her spirit as she began a novel that she had been hoping to start reading since she had purchased it several weeks ago. Mary read slowly from her book, savoring the relaxation, the sun, and the breeze as she began the fourth chapter. She caught herself getting sleepy and she allowed herself the luxury to doze off, basking in the afternoon sun. She slept for almost an hour, waking up as the tide came in. The beach on the Isle of Palms was a dark brown in color and very flat, which resulted in the water being almost one hundred fifty feet closer to her, due to the rising tide, than when she originally arrived. The water was now lapping at her feet as she slowly awoke from her slumber, enjoying the relaxation of the day and her restful repose.

Mary watched the sun begin to slowly shift towards the western sky, checking her watch noting it was a little past six. Mary knew her parents were not expecting her until eight in the evening and was enjoying her nice leisurely day and the way that she felt. Running her hands through her hair she relished the blowing, gentle breeze. Deciding to take a little extra time for herself, Mary opted not to hurry over to her mother's but instead decided to leisurely drive over to the home that the Charleston Historical and Preservation Society was raising money for. Mary thought how much she might like to spend a little extra time studying the home and to contemplate the upcoming fund-raiser. The event was now just three weeks away and there were yet still a few details left to resolve. Mary loved the planning of the events as much as the actual fund-raiser itself. She knew that her attention to detail and pursuit of perfection were well appreciated by the society and she really enjoyed her time and efforts spent there. As with most of the homes the society helped raise money for, a key was made available for Mary and other society personnel to use as needed for access to the home. As usual, it was Mary who was at the fund-raiser homes most often, accordingly, she would usually keep the key; she already had the key on her key chain as she headed over.

As Mary headed back over the Cooper Bridge towards Historic Charleston, traffic was about average for that time of day, heading back into town, and moved relatively quickly, especially as she was driving against the rush-hour traffic that was just beginning. Within twenty minutes of leaving the beach parking lot, she neared to within a few blocks of the home. Foot traffic in the area was beginning to pick up as the day was starting to cool off and headed toward early evening. People were walking about enjoying the ambiance of the weather and as always the majesty of Charleston herself. Mary pulled in front of the home, choosing to park in the street. As she walked toward the residence, she observed the home's inner courtyard. The courtyard had been well maintained despite the renovations that the home needed. One of the charms she enjoyed the most about the city had always been the elegant courtyard areas where people could relax and gather to enjoy the ambiance of one another's company. Walking up the front steps to the home, Mary paused and then slowly put the key in and opened the door. The door creaked as it slowly swung out into the room.

Joseph suddenly stopped what he was doing, becoming painfully aware that he was afraid and shaking. He knew that he was sitting safe in his office working late and yet he was frightened. He sensed tension in the air as the hairs on his arm stood on end. He knew that something was amiss and yet not knowing what to do in turn, he prayed, "Dear God, in you alone I place my trust, in you alone I have my faith. Though I walk through the valley of the shadow of death, in you I know I will find no turning. Dear God, I do not know why I find myself afraid but yet I know that I am never alone and that you are here and that in you alone, I trust. In Jesus' matchless name, I pray. Amen."

Mary walked slowly into the room as the door creaked as it swung further open. The foyer was still dusty and musty from the years of neglect, but Mary knew that once restored, the foyer would indeed be the centerpiece of the house. Mary walked into the foyer, studying the details that had been handcrafted into the home's woodwork by its original owners. Mary knew the painstaking effort that they had put into the house as she had watched the workers restore and reconstruct homes and knew the exacting standards required to recondition a home to its original luster. Mary walked down the hall and into the master bedroom, which was about twenty feet from the main foyer and the front door. She remembered that she had left the front door open as she stopped and slowly turned as she thought she heard the hardwoods squeak.

Joseph finished up his prayer believing in faith and knowing that he worshiped the one true God of the universe and that He was in control of all things past, present, and future. Though Joseph trusted and believed in God, he knew that God controlled all, that God wanted him to trust in Him alone, and that God expected Joseph to do his part, no matter what that might be. Joseph thought about whether or not he should call to check on Mary when one of his employees headed into his office for a question.

It was approaching seven and David and his grandparents were having a big evening. They had just finished up dinner and were planning to spend the evening out on the front porch overlooking the Battery and the harbor watching while the day slowly ended and the sun set. The sun sparkled as it eased into the horizon with the light shimmering and dancing on the waves as they gingerly lapped toward the shore. Only God Himself could have imagined such beauty and created such a wondrous setting and a beautiful world. Yet, since the day of Adam and Eve, free will and man's own pride tried to destroy or diminish every good and perfect gift that God gave. God's mercy and compassion and His desire for us, causes Him to continue to pursue us though man continues to fail Him over and over. Man does not want to accept His gift of love, and man, though created in God's own image to be with and to worship God, continues to seek His own way. Christ himself offered a perfect sacrifice of His own life so that we could be and live with him forever. No greater love can one have than to lay down his own life for another, and it was that love that He freely gave of himself.

Mary turned as she heard her old cell phone ring from another room and she began walking back towards the front door, trying not to make a sound as she moved. As Mary walked from the kitchen toward the dining room, she suddenly stopped, sensing in horror, the same fear she felt that night someone broke into her home, knowing that she was no longer alone. Just then a car drove quickly past the front of the home. Mary was startled as she slowly turned as the car driving almost double the posted speed limit.

The sun was setting and soon it would be dark and David and his grandparents retired into the home for the duration of the evening. Mary was due home soon with David hoping that she'd be there in time to read before his bedtime.

Mary resumed walking toward the open door, just over ten feet away. As she turned into the dining room, she began trembling. Mary felt a rush of wind and then an arm wrestled her from behind clasping something over her mouth. As she fought to escape, she kicked backwards with her right foot and leg and bowed her back in an effort to free herself from the grasp that seemed to be ever tightening. Mary realized that the assailant was holding a cloth over her mouth and she was able to bite at his fingers, causing him to let go, and let out a muted yell of pain.

As Mary turned, she felt herself losing consciousness. It seemed slow at first as she lost her balance and tried to scream. All she could do was to form her mouth to begin to cry out for help but she could not mutter a sound. Although it seemed like several seconds, almost as time were standing still, in reality it was a little more than a second or two as she lost total consciousness.

Chapter 8

THE ETHER IN THE RAG over Mary's mouth and face had its desired effect as she slumped to the floor. Mary was totally unconscious as he dragged her by her arms and shoulders towards the garage where his car was hidden. The dust and dirt left a trail of where she had been pulled towards his awaiting vehicle. Opening the door to the garage and then to his car, he pushed the trunk release, opening the trunk so that he could place her body inside. He easily lifted her one hundred fifteen pounds over the back of the car and into the trunk. Taking no chances, he dabbed a little more ether on the rag and placed it over her nose and mouth, causing her to breath even more. He estimated that it would be at least three to four hours before she gained consciousness, which would allow him more than enough time to transport Mary to another location.

Opening the garage from the inside, he headed out into the street. Leaving his lights off as he started up the street so as to try to leave covertly as possible. After he had passed several blocks from the home, he turned on his lights and headed up Meeting Street. He knew that there was no way, given the amount of ether she had inhaled into her body, that she would be awake anytime soon, so he did not bother to tie her arms and feet nor to even gag her mouth. Also, he knew his destination was only about an hour or so away and he did not want to stay at the home any longer than absolutely necessary. So that he might escape undetected, he made sure to carefully obey all traffic signs and speed limits so as to not draw any attention whatsoever to himself. He was aware that many people had been apprehended simply as a result of minor traffic violations, often even as simple as a failed bulb on a taillight. Situations had occurred where individuals had been stopped for something extremely minor and in the process of running routine identity checks, they had been detained and subsequently discovered that they had committed a much more serious offense.

As he neared his destination, he thought about his next steps of the plan that he had already set out. So far, everything had worked like clockwork and he wanted to make sure that he followed his plan diligently. He knew that he needed to follow the steps he had laid out exactly, lest he make a foolish mistake. Some thirty minutes ago, he had left the heavily populated areas of Charleston and had reached the beginning of the city's outer rural areas. As he pulled off the road, he doused his lights and then slowly pulled up the long gravel driveway. He drove approximately two hundred yards through thick woods on either side of the drive and then pressed the remote control to open the garage door as soon as he neared the structure. Before he left, he had taken care to leave all the lights off and to remove the bulbs from the garage and from its opener to remove any opportunity of detection. He slowly backed his vehicle into the garage and then as soon as he was safely inside, he concurrently turned off the car and pushed the remote again, closing the garage door behind him.

His ultimate destination was deep within the woods off the road. On the other side of the property lay a small marshy area of approximately a quarter of a mile and then lay the vastness of the Atlantic Ocean. He knew that he was in a location that was so remote that not even the loudest screams for help could possibly be heard. As he stepped out of the car, he headed back towards the trunk, saying aloud, though Mary was still deep asleep from the effects of the ether and though he knew no one else could hear, "Come here, my pretty."

As he picked her up, he carried her inside into a room that he had prepared. The room had no windows and but a single bed with a bedside table with a single lamp. He laid her in the middle of the bed and then left the room to gather a small portion of food and water for Mary for when she awoke. When he returned he tied her hands and arms together with a one-and-a-half-inch-thick rope. He knew there was no way Mary might untie herself as he grimaced as he tightened the rope well beyond what he needed to in order to keep her secure.

He did not bother to gag her as he knew that there was no way that any scream could be heard through the three-inch-thick hardwood door and half-foot-thick walls. Several weeks ago, he had taken care to test the adequacy of the sound-insulating capability of the structure by placing a boom box in the room, closing the door and playing the music at close to concert sound levels. As he walked outside of the structure, he noted that he could only hear the extremely muted sounds of the bass as it reverberated within the room's stout walls. The room Mary had been placed in was an internal room inside the building's structure and as a result of the sound test, he knew that there was not way any sound could be detected as a cry for help, especially given the location's remoteness.

As he prepared to leave the room, he triple-checked to ensure that there was nothing that could be utilized either as a weapon or an instrument in the room that Mary might use to free herself. He had taken special care to place just the mattress in the room and a very flimsy pressboard end table. He had also taken care to ensure that the hinges on the door had been reversed so that it opened toward him rather than toward the inside. This had the advantage of being able to add two large wooden boards as well that he could swing down into place to further barricade the door to ensure that the room's contents, namely Mary, remained inside.

As he left, he made sure that all the lights were out and with that he left his cars lights off as he slowly headed back down the gravel driveway. When he neared the road, he slowed down even further and then stopped and got out. He walked behind the vehicle, pulling two large and rusted chains together and padlocking them tight. "No Trespassing" signs hung from the chains to further eliminate anyone inquisitive from potentially entering. He got back into the car, closing the door gently behind him, and drove out onto the main highway. After he was a ways down from the turnoff, he turned back on his headlights, being sure to continue to carefully obey all traffic laws so as to not be unnecessarily delayed or stopped.

Mary's parents were beginning to get more than a little concerned. It was almost eight-thirty, a half hour past the time that she was due home, and they had still not heard from Mary. After putting David to bed, Grandpa Billy decided to call her cell phone. It rang and rang but to no avail; Grandpa Billy double-checked to make sure he was calling the new cell phone number and not the old one, as he was aware that Mary had lost her old one. Grandma wanted to immediately call the police to report her missing but Grandpa Billy was able to convince her to wait before calling the authorities. However, he had to do something, so he opted to drive out to Isle of Palms beach and to see if perhaps Mary might still be at the beach or perhaps one of its nearby restaurants. Grandpa Billy knew that it was not uncommon for Mary to make an additional stop on the way home but he also knew that she kept her cell phone on and near her most all the time. As he drove out of the driveway, he prayed that perhaps her battery had died or that he would pass her as she was driving on the way home. The roads seemed unusually quiet; Grandpa Billy tried to stop himself from thinking about it, but if he had to be honest, he was frightened and afraid for Mary's safety.

After locking up and leaving his office at the harbor, Joseph's day had been a long one and he was excited about getting home and going to bed a little early to rest up for tomorrow. As was his custom, he called Mary on his way home, on her cell phone, but received no answer. Joseph assumed that Mary was putting David to bed and perhaps doing a little extra reading with him before bedtime. He resigned himself to calling her after he got home and got settled. He knew Sara would probably be asleep by the time he got home, as her bedtime was nine and Yana would already have most likely put her down for the night.

Grandpa Billy approached the Isle of Palms beach parking areas, driving through each and every lot he knew of to no avail. Leaving his headlights on high beam to heighten the car's headlight illumination, he circled back around through the lots as his cell phone rang. Excitedly he answered hoping that it was Grandma telling him that Mary had arrived home safely. It was Grandma, but as of yet, there was no word from Mary. It was now approaching nine-thirty and although Grandpa Billy tried still to put her to ease, he was beginning to fear the worst himself. Grandpa Billy kept talking to Grandma as he drove through all the lots trying to be strong for her and promised to call her back after he drove by the local restaurants to look for her car there.

As soon as they hung up, Mary's mother received a call from Joseph who had just arrived home and had called the home to see if Mary had finished putting David to bed yet and could talk. Joseph had called from his kitchen where he had begun to make himself a sandwich before retiring for the evening. Immediately Joseph tensed and his stomach tightened as Grandma told him how Mary was due home over an hour ago and where Grandpa Billy had already looked. As they were talking, Grandpa Billy called to report in and upon finding nothing, they all agreed that it was time to call the police and report her missing. During normal times, this would have never even occurred to them but there was a killer loose on the streets of Charleston and it was now approaching ten. Grandpa Billy and Grandma had held out hope that maybe she had stopped by to spend time with Joseph, but upon knowing that she was not with him, they all agreed it was now time to call the police and to request that they put out an APB—an all points bulletin—to begin to search for her whereabouts.

Detective Stone was still working in his office and was immediately notified of their 911 call. After meeting briefly with his detectives and key members of his task force, they unanimously agreed to call an Amber Alert. Amber Alerts was a recently passed piece of federal legislation that came about as a result of a young lady that had been missing several years back and was never found alive. From prior investigations of hundreds of cases nationwide, it had been learned that for every missing person that was kidnapped, the likelihood of finding them alive dramatically decreased with each and every passing hour. Amber Alert procedures were detailed such as to have authorities to set up roadblocks and establish a perimeter around the last known location of a missing person. Detective Stone made the order himself and ordered the last known location to be the Isle of Palms beach area.

Within moments of the order, the three main roads in and out of the Isle of Palms were blocked and police began stopping, searching and questioning each and every vehicle that was approaching or leaving the Isle of Palm area. The roadblocks were initially set at a three-mile radius of the beach to have the maximum amount of exposure and opportunity to find Mary alive. Then, as time elapsed and more officers called in, the ring of the roadblocks was extended as well as, unfortunately, the likelihood increased of someone being further away from the last known contact location. Detective Stone also ordered a squad car go by Mary's home and then to drive the probable route that she would have taken either going to or returning from the beach. The task force office was abuzz with activity and everyone feeling the pressure of trying to bring the case to a swift close, to bring the perpetrator to justice and, most of all, to locate Mary McCarey alive. Detective Stone immediately remembered that Mary and Joseph were seriously dating and personally called Joseph on his cell and then Mary's parents' home to ensure that they knew what was going on and that they were doing all they could to locate her as soon as possible.

Joseph had just hung up the phone when Detective Stone's call came in advising him of what they were doing. With Detective Stone remarking, "We are doing all we can, I want her found alive just as much as you."

"I'm sure you do," Joseph murmured, thinking, *If you only knew how much I love Mary and how important she is to me, then you'd really know how much I need to find her and how it is to truly love.*

As they hung up the phone, Joseph knew he could not spend the night idly by and just wait. He decided to go meet Grandpa Billy and join him in his search at the Isle of Palms beach area. He quickly told Yana what was going on and that he did not know when he would be home and dashed out the door. Nothing he had ever faced before prepared Joseph for what he now felt and he prayed, "Dear God, Father who art in heaven, I know that I am a sinner, not deserving of your grace. I know that I have sinned and fall so very short of the glory and power you have laid out for me in my life. I am not going to bargain with you as I do not want to insult you and I know that as a man I will never be able to prove worthy or to be able to guarantee that I will be always able to do what I'd like to commit to. Dear God, I know you know where Mary is. You know whether or not she is safe. I pray that you bring her back to those that love her and especially to me. I believe we are supposed to spend our lives together and I believe together we can do more for you than we can ever do apart. Please forgive me for my many sins and lead me closer to you. Please take whatever course you need in order to accomplish the work that you have started in me. Lord, lead me to be more like You, prune me, mold me, and please, Oh God, bring her safely back home."

Joseph caught up to Grandpa Billy at the fire station in the Isle of Palms. Joseph went inside, where Grandpa Billy was already talking to the station chief about possible beach locations parking areas and restaurants that he might have missed. The fire station had heard the news on the police scanner as well as through normal channels and procedures. They had already, in fact, dispatched two of their vehicles and called in all off-duty personnel so that they could dispatch three other trucks to be utilized in the roadblocks when they arrived. These personnel would be used in assisting the police in what amounted to setting up a perimeter around the area. The firefighters were to provide additional personnel to help stop, screen and search vehicles entering and exiting the area. The firefighters were well trained in utilizing the procedures they were to be following and were dispatched as quickly as they arrived at the station. Only the fire chief remained at the station now along with someone in dispatch to help coordinate their efforts in assisting the police and the task force in their search.

Joseph and Grandpa Billy discovered from the fire chief a few extra eateries and perhaps a parking lot or two that they could search for Mary's car. It was now about eleven-thirty as they headed out into the night to search for Mary. Joseph had come to truly respect and admire Mary's father and he deeply appreciated how warmly and quickly they had accepted him and Sara. Joseph knew he could trust Grandpa Billy with anything and he was honored to be alongside him at this time, even though it was a deeply painful moment for the both of them. Grandpa Billy spoke first after they headed out, "I'm glad you're here. I hope nothing has happened. No one had better have hurt my baby."

Joseph, upon hearing Grandpa Billy talk with such passion and a crackling in his voice, realized that Grandpa was hurting as much as he was. Joseph replied, "We will find her and she will be okay. I just know it." He mustered all the confidence that he could but inside, Joseph knew he was deeply afraid he'd never see her alive again.

Together they found each and every restaurant the fire chief had referred them to, as well as the additional parking areas he had suggested. For each lot and establishment they approached, they silently hoped that this would be the one they would find her in, perhaps with the hood up on the car and her looking in. They checked each area carefully and then they checked them again as well as all the other areas Grandpa Billy had already double-checked on his own. Though he knew they were doing everything they could, Joseph believed Mary was no longer in the Isle of Palms area and his heart sank. It was now approaching one-thirty in the morning and they decided to leave Grandpa Billy's car at the fire station and ride over together to look for her on the way that she would have driven home from the beach. Like every car leaving the area, they were also stopped at the roadblock. Quickly explaining who they were and that they had just left the fire station, they were sent on their way. They were careful to drive slowly and in the far right lane so as to be sure to see any car in the dark of the night that might have pulled over due to needing roadside assistance, but they found nothing. They opted, as well, to drive by Mary's home to see if perhaps she had stopped by for something, but again, they found nothing. It was now almost three o'clock and they decided to catch a few hours of sleep and to resume their efforts early in the morning.

Fighting to regain consciousness, Mary slowly blinked her eyes and then squinting extra hard, she looked around the room saying to herself, "Wow, where am I?"

As she slowly awoke, she realized that she was lying on a twin mattress in a small room with a dimly lit lamp on. Trying to sit up, Mary realized that her hands and feet were tightly tied. Thankfully, she discovered that her hands were tied in front of her so she was able to push herself in order to sit up. Mary sat on the edge of the bed and tried to remember how she got there. Rubbing her eyes with her bound hands, Mary realized that the last thing she remembered was someone startling her and grabbing her from behind and then placing something over her mouth. Mary remembered struggling to get free and wanting to cry out only to almost immediately fall fast asleep and unconscious. Mary looked around the room and quickly realized that the room was sparsely furnished with only a twin bed and its box springs, a coffee table, and an old lamp with dimly lit bulb.

She took the lampshade off the lamp, which added almost twice as much illumination as before. Mary was afraid to cry out because it might cause her captors to come in and perhaps beat her or worse. Mary walked slowly over to the door, turning the knob slowly and finding it locked from the outside and then immediately noting that the hinges were on the outside of the door. Mary took little steps, with the rope tied tight around her legs, near her feet, back over to the bed and slowly sat down and wondered what to do next.

Mary tested the ropes both around her hands and her feet. They were pulled so tight that she did not think she'd ever be able to loosen them enough to free herself unless she could find something sharp enough to do so. She looked into the drawers in the nightstand and upon opening and searching the drawers, and finding a Bible, just sat down and cried. She looked at her watch noting it was almost five o'clock, but with all light from the outside blocked off, she could not tell if it was five in the morning or five in the afternoon. Other than the lamp there was no illumination in the room at all, which led her to wonder if the room was located in a basement. Mary had been out cold for what felt like ten plus hours but she had yet to fully regain her senses and being totally shut out from any outside light, it was difficult to regain her senses. The walls appeared to be made out of concrete and she could tell they had been painted over several times. Mary realized that for at least the time being, there was nothing she could do to escape and that she was trapped. Not knowing what to do, she lay back on the bed and closed her eyes in prayer. "Dear God, I do not want to die. I am afraid. I want to go home. I want to live. Only you know what my captor's motive is. Please set me free, let me walk away from all of this safely. There is so much I want to live for. Please, dear Jesus, hear my prayers, know my heart, and protect your child. In Jesus' name I pray, Amen."

Still feeling groggy from the effects of the ether, Mary began feeling very woozy. As she lay slowly down on the bed, she fell deeply asleep by the time her head hit the pillow.

Joseph awoke suddenly at six in the morning after just a couple of hours of sleep. Nothing before had prepared him for how he now felt. Right before his eyes, Mary had almost magically appeared several months ago, and now almost as quickly, she was gone. Joseph felt that they were meant to be together as if God alone had ordained their meeting and now with so much for them to live for together, she had been taken away from him. In his anxiety and fear, Joseph mused how much joy he had felt with Mary since they had met and how close they had grown together, and now Joseph did not know if he would ever even see her again. It just did not seem fair but Joseph respected God, the sovereignty of God; yet he still had to cry out in his pain. "Bring her home, bring my Mary home. I love and I adore her. Please bring her home."

He cried, not to challenge God or His ways, but cried to just bring her home, to let me hold her, to let us just be together! Joseph's mind wandered to his past sins and prayed, "Father, I know that I have failed you and that I have not always lived for you as you would have me. Please forgive me for my sins. Help me see all that you would have me see."

As Joseph prayed, God heard and answered his prayer and it was revealed to Joseph all the many times he had not lived up to God and his commandment of love. Joseph saw how he had failed God over and over again. As Joseph lay there, God revealed to him as Joseph had asked, every sin throughout the whole of his life, he had ever committed. Joseph felt the pain that Jesus faced while hanging on the cross as he paid the price for all sins past, present and future. The day of the crucifixion, the sins were so numerous that they blocked out the sun and yet Jesus stayed true to what his Father had commanded and cried out, "Forgive them, they know not what they do."

Jesus was there hanging and dying on the cross and yet he prayed for his prosecutors so that they might become fellow heirs of the throne. Jesus loved so greatly that all he thought of was us, and yet Joseph when dealing with only the sins he alone had committed, could not alone endure the pain.

In tears, Joseph cried out, "Father, Father, Please forgive me, reach out your hand to me, oh Lord. In you alone can I find peace. From the depths of my soul I see the wickedness of my thoughts and shame. I am sorry for how much I have failed you. I know I have not always put you first. I know I need more of You in my life. Please help me to see what you would have me to see. Please help me to be the man that you would have me be. Help me to be more like you, help mold me to be what you want me to be. Please help me decrease so that you might increase. Dear Lord, please forgive me."

In pain and shame, Joseph cried deeply and loudly. Holding his hands to his eyes, and the top of his head, Joseph felt both his tears and his shame.

Detective Stone was sitting in his office when he got the call. Mary's car had been discovered on Meeting Street by a squad car that was coming off his shift and heading back to the precinct. The officer was there now at her car and had found it unlocked. Fearing for Mary's safety and well-being, the officer immediately pulled the trunk release, finding it empty. It was at that point that the officer had called in and reported his findings. Detective Stone ordered five of his best investigators to the scene along with a large complement of numerous uniformed officers who would seal off the area and begin canvassing door-to-door questioning the neighbors and businesses in the area.

Detective Stone arrived at the scene within ten minutes of the call, noting that they had already started to cordon off the area. He was a little surprised that the press wasn't already there as their office was just a few blocks away, and they constantly monitored the police ban and this was the biggest story to rock the city of Charleston in years. The detectives immediately began the process of thoroughly dusting each and every surface of the vehicle for prints and then examination of the vehicle for any fiber evidence that might be obtained. Hundreds of pictures were taken to carefully document each and every item at the scene. Detective Stone immersed himself in the collection of potential evidence, as he did not want to take any chances of missing anything that might give him a lead toward recovering Mary alive. As soon as he arrived on the scene, he called Joseph and told him the news, "We've found her car. I'm at the scene and it's here on Meeting Street."

Joseph, without hesitating, asked the address and upon hearing it, stated, "That's where the society's fund-raiser house is."

Joseph ran out to his car and headed over. Detective Stone called the Charleston city's court office immediately and asked for a warrant for the fund-raiser house and advised of the emergency search at the scene of Mary's car to determine if she was in the immediate area or perhaps in the car itself. His request was immediately granted and he was given full and complete authority to search the house and car as needed. Officers were already starting their door-to-door canvassing and were each equipped with several pictures of Mary and a full description of her vehicle. The last anyone had heard from Mary was mid-afternoon on the prior day. Detectives concluded that the car had been there for at least three hours as the engine had totally cooled down by the time it was discovered and had also been coated with morning dew. Detectives were asking specifically about approximately a twelve-hour window from three in the prior day's afternoon to three or four o'clock in the morning. Detective Stone decided that the initial canvassing would be set at a five-block radius of the home. These door-to-door conversations would take until very late in the afternoon, especially since most of the people would not even be at home until after five as it was a workday.

Detective Stone had to wait on the search warrant to be in his hand before entering the house. Due to the priority of this investigation, the warrant arrived in just under fifteen minutes. Officers had already taped off the entire area now and the whole lot so as to clearly mark the house and search area. Detective Stone was the first one inside the home. Not taking any chances, they entered the home with guns drawn. Detective Stone was careful, as were the other investigators, not to disturb anything inside the home. As Detective Stone entered the home, he feared what he might find. As he entered the foyer into the dining room, he saw what he believed to be track marks from something being dragged across the floor towards the garage. Detective Stone followed the markings out into the garage, where they stopped towards the back of where a parked car would have been.

As he did not see Detective Stone outside, Joseph arrived at the society's fund-raiser house and rushed towards the front door. Officers stopped him with their arms outstretched as he neared the porch. One of the investigators immediately recognized him and went inside to see if Detective Stone might come outside to speak with him. Joseph waited outside for the detective to go inside and to bring Detective Stone out. As Detective Stone approached the door, seeing Joseph, he remarked, "We are not done with our investigation by any stretch. We'll be here for hours or as long as it takes. It seems as if she was incapacitated in some way and drug to the garage. We suspect that she was removed from the premises via the garage in the trunk of a car. We have officers going door-to-door asking everyone in a five-block area if they have seen anything at all. So far, we have not discovered any signs of a struggle. We don't know where she is or even where she might be but right now we will be searching for her non-stop, morning, day, and night."

Detective Stone wished there was more he could say or that he might even be able to provide Joseph some comfort, but there was nothing he knew that he could say at this time that would bring any relief.

Joseph stood listening intently as Detective Stone talked. Each and every word pressed through to his heart and soul. Even though he had expected the worst, and yet not heard it, the present state of affairs was hard to take. Mary, the person that he loved the most, had more than likely been kidnapped by a killer. Within the pit of his inner being, he grieved deeply. Trying to regroup and wanting to be of assistance, he asked, "What can I do to help? I need to be able to do something. Anything!"

Detective Stone immediately listed all the things he could do help. They ranged from ensuring Detective Stone knew all of Mary's work habits, her schedules, her circle of friends and the nature and present status of Joseph and Mary's relationship. Detective Stone asked, "Please be as specific as possible, as anything might be the key to resolving the crime. Perhaps there was someone, anyone at all that you can think of, who might have an axe to grind or perhaps some sort of grudge against Mary."

Although Detective Stone believed Mary's disappearance to be the work of the serial killer, he could not afford to overlook any nuance that might lead to discovering her whereabouts and hopefully finding her alive. Detective Stone then gave Joseph one of his personal cards, taking care to write his cell phone number on it.

"Please feel free to call me at any time with any advice and direction that you can assist with," Detective Stone advised Joseph.

Detective Stone could see the throng of newspaper and television reporters gathering just outside the cordoned-off area of the crime scene. Detective Stone knew that soon he would have to face them and answer all the questions that seemed to him rhetorical. Yet he knew that this was a critical part of an investigation. By keeping the public informed and seeking their help in solving a crime, he was often able to propel the investigation much faster. During each interview, he always had to walk a line of telling enough in order that the public might have enough information that they needed to know to protect themselves and yet he had to be discerning so as not to reveal any of the specific or confidential details of his investigation. Critical information might unduly implicate someone that they were investigating, or worse yet, might alert a felon or criminal as to the status of the investigation or perhaps even the potential of their imminent discovery.

The local news press continued to be supportive of the status of the investigation and the efforts and had to date been an asset in helping solicit support and needed information for the task force to help solve the crime. Yet now, support was beginning to unravel a bit as two of Charleston's citizenry had been murdered and now one apparently kidnapped by the killer that stalked her streets unscathed. As this could now be potentially the seventh murder, counting the four that had occurred in Wilmington, NC, there was intense pressure to solve the case. Mayor White's latest assignment of additional personnel and resources were deeply needed and appreciated, but they had also inadvertently added pressure to have the case quickly resolved. Many of the questions had an edge of impatience to them as both the public and the press were demanding and crying out for this case to result in apprehending the perpetrator now. Detective Stone handled the questions as well as anyone might with a serial killer on the loose, but he knew that he needed to make real progress on solving the case, and soon.

After watching the interview for a while, Joseph decided to leave his car there and walk over to Mary's parents' home, eight blocks away. Grandpa Billy saw him walking up and met him at the front door and they embraced. They opted to sit out on the porch to talk and just be together, neither knowing exactly what to do or say. As of this morning, Grandpa Billy told Joseph that they had decided not to tell David of Mary's abduction and had opted to send him on to school. To protect David from being upset, they said that Mary had stayed at Tracy Barnes', her girlfriend's, home overnight. Soon after they began talking, Grandma joined them out on the porch, bringing some coffee and homemade biscuits with her.

Joseph brought them up to speed on his conversation this morning with Detective Stone and his efforts to assure him that they would find Mary and bring her home alive. As he talked, Joseph just wished he were as confident as he tried to sound. Joseph was deeply hurting and afraid but he knew he could best help Mary's parents by striving to put on a good face and by being positive. Joseph shared with them the request that Detective Stone had made to provide any and all details that he could to assist him in his investigation. Joseph reiterated that Detective Stone had mentioned that he'd stop by to see them himself probably mid to late afternoon. Joseph stayed on until past lunch before heading home for the rest of the day. Before Joseph left, he huddled with Mary's parents and prayed for Mary's safety and her return. Joseph's eyes misted as he prayed and Mary's mother wept openly. Grandpa Billy finished up the prayer, his voice trembling with every word, while seeking God's help in bringing his baby home.

Chapter 9

MARY AWOKE VERY slowly and still groggy. The effects of the ether were now predominantly gone and she slowly regained her wits about her. When she awoke, she slowly looked around the room unsure of both what happened and where she was. Mary guessed she had been asleep for twelve plus hours but with no window in the room, she was unable to tell if it was day or night outside. Looking at her watch, she could see that it was two o'clock but between the effects of the ether and no view of the outside world, she could not tell if it was day or night, causing her to be unable to get her bearings.

Mary looked around the room, noting that it was a third smaller than her bedroom back home. Mary wished silently to herself that she could be there now. Mary slowly sat up, being careful not to move too quickly for fear of losing her balance or consciousness. Mary sat on the edge of the bed for a moment before she felt she had regained enough of her equilibrium to stand. Carefully bracing herself, Mary stood again while hesitating to ensure she was conscious enough to take a step. Her first step or two were very deliberate, to be sure that she did not fall or lose her balance. Mary estimated that the room was about twelve feet wide as well as twelve feet long. Quietly tapping on the wall, so as to hopefully not alert her captors, she quickly found, as she feared, that the walls were extra solid. By hitting on the wall with some force, she received a resounding thud with each impact, leaving her to estimate the wall to be at least eight inches thick. Easing over to the door, Mary repeated her tapping process while striving to hit a little lighter than before so as to not make the resounding noise that wood does when knocked on with any force. Mary then gently pushed on the door and then by applying some force, she estimated that the door was a solid hardwood. Though well aged, Mary believed it to be very solid, at least four to five inches thick and perhaps a hard maple or a walnut. The door was fitted snugly in its frame as she guessed that it had multiple locks on the outside even though she could only see the one door handle from the inside.

Moving back to the only other piece of furniture in the room, the nightstand, she first opened the top drawer, finding nothing, and then the bottom drawer, finding a well-worn Bible. Deciding to sit down on the corner of the bed, Mary flipped through its pages, finding it well marked with notations off to each side of its pages. Guessing the Bible to have been at least fifty years old, Mary opened it to the first few pages and found the copyright and print date to be 1952. Mary looked to see if there was a name or notation in the front which might reveal its owner, and on the first page, she found the words, "To my beloved son. Happy Birthday. Love, Mom."

She briefly scanned the notations as she turned the pages looking for any clue of who its owner might be, and upon finding none, put the Bible on top of the nightstand beside the lamp. Mary slowly lowered her head, placing her hands over her face, and wept. Slowly at first and then intermittent sobs as tears cascaded down her face. At first, Mary tried to hold it in so as to not make a sound, and then, no longer being able to, Mary wept aloud and completely. Letting it all out, Mary cried deeply with huge tears cascading down her face as she wept. Never having been so afraid and at such a loss to control or even influence her captivity or what might happen to her, she wept. Though intellectually Mary knew she would die at some point in her life, she had always believed that she would pass in her sleep in the later years of her life. Now Mary knew that, perhaps in a few moments or hours, her life might indeed be over. As she cried, her eyes reddened and became swollen, almost shut, and yet the tears continued. She cried for what seemed like hours and after having finally exhausted herself, fell asleep.

Grandpa Billy and Grandma picked up David from school and then headed back to the home. On the way home in the car, it was a little quieter than normal as they waited until they got home to tell David about his mother. After they arrived at the home, they opted to head into the living room to talk so that hopefully David might be as comfortable as possible so they would not be disturbed. Sitting on either side of David on the couch, Grandpa Billy began, his voice wavering as he spoke, "David, we were not entirely honest this morning. Your mother did not spend the evening with her girlfriend. She's been missing since yesterday. The police believe that she's been kidnapped. They are doing everything they can to find her." Grandpa stopped, trying to regroup and sound convincing. "God will take care of your mother and He will bring her safely home. Our job here is to continue on, not let this beat us, to have faith and to pray."

David leaned back deeply into the couch. Being just nine years old, it was very difficult for him to take all this in. He hesitated and then asked, "What does this all mean? When will Mommy be home? Does the killer have her?"

Grandma began to speak but emotion overtook her and she could not get out a word, so Grandpa responded, "We do not know ourselves yet what this all means. We are praying that she will be brought home to us soon. They have found her car and the police are doing everything they can. I choose to believe that she will come home and until God proves otherwise, that is what I am going to believe."

David, beginning to sense the severity and enormity of this news, laid his head in Grandma's lap and began to cry. Grandpa Billy, trying to soothe David, held him while he lay in Grandma's arms as he cried and said, "There, there, it will be okay. You just wait and see." Grandpa Billy held both of them close to his heart.

They all jumped as the doorbell rang. Remembering that Detective Stone was due to come by the home, Grandpa Billy walked quickly to the door and answered. Though he would never admit it to anyone, Grandpa Billy privately feared that he'd never see his daughter alive again. As he opened the door, he invited Detective Stone into the home with a wave. Grandpa Billy asked Detective Stone to wait in the study for a moment while they got David settled. After Grandma felt like David was calmed down a bit, she joined them in the study. To help settle David down, she took him into the kitchen and gave him something to eat and turned on the television.

Detective Stone reiterated the questions he had asked Joseph, asking for any and all details whether large or small, that they might be able to provide. Gaining their permission first to tape the conversation so that he would not miss anything, Detective Stone turned his recorder on and laid it on the desk. Detective Stone asked about Mary's work habits, her friends, and if there was anything at all they might be able to tell him that seemed unusual or perhaps even out of the ordinary. The questions seemed endless until at last they were over. Grandpa Billy hoped that something they might have said might be helpful but he could just not imagine how. Leaving, Detective Stone gave Grandpa Billy his business card, asking that he call him personally if they thought of anything else at all that might be useful.

Joseph awoke the next morning after getting just a few hours of sleep the night before. Between his bouts of sleeplessness, Joseph prayed to God to protect Mary and to bring her safely home. Feeling helpless no matter what he did, he opted to go into work for a few hours to see if he might get something positive accomplished there. On the way into the office, he drove by Mary's home, stopping briefly for a moment and then driving over to the fund-raiser house where Mary had been kidnapped. The police tape was still around the house warning people to stay away. There was one detective car with two officers there, he assumed, in an effort to clarify any evidence gained yesterday or to find anything they might have overlooked. Joseph hoped that the plethora of detectives and officers that were there yesterday were busy at other locations still diligently looking for her.

Mary awoke now feeling fully recovered from the shock of her abduction and the effects of the ether. Had her arms and hands not been bound, Mary believed that she might have even felt refreshed. She was thankful that her mouth was not taped or gagged as the tight ropes around her arms and feet were causing enough discomfort on their own. She pulled on the ends of the rope around her hands trying to free herself, but the rope was too thick and the knot pulled too tight for her efforts to be of any benefit. Also, the ends of the rope had been cut, she imagined, after they were tied taut, as there was only a quarter of an inch or so beyond the knot. Looking at them further, she noticed that the ends had been burned or singed together, helping to keep them from being frayed and then loosened.

Mary figured she must have slept soundly as she noticed that there was bottled water and a peanut butter and jelly sandwich set beside the door. Apparently her captor had placed these just inside the room while she was asleep. She realized how hungry she felt and noticed that her watch said twelve o'clock but again, she could not tell if it was noon or midnight. After estimating the times in her head, she thought that it perhaps was midnight the day after her abduction. Mary walked over to where the food had been laid by the door. Kneeling down she picked up the water and turned the cap noticing that until now, the safety seal had not been broken. Indulging greatly, she took a large gulp of water and let it sit in her mouth so as to savor its moistness in an effort to refresh her. Grabbing the sandwich next, she noted that it was in a Ziploc bag. Although she knew that the sandwich might be laced with anything to drug her, she knew she had to eat to keep up her strength. Taking a small bite at first to see if she might be able to detect anything amiss and then noting nothing but the taste of peanut butter and grape jelly, she quickly ate the rest. The sandwich and water placated her physical needs for the time being and she was grateful for the nourishment they provided.

Being more rested and now fed, Mary felt more cognizant of her surroundings. There was a heavy, musty order about the room that seemed to permeate everything, even seemingly clinging to her. Having come directly from the beach to the fundraiser house, she was still wearing her bathing suit with shorts and a t-shirt over them and had on a pair of sandals. Hearing rustling outside the room, she stopped cold. Fearing to breathe aloud, she took shallow breaths and did not move. Even though she desperately tried to stop herself, she could not help but tremble. The noises outside continued for perhaps ten minutes. Mary wanted to cry out in case it was someone who might save her but she believed the noises to be coming from her captor. She could not help but think about the irony of it all. Here her captor was holding her against her will and yet she was afraid to cry out from fear of being discovered. The steps came closer to the door and she could hear the locks being undone on the door.

Grandpa Billy and Grandma Mary Sue had a long day and night the day before trying to deal with the pain of Mary's abduction and in trying to console David. They both tried to put on a good face and to be strong for him but with every passing hour, the strain of not knowing exasperated their spirit and tried their faith. In an effort to take David's mind off events as much as possible, they decided to send David on to school. Although everyone, including the children, knew of the kidnapping, due to the extensive news coverage, they hoped that the structure of the day might prove to be a positive distraction for him. Though they realized David would be thinking about his mother all day, hopefully there would be enough things that he had to do that he would not have the chance at least, to dwell on his mother being gone.

Mary imagined that there were deadbolts on the outside of the door as there was not any trace of them on the inside. Mary then heard the sound of wood sliding against the wood door as he removed the heavy boards that barricaded her door. By this time, Mary was so frightened she was hardly breathing at all.

After Grandpa Billy returned home from taking David to school, he decided to try to do something to take his mind off the situation. He began by sitting down with a cup of coffee to read the paper. Taking the rubber band off the paper, he opened it to the day's headline, "Real Estate Agent Still Missing." He tried to read beyond those words but he found that he could not focus and had to put the paper down. After sitting quietly for a few minutes, Grandpa thought that perhaps logging onto the Internet and checking his e-mail might prove an adequate distraction, so he headed into his study where he kept the computer. Sitting down at his computer to log on, Grandpa Billy went directly to his homepage that had local weather, stocks, and news. Grandpa Billy liked the distraction that the Internet provided him, and he would often spend an hour or more online responding to friends and associates and occasionally doing research on a particular subject that might have piqued his interest. The Internet seemed to be moving a little slower than normal today as he first reviewed the market price of a few stocks that he had invested in. Noticing that the market had recorded a slight up-tick over the last couple of days, he decided to check to see who might have sent any e-mail.

As Grandpa Billy logged onto his e-mail, the words jumped off the monitor as he read, "If you ever want to see Mary again alive" in the subject section. Saying a brief prayer for her safety, he clicked in order to see the message itself as he yelled to Grandma, who was in the kitchen, "It's about Mary, come here quick!"

The message came up about the time Grandma entered the study and as she did so, they began reading the message together. "Mr. Loudermilk, your daughter has offended the Lord and for that you or she will pay deeply. If you wish to see her alive again, I demand that $200,000 be placed into an unmarked Swiss account within one hundred hours, the details of which are below. If you fail for any reason, then just know that you alone have chosen. This is the only message you will receive."

Numb, they both just sat there and stared at the screen and Grandpa Bill finally broke the silence, "What does this all mean? What are we supposed to do? I want to believe this means she's alive and that we'll be able to help bring her home."

Although the message said nothing of involving the police or not, Grandpa Billy and Grandma discussed whether or not they should share the message with Detective Stone. They feared that if they did that the kidnapper might do something rash. They decided to call Detective Stone, as they feared that they knew nothing of how best to handle such matters. They called Detective Stone and told him of the ransom note, with Grandpa Billy exhorting, "We'll do anything we can in order to bring Mary safely home."

Detective Stone listened intently as perhaps he had received the first a big break in the case. For the first time, he believed that maybe the killer had slipped up and let his guard down. He knew that e-mails were traceable from wherever they might have come from and now all he had to do was simply track down its source.

The door slowly opened revealing Mary's captor. He was dressed in long blue jeans—baggy pants that had to be at least two sizes too big—and an extra-large navy blue sweatshirt hanging loosely from his frame. He was wearing a black ski mask that caused Mary to gasp in fear as he stepped into the room. Over his eyes, he had placed an extra-large pair of mirrored sunglasses so as to further hide his identity. She thought he had on a pair of extra-thick brown work gloves, no doubt to avoid any possibility of leaving any fingerprints. Clearly striving to disguise his voice, he walked up to her and held her left arm firmly in his right hand. As he did so, he murmured in a very hoarse voice, "Come on, you are going with me."

Detective Stone's instincts told him the one-hundred-hour deadline and ransom request were real. Often in such cases, copycats or thrill seekers would perform random acts to either emulate the perpetrator or as some sort of sick joke to confuse the police. One of his first challenges in any such case with such an apparent new piece of information was to attempt to determine its authenticity. Detective Stone believed that his swift and gauged reaction would result in either Mary's life or that of her death. At one in the afternoon, Detective Stone called a meeting with his key detectives and staff members and the FBI liaisons to strategize on how best to proceed. At his disposal were some of the best forensics people and seasoned investigators in the nation, and a hostage negotiator was at his disposal should the need arise. Detective Stone knew that in order to overcome the obstacles that lay ahead, he was marching against a ransom note and a deadline that he believed was real and he knew that Mary's life hung in the balance.

News reports were now also reporting that a Category 4 hurricane name Janet had, in just the last hour, taken a dramatic easterly turn and was now headed directly towards Charleston. Previously, it was believed that Hurricane Janet was headed due north and was to stay harmlessly out at sea, but now with the storm's turn it was headed to the city's center. The eye of the storm was very tightly formed and with sustained winds of one hundred forty miles per hour with gusts to one hundred fifty. Although no substantive effects, absent slightly elevated surf, were being felt in the city at that time, the storm was moving at a speed of twenty-four knots and was three hundred miles offshore. If current conditions continued, Charleston was expected to get a direct hit in approximately thirteen hours.

The Hurricane Service ordered an immediate evacuation, as a direct hit from Hurricane Janet on a heavily populated area such as Charleston would threaten anyone in its path and cause millions and perhaps billions of dollars of property damage and a life-threatening environment.

As Mary's captor began to lead her out of the room, she froze with fear. Unable to move a muscle, Mary stood motionless. He pulled firmly on her arm, nudging her strongly to move forward, so she complied. Racked with utter panic about what was to happen next, Mary shivered. Mary wondered if she'd ever see David again or if she'd live even another hour. Not knowing what to do or if to say anything or cry out. In fear, she held her head low and silently prayed, "Dear God, I come to you as your humble bond servant, please hear my prayer. You and you only know what will happen and into your hands I commit my life. There is no way that I can repay you for what you have done for me. Thank you for dying on the cross for my sins. I know and feel that I have failed you. I have not done the work that you have laid out for me. I know that I am a sinner deserving eternal separation from you, yet you have loved me. Save me, your child. Dear God, I am not worthy to even untie your sandals but no matter how long I live, be it only a few more moments or fifty more years, I want to live for you. Please forgive me for my sins. No matter what happens next, I want you to be my King. I love you. In the matchless name of Christ, I pray. Amen."

As Mary's captor led on, he stopped about halfway down the hall and draped not one, but two towels over her eyes, blocking out all light and any chance of seeing anything. As he continued down the hall, Mary continued by taking very small steps, as her feet remained bound. As she trudged on, Mary sensed the very presence of Jesus with her and though inaudible, He spoke to her just the same, "Be still, my child. Be still. I am here. I will never forsake you." Mary smiled, walking on perhaps to the very end of her days but knowing He was there and that He would comfort and take care of her, Mary spoke back to Jesus, saying, "Into your hands I commit my spirit."

Chapter 10

DETECTIVE STONE now not only had a ransom note to contend with, he had a Category 4 hurricane breathing down on him. He knew that the killer was serious about the ransom note and that he would kill again. Mary's life hung in the balance and that the next one hundred hours would dictate if another victim would be added to the killer's list. Detective Stone knew he needed to be both accurate and fast.

Joseph phoned Detective Stone after he had discussed with Mary's parents about Grandpa Billy's receiving the ransom demand via e-mail. Joseph asked, "Please let me know what I can do? I want to help. I want to find her. I'll do whatever you ask."

Just as Joseph finished his sentence, one of the detectives on the task force rushed in. "It's Mary; we have a fix on her location. We just had her cell phone show up as being active."

Finally Detective Stone had the break he had been hoping for, a chance to quickly solve the case and find and return Mary alive to her family.

Joseph was still on the phone and, having overheard the conversation, exclaimed, "Where is she, what can I do?"

The initial locater devices had put Mary's location actually out in the middle of the Charleston harbor headed out toward the vastness of the Atlantic Ocean. Detective Stone knew that he needed to act and that he needed to act fast. Detective Stone asked Joseph to meet him at the harbor docks and then by using the tracking devices on board the harbormaster's boat and the last location of her cell phone usage, Detective Stone knew that he would be able to track Mary's location and rescue her soon. He and Joseph were both at the dock in a little under ten minutes and the crew was ready and pushed off as soon as they stepped on board.

Detective Stone was not taking any chances this time. He had his people put in a call to the Coast Guard and as well, asked them to see what they could do to make available satellite coverage of the area. By coincidence, the Coast Guard had a satellite that had just come overhead and would be available for their use for the next ninety minutes. Detective Stone said, "Finally, I have the break that I've been waiting for."

Detective Stone and Joseph sped at thirty knots toward Mary's rescue and returning her to Joseph and to her family. For the first time in the case, Detective Stone allowed himself to feel a little relief. They should be overtaking the boat that Mary was on in less than fifteen minutes. Photos from the Coast Guard satellite were now being downloaded to his task force's command center and within a few minutes of leaving the dock, he had a picture of his prey in his hand. It appeared to be a thirty-five-foot fishing vessel that was cruising at a speed of twenty knots, apparently unaware that soon they would be surrounded about the time they would be approaching the deeper water of the Atlantic. Detective Stone, though confident, was taking no chances; he ordered two police boats to join in their pursuit as well. In another stroke of good fortune, the Coast Guard had a ship within just four miles of where he calculated that he would overtake the ship Mary was on. The captain of the Coast Guard vessel quickly agreed to help vector his vessel and armed personnel in on the kidnapper's vessel.

Speeds and times were coordinated so that all four ships would arrive near where Mary was being held and at staggered intervals. Joseph studied the blip on the radio as they steadily closed in on Mary and her captor. For maximum effect and to hopefully surprise the kidnapper, it was decided that the Coast Guard vessel would approach first with all hands at battle stations. The Coast Guard ship was extremely well armed and heavily plated and would intimidate anyone other than perhaps a like-armored ship. Coast Guard personnel were already poised at their battle stations in the hope that the kidnapper would be so overwhelmed that he would immediately surrender and not try to hold Mary hostage.

All of the five approaching ships were now in visual range of the kidnapper's vessel. Satellite reconnaissance had continually tracked the vessel visually and on radar. Also, the Coast Guard and Joseph's harbor vessel had tracked it on radar. There were no other ships in the immediate area and there was no doubt this was the vessel that the cell phone signal had originated from. If everything fell just right, this horrible nightmare would soon be over and Mary would soon be on her way safely home. Detective Stone knew not to celebrate until all the cards had been counted and all the hands revealed, but he felt that this time, lady luck had finally shone favorably on him.

The Coast Guard vessel with all of its crew, armed and ready, came within close visual proximity with the kidnapper's vessel that seemed to be plodding on as though it were just another day. All of the Coast Guard guns were trained on the unsuspecting vessel as it came into the kidnapper's direct path and on both loudspeakers and on the maritime radio, the Coast Guard captain bellowed, "You are surrounded! Stop your vessel immediately. If you do not, you will be fired upon and forcibly stopped."

Detective Stone watched as the Coast Guard closed to within a hundred feet of the kidnapper's vessel. To think that just a few hours earlier today, he had received a ransom note and had little if any direction or leads to solve the case. He tried to always keep in mind that every case seemed to hinge on one piece or shred of evidence that seemed so trivial but would wind up being critical to a case's resolution. Often detectives would refer to this as "breaking" a case because it seemed as if all at once, a case was solved, almost as if magically. To imagine that earlier today, he was in his office working diligently and now the case might be over in just a few moments. Detective Stone imagined that Mary was down in the hold of the galley that they were approaching. Thinking that perhaps Mary had somehow worked herself free or briefly gotten just far enough away from her captor or alone enough to utilize her cell phone. Current technology allowed trackers to know the exact location of a cell phone when being activated or used. Somehow it seems many perpetrators of crimes still were not aware of this technology that was available. Detective Stone believed in using every tool in the toolbox to solve a crime and soon he hoped to see the fruits of his efforts and success.

Joseph did not normally drive the harbor boat when on board, as he preferred to usually allow the crew to handle the helm so that he could concentrate on other matters. But today, as they headed toward Mary, following his natural instincts to lead and to care for those he love, Joseph took the helm. Joseph thought intently of the deep abounding love he had for Mary, as he drove the harbor ship closer and closer. These past few months Joseph knew He had ordained their meeting, the fun and closeness that he felt when Mary and their two kids were together, their courting, and their abiding love in each other. No one had ever made Joseph feel the way he did when he was with Mary. He knew there would always be bad days ahead but he knew that he wanted to spend each and every one of them with Mary.

As they neared to within approximately a mile of the chased vessel, he quickly calculated and slowed his speed. Joseph knew that they wanted the heavily gunned and armored Coast Guard vessel to arrive first and then for the other three ships to arrive just over a minute after. Joseph slowed the speed to just over twenty knots so as to be sure to arrive at precisely the correct time. Although Joseph had been in the Navy, he was not familiar at all with police tactics or those strategic operations and procedures that they might follow when working with a hostage situation. In the Navy, Joseph's training was focused on gaining a tactical advantage. On that front, he believed that police and naval practices coincided. But he imagined after that point, the similarities ceased. In the Navy, they were charged with gaining a tactical advantage and then in using that with as much strategic and overwhelming firepower as to overwhelm and therefore overcome an enemy. It was certain; Joseph's Navy training was intensely and keenly trained on protecting innocent civilians. But to be frank, he could not remember anyone even telling him of any specific situation ever where civilians were out and about just walking when a major firefight developed. Joseph prayed that God would lead the Coast Guard personnel and that their training and skills were exactly poised for those specifically needed today in this circumstance.

The waves were beginning to pick up as Hurricane Janet approached. The waves were now developing into five- to eight-foot swells that were almost fifteen feet wide. Normally the seas here would have been two to four feet and relatively narrow, but with the influx of the storm, the seas had picked up dramatically. They were now out of the relative safety of the harbor and exposed to the elements of the open seas of the Atlantic Ocean. Detective Stone feared that the waves might impact their approach as they neared the vessel and attempts were made to board her. As the Coast Guard vessel approached within fifty feet, Detective Stone watched; swells would first substantially raise one boat and substantially lower another. As the Coast Guard vessel approached even closer guardsmen standing at battle stations at the forward fifty-caliber machine guns noted that what was believed to be a woman had just entered below deck with someone behind her. Detective Stone's biggest fear was not the weather or his lack of ability to oversee the action of the Coast Guard personnel. Detective Stone was most afraid that an obviously sick and twisted individual who had committed multiple killings was holding Mary captive and that her life was in grave danger.

Detective Stone knew this kidnapper was capable of cold-blooded murder and that he would not hesitate to do it again with what had so far proved to be random acts of violence with no link between them other than that they were real estate agents. Detective Stone knew he was dealing with someone without a conscience who would both quickly and easily kill again. As hard as he tried, Detective Stone could never understand why someone would do such a heinous crime to anyone for any reason. Knowing that the next few seconds would determine Mary's plight, Detective Stone held tight to the railing in the harbor boat's cockpit due to the rough seas and his own anxiousness about what would happen next. Detective Stone's knuckles whitened as he clenched tighter and tighter. Briefly, he tapped his nine-millimeter handgun almost as if to confirm what he already knew: it was there. He believed that the ultimate disposition of what would happen would be over by the time they got there but he had to be on guard to help if needed.

Detective Stone listened intently to the radio as he tried to hear what was happening as the Coast Guard vessel approached. Everything was happening so fast that nothing was truly understandable or legible as voices yelled demands and responses in rapid succession. Closing his eyes briefly, Detective Stone concentrated on what appeared to be multiple mutterings over the radio and then he heard shots being fired. Detective Stone immediately exhorted, "Joseph, hurry! We have to get there now!"

Although the distance was now less than two tenths of a mile, Joseph went to full throttle. The dual 2,400-horsepower diesel engines roared to maximum power and then they quickly surged ahead. As they neared the vessel, Joseph prayed, "Dear God, Please let her be safe!"

As they approached within one hundred feet of the kidnapper's vessel, Joseph saw the Coast Guard personnel with guns drawn and trained on the perpetrators. The Coast Guard vessel was now alongside the other vessel and a rope being quickly thrown and tied off so as to close the proximity of the two vessels to within a few feet. Coast Guard personnel were well trained on how to board other vessels and to do so, if necessary, when under fire. Within seconds, four Coast Guard personnel were aboard the ship and had the perpetrator pinned on his stomach as they quickly handcuffed him. The bullet wound was to the kidnapper's right thigh and had slowed him down just enough to allow the Coast Guard personnel to quickly overtake him. Still with guns drawn, two more soldiers boarded the boat and kicked the door open to the galley. Taking turns entering, first one, then a second, and then a third soldier entered the galley. Joseph looked on, hoping to hear no more shots and to see soon, the head of his love, Mary, exiting from the galley alive and to freedom. Joseph knew the solders would first have to ensure that they had secured the area to avoid any one of them being killed or shot and then they would free Mary from her captivity. It seemed like forever as Joseph waited to see her. A lady emerged from the galley and his heart leapt for joy. "It's finally over!" Joseph muttered.

Detective Stone boarded the boat first as the harbor vessel pulled alongside. The Coast Guard personnel had quickly secured the area and now Detective Stone's responsibility was to be sure that the victim was safe and finally free. Detective Stone first noticed the blood that was coming from the perpetrator's leg. After searching the kidnapper completely, the soldiers finally turned him around so that he was face up. Finally, Detective Stone was able to see the face of the serial killer who had tortured his soul for so long and took the lives of many innocent women. The killer's face was hard and worn and his clothes were that of a workingman. He looked to be in his mid-fifties and a little over 180 pounds, just as Detective Stone had expected.

Detective Stone felt no satisfaction from the capture like he had thought that he would. He felt only deep regret for the women who had lost their lives and the ones left behind who had lost their loved ones. Looking into his face, Detective Stone almost yelled out, "Why did you do it? Why did you kill them?"

The killer retorted, "I do not speak good English. I did not mean to do wrong."

As the killer spoke, Detective Stone looked up as the soldiers led her out into the open. Her long blonde hair was mussed about her face. She held her head down as she came out into the open almost as if afraid. When she finally lifted her head and Detective Stone looked upon her face, he saw the same as Joseph did at exactly the moment. "It's not her!" Joseph and Detective Stone said in unison.

Detective Stone barked orders, "Get down into the galley and find her!" The soldiers immediately headed back down only to return moments later with a puzzled look on their collective faces. The first lieutenant remarked, "There's no one else here."

Detective Stone immediately sprang into action yelling out orders as he went, "Check to see if there are any secret holds, any secret compartments; I want every inch of this boat checked and then rechecked. See if there are any lines of any type attached to the back of the boat or underneath. I want divers in the water now! Check the boat's registration. See who it belongs to. Get me a search warrant for the house of whoever this guy is. Find his identification. I want answers and I want them now!"

Immediately detectives, officers, and soldiers sprang into action. One called the judge to get a search warrant, boater's registration, and a call to get divers to their location as soon as possible.

Joseph feared the worst. He had watched with great apprehension as they had approached the perpetrator's vessel. His biggest fear was that a stray bullet might accidentally go awry. Then, when he saw what he believed to be Mary emerging from the galley safe and unhurt, his pulse quickened. This joy immediately turned to confusion as he looked on. He was the first to suspect that it was not Mary that emerged from the galley. Looking on as events evolved, Joseph feared, as the soldiers stormed back into the galley to look for any sign of Mary, that there would be no trace of her, or worse, that they would find her dead. As the soldiers re-emerged without Mary,

Joseph felt the pain again of not knowing and of being afraid for Mary and for her safety. Joseph knelt, at once, in prayer asking God, "Please bring her back. Please give me one more chance. Please help me to live only for you. Guide me as you would have me go. Let me be a lamp for you to all that I meet. God, I love you. Please forgive me as I strive to surrender all to you. Dear God, I know and appreciate your sacrifices for me of death, even death on a cross; I know that I am not worthy of the kind of love that you give me. Dear God, please forgive me for all my sins past and yet to be committed. I love you with all my heart. Be my center. Be my true north. Please keep me centered. You know that I love you and that I believe I need her to help me serve, as you would will. I want to submit to your will for my life. Please bring her back to me and let me love and care for her just as you, Christ yourself, loved the church. I love you with all my heart. Amen!"

"Dear God," Joseph prayed, "Please know that I believe that you are here. I feel your presence. I know that you are the God of Abraham, the Great I AM! You alone are the creator of all. I praise you for the wonders and the majesty of your world and your love. No one is like you, no not one. No one knows how the heavens and the earth were created. No one knows where wind comes from or to where it goes. There is none like you. You created the world in seven days. You created man from dirt and woman from the rib of Adam as he slept. You threw open your blessings to your people. Through your bond servant Joseph, you protected your people in Egypt during seven years of famine. Moses used his staff and the grace of your power to bring your people out of Egypt and into the Promised Land. You divided the Red Sea to save your people and then allowed the seas to close, killing all those who would persecute your people. You rose up a great king to unite your Kingdom. King David as a boy slew a Philistine giant, Goliath, with nothing more than a rock and a sling. You created King David, who was a man after your own heart. Perhaps the man who fell the most frequently and the hardest was a man but yet you called him a man after your own heart. The majesty of your ways beckons my name, pulls on my heart, and fills my every moment. You alone are the author of my life and in you alone I put my trust. There is no other God before you. There is no one like you. You alone are the king of kings, the lord of lords, the alpha and the omega. In you alone, I put my trust. You created me, a man, in your image. You felt the pain that I feel. You walked the trials that I face and yet you conquered all of them. You have taught me to abide deeply in your love and to trust you to have faith like that of a child. Father, I come to you. I place my life in your hands and my feet at your cross. Forgive me for my sins; please forgive me for the nails that I alone pierced through your hands and onto your cross. I alone am unworthy but with you I am protected by the lion of Judah, the truth and the light, a piece of the heavenly host. With your power, I can bind things on earth that will also be bound in heaven. With your faith, I can, with simply the faith of a mustard seed, move great mountains in your name. In you alone, I trust. Thought I walk through the valley of the shadow of death, my head will know no turning. Towards you and you alone, I will look, I will see, and I will follow. There is no one like you. You are the creator, Abba, Father, the lover of my soul, and my deliverer. I will follow you all the rest of the days of my life and in your peace I will rest. I will write your name on my door. I will teach my children your precepts so that when they are older, they will not stray. I will teach them as I walk, as I work, and as I play. They will seek your face; they will seek your Kingdom. I marvel at your works. I am astonished at your ways. Although you are a God that I fear because I know your teachings are true. I know that you desire that no one perish, no, not one. I know that you will work all things for good and in that faith I safely rest. Dear God, you have led me to this specific place and time. I am here. I am open. I want your will for my life. Dear God, fill me to overflowing; fill my heart abundantly with only you. I love you with all my heart. Amen!"

Joseph got up off his knees from his prayer feeling refreshed and invigorated by his communing and adoration of the Most High God. Joseph felt as if the shackles that had bound him all this time were gone and that now he was finally alive and living in the peace and love of His abiding spirit. Joseph knew that he had been washed in the blood of Jesus and that now with His guidance and leading that he could indeed do all things. Joseph knew that from this moment on, all he had to do was to live for Him and that if he did so, God himself would work all things for good.

Detective Stone was still aboard the perpetrator's boat collecting evidence when one of the Coast Guard personnel yelled, "I found something. Come here quick." It was Mary's phone. One of the soldiers leaned over to pick it up as Detective Stone approached the location in the hold where the phone was found. It was lodged behind a chair totally hidden from sight unless one were to lean well over the back of the chair to see it. As the soldier stretched out his hand to touch it, Detective Stone yelled out, "Don't touch it! I don't want to smudge any fingerprints." Reacting immediately to his command, the soldier pulled his hand away and moved away so that Detective Stone could approach. As Detective Stone's eyes adjusted to the lack of light behind the chair, it was then that he first saw it. He immediately asked for a flashlight so as to get a better look. Being careful to pick up the phone with latex gloves, Detective Stone immediately noticed that the phone was on and that it indicated that there was a message on it. After carefully peering further behind the chair, Detective Stone satisfied himself that there was nothing else to be found there. Carefully he held the phone, noticing that the signal strength was low, and pushed the play message on the button while holding it near to his ear as it played.

"So… you… you… am… ahead of you… If you… see… you'll… what… you've… told. This is your… warning." Detective Stone was both puzzled and frustrated as he listened, as not all the message was audible. Coming back topside, he again held the phone high and out in the open so as to strive to obtain a stronger signal and pushed the play message again.

Mary was being led now several feet from the door where she had been held captive. Once again, fear overtook her and she began to tremble, slightly at first and then uncontrollably. She took each step knowing that her next could be her last. His grip tightened on Mary causing her to grimace in pain as they walked down a hallway. Mary wondered if she would ever see the light of day.

They passed two rooms though she could tell nothing due to her eyes being blindfolded twice; she could feel the warmth of the outside air and could hear the wind blowing as if just before a storm. "You're here," he said gruffly.

Mary waited for the blow or gun blast that she knew was to come. Mary tensed, waiting and holding her breath tight, feeling that the inevitable would soon happen.

Holding the phone up in the air, seeing that the signal strength was much improved, Detective Stone pushed the play message again. Although he had to strain against the noise of the idling engines of the boat and the wind that was now picking up, he now heard his each and every word. "So you think you found us. I am way ahead of you. If you ever want to see her again, you'll do what you've been told. This is your last warning."

Stunned, Detective Stone leaned against the side of the boat and put his right hand over the top of his head down his face to his chin and sighed deeply. Pausing as if trying to be a thousand miles away, he yelled just loud enough to be heard over all the noise, "It's him. He duped us."

Looking down at his watch, Detective Stone remarked, "We have only ninety-six hours left, and we have a Category 4 hurricane breathing down our backs. We've got to find her. I want everyone at their best. Let's get on this. He started this and now I'm going to finish it. This has become personal."

Waiting for the blow or blast that would end her life, Mary steadied herself. Whispering amid her tears, she prayed, "I have always been yours and I am yours now!"

Gripping her even tighter, he pushed her forward saying, "I bet you're ready. It has to be time." Mary clenched her teeth tightly waiting to see Jesus when he said, "It's the bathroom." He continued, "I'm sure you have to go."

Chapter 11

DETECTIVE STONE had gone back to his office and was sitting at his desk furious. He was being played for a fool and he knew it and so did the killer. Never in his career had someone played him as well, much less for as long. Sure he had chased down bad clues or followed bum leads to dead ends, but never before had someone seemingly held such an upper hand. Detective Stone determined that this would not stand and that he would return Mary alive, or if God willed, he would die trying. So far, every hopeful lead or possibility had proven fruitless. The e-mail that had been sent had been traced down to a public library and it was determined that the real identity of the sender was a phony. Evidently, either the killer himself or perhaps someone he had hired entered a public library over a week ago and had set up a phony e-mail address for the ransom message to be sent for a certain day and a certain time. Evidently the killer was certain enough of the time and the place of the abduction that he was able to pick the exact moment that he could with certainty plan the timing and the delivery of the e-mail message. He had the message sent from Charleston's largest and busiest library where over a thousand patrons visit daily. Since that time, almost four thousand patrons would have visited the library, and there was nothing unusual that any of the librarians had noticed or observed on the day in question. Also, Detective Stone learned that the call that was made to Mary's cell phone was made from a very remote public phone. It was immediately dusted for fingerprints as well as her cell phone, which returned nothing but traces of Mary's very own prints. The public phone from which the call was made, was so remote and used so infrequently that it had already been slated to be removed next month by the phone company. People who lived and worked in the area near the phone had been canvassed and questioned only to find that no one had even been seen in the area for the last several weeks. The phone company confirmed that the time that the call was placed matched that of the time on Mary's cell phone but could only trace the call's date, time and origin from being from that of a public phone.

Every single lead Detective Stone had was turned for naught and Detective Stone did not know where to turn. He believed in his heart that he could and would find a way to solve this case but for now he knew not what to do. Detective Stone leaned his head down, burying his head in his hands and then rubbing his hands up and down on his forehead lamenting in anguish, "I'm going to get him if it's the last thing I do."

Joseph wanted to go home to spend the rest of the day there but with a Category 4 hurricane bearing down on Charleston, he had plenty at the office to do. As Charleston's harbormaster, it was his responsibility to get the whole of the harbor ready for the hurricane's impact. Several of the larger ships were readied and immediately ferreted out to sea to ride the storm out there, as most of the bigger ships were able to survive the storm more safely at sea. Almost all of the ships that were less than fifty feet in length had to be left where they were and tied up as best as could be, as they were too small to survive a storm of this magnitude out at sea. Often these ships in other harbors could be moved to other locations where natural barriers like big hills along the water could provide protection from the high winds and seas. Charleston's terrain, however, was very flat and there was no place for those smaller ships to hide. Therefore, the only security that could be offered was to attempt to ensure adequate tying, moorings and additional cushions along the sides and fronts of the ships so as to hopefully sufficiently protect them. Joseph had very specific guidelines for a Category 4 hurricane that he was required to follow to get the harbor ready. These procedures were constantly updated so as to ensure they remained applicable and that new procedures and nuances could be added to help ensure they remained as relative and functional as could be.

Due to the size of Hurricane Janet, an immediate evacuation had been ordered, with only fire, police and emergency personnel being allowed to remain in the area. Already relief efforts were being organized so that they could be on the scene as soon as the storm cleared the area. Large amounts of food, ice, water, and medical supplies were already being assimilated in preparation for the huge logistical issues that lay ahead. This storm was expected to be far worse than Hurricane Hugo, and the whole of the city of Charleston was busy boarding up their homes and businesses and then evacuating the city.

Mary was now being led back to the room where she had been held for almost two days. Having to still take little steps, as her feet were still bound, it seemed like she was getting nowhere as she was reduced to taking lots of three-inch steps. Mary could not help but see the irony of the fear she had felt as she had been led to the bathroom. She had feared that she was being led to her own slaughter. Mary was thankful that her hands were tied in the front of her body so that she could still do some little things for herself. She knew that the little acts of decency that had been afforded her were just that, and she believed, absent God's intervention, that her life was in immediate and dire jeopardy. Mary's captor had been careful to hide his face, to blindfold her as she had left the room where she had been held and to continue to disguise his voice. After leading her back into the room, he shuffled about as if he was moving something into the room. Mary hoped that it might be something to eat and drink, as it had been several hours since her body had last been nourished. He led her to the center of the room and then faced her toward the back of the room as he untied both of the blindfolds that had covered her eyes. As he left the room, Mary turned slightly to get a glimpse of him as he was closing the heavy door. Shuddering as she got a brief glimpse of her masked kidnapper. Mary heard him moving back into place the large boards that blocked the door and heard the locks being shut and closed tight. Mary was thankful that, at least for the time being, she was alive and that maybe God would somehow yet intervene. Mary noticed the water and sandwich near the door and took baby steps over to pick them up. Opening the sandwich up, Mary sat down on the side of the bed, savoring her peanut butter and jelly sandwich.

Although the grape jelly was not her favorite, she enjoyed that the sandwich was made with a creamy peanut butter, which had been applied liberally. Savoring each bite as she chewed, Mary knew that God cared about all the little things in her life as well as the larger ones.

Joseph knelt at his desk and prayed, "God, you know and see all. You know how and why our lives began and how they are yet to be lived out and how they will yet end. I believe that Mary and I were meant to be and to live as man and wife and to serve you and your Kingdom. Please guide me in helping to secure her freedom and to be a light of you in this world to those I meet and know. Let me seek out ways to serve you and to share your love with others. Dear God, I know your teachings and I hold them dear to my heart. Please bring Mary home safely so that we might serve you together as one. Jesus, I love her. I want to help bring her home. I am your bond servant. Send me! Please, Dear God, hear my prayer. In Jesus' name, I pray. Amen."

Grandpa Billy and Grandma were at home making some final preparations for the storm that was headed their way. They remembered the damage that Hugo had done to the whole of the Charleston area, and Hurricane Janet was expected to be even worse. Grandpa Billy was luckily able to find someone to come over and board up the windows and to help move the keepsakes that were on the lower level of the home upstairs. The storm surge was expected to still arrive at high tide and the weather alerts were still anticipating a surge of historic proportions. Grandpa Billy and Grandma had decided to ride out the storm at a city shelter. Normally they would have left Charleston with the storm bearing down on them, but with Mary still missing neither of them felt comfortable with leaving with her not yet being found. Since her disappearance neither of them had enjoyed a good night's sleep and Grandma especially was not holding up well. Through the storm Grandma knew she could survive well enough, but she was deeply afraid for the safety of her daughter Mary.

After Mary had finished eating, she decided to open up the Bible that had been left at the nightstand by the bed. There were lots of markings throughout the Bible in all types of different colors and annotations with notes made beside many of the verses. Mary noticed that most of the verses underlined had been done with a black or a blue pen. Mary noticed that there were a few verses throughout the Bible that were done in red, and the notations beside them seemed to be done more emphatically than the others. The writer appeared to be angry and had taken and interpreted the verses out of context from the way she had understood the passages, particularly the way God laid out the world and the book of Genesis. To Mary, it just all seemed so simple as God had made earth for man and for him to care for it and had also given man a woman as a helpmate so that he would not have to be alone. Mary imagined that life in the garden would have been grand as man was placed in charge of all the animals there and had the opportunity to commune, walk, and even talk with God himself.

God had but one command, and that was for man not to eat from the tree of life, and when man failed to live up to this command, God banished man from the Garden of Eden. As a consequence to man's sin, God also added several crosses for man to bear that otherwise they would not have had to. Among those, God cursed woman to have pain in childbirth and that her desire will be to rule over her husband. God added curses to Adam that the earth's ground would be cursed and that man, only through painful work and the sweat of his brow would he eat of it.

Mary thumbed ahead through the books of the Old Testament to Numbers chapter 33, finding more verses in red with angry notations made where God commanded the Israelites to take the land and to live in it as God gave them the land to have as their own. God commanded the Israelites to drive out the people who had lived in the land and that if they did not that they would become "barbs in your eyes and thorns in the land where you live. And then I will do to you what I plan to do to them."

Mary read on to Deuteronomy chapter 20, where God gave the land over to the Israelites, commanding that all the inhabitants be killed by the sword taking all of their plunder and making sure not to leave anything alive that breathes lest the Israelites learn their evil ways and in doing so, would sin against God. God told the people of Israel not to destroy its trees because of the fruit that they would bear.

Mary had always believed that God was a just and fair God who loved his people and worked all things for their good. She believed that these verses laid out man's consequences that occurred as a result of his failings to live in accordance with God and His will. The red highlights and the handwritten notes written beside the verses were very cold and terse and seemed to belie an underlying anger that she could not put her finger on. One of them in particular disturbed Mary when it said beside one of the red underlined verses, "death to all who would destroy our environment."

Mary shuddered, wondering if the writer of these notes had taken these verses of God's discipline and love to be one of vengeance and anger. Beginning to shake again in fear, Mary put down the Bible and lay back on the bed trying to regain her wits about her and to rest. Mary had wondered why the killer had only selected real estate agents, and now she wondered if it was because agents assisted in developing raw land into subdivisions and communities. She had always prided herself on developing and selling in communities that were in harmony with nature and that added to an area's ambiance rather than detracting from it. Mary was also an active and integral member of the Charleston Historical and Preservation Society, which helped to restore homes and communities to their original luster. And now for what she felt was her having been a responsible citizen, Mary was being held captive against her wishes by a serial killer. Mary wondered if those who were victims in the past had ever been held here and for how long before their ultimate murder. Mary knew that no one in the past had ever escaped and she did not see any way for her to do so now. Perhaps now, Mary alone had discovered the reasons for the past murders and she wondered how she might be able to help the police quickly discover the who before it was too late.

Chapter 12

DETECTIVE STONE sat in his office contemplating his next move. His pulse, as well as his blood pressure, was still at elevated levels from the chase and its disappointment. Detective Stone had never been toyed with like this before. He felt like a mouse being played with by a cat right before it made its final pounce and before devouring its prey. Detective Stone knew he had been played as the fool on this case so far, but he believed truth and good would always triumph over will.

The door-to-door canvassing at and near the Charleston Historical and Preservation Society's restoration home had so far resulted in pretty much a dead end, but had prompted some initial excitement. One of the neighbors several doors down from the restoration house had seen a car leaving slowly that evening approximately thirty minutes after dusk. They had seen the car pulling away with its lights off and then after it had passed several homes, turned its lights on and proceeded down the street. The neighbor reported nothing else unusual about the vehicle other than perhaps a neighbor who had initially forgotten to turn on their lights. They reported that they believed it was an American-made vehicle and perhaps a four-door with dark blue or gray paint. Tire tracks in the restoration house had been analyzed and determined to be a match of commonly used steel-belted radials sold on almost three million mid-size American cars annually. Detective Stone resolved to not let this kidnapping stand and to bring Mary safely home to Joseph and her family.

Hurricane Janet was still classified as a Category 4 hurricane and was due to officially hit the city within six to eight hours. Seas and winds had both dramatically picked up in the last two to three hours, and soon hurricane-force winds and seas would be buffeting the whole of the Charleston area. Hurricane Janet was expected to intensify and the eye of rotation of the hurricane itself to tighten as it neared and landed on the shores of Charleston. The eye of the storm itself ranged from approximately fifty to seventy miles across with the whole of the most dangerous areas of the storm approximately two hundred miles wide. The eye of the storm was still expected to be a direct hit on the whole of Charleston proper. As Detective Stone sat at his desk contemplating the effects of the storm on his investigation, he realized that when it hit there would be no investigative progress made during the storm at all. Detective Stone still believed that the one-hundred-hour ransom note was real and that he now only had eighty hours to find Mary and to find her alive.

Mayor James White came on regional news coverage again reiterating the mandatory evacuation of the whole of the Metropolitan Charleston area. Mayor White discussed in brief detail, safety procedures, but with the hurricane now only a few hours away, he focused mainly on evacuation efforts and procedures. Police and emergency personnel were canvassing the streets, neighborhoods, and businesses, ensuring that everyone was leaving and assisting anyone who needed special help. Mayor White made it very clear that this was a mandatory evacuation and that everyone must leave at once.

Only after Mayor White covered the details of the evacuation did he then turn his thoughts and words towards solving the case of the serial killer. "As you know, there is yet a serial killer in our midst. As you are aware, we have recently redoubled our efforts to solve the case and to bring the perpetrator to trial and justice to light. I stand along with the fine people of the citizenry of Charleston in their fervent desire to bring peace back to our fine community. The timing of Hurricane Janet could not have been worse. But, we will not cease in our efforts, and we will continue to work around the clock throughout even the eye of the storm. I, along with police and emergency personnel, detectives of the task force, the FBI, and other federal agencies will remain here and on task as long as it takes. I pledge to each and every one of you that I will not rest until these terrors that beset our city are resolved. I am and will forever be on watch looking out over our fair city, and we will persevere."

Joseph listened intently to Mayor White as he spoke. Although Joseph was relatively new to Charleston, he sensed Mayor White's words and intentions matched that of his heart. Joseph heard the procedures Mayor White detailed regarding the evacuation for the oncoming hurricane, but he did not listen intently until Mayor White began his addressing the details of the search for Mary's kidnapper. The airwaves had been flashing hourly updates on the search for the serial killer and Mary's picture, her physical description, including the clothes she was last seen wearing, and her last known whereabouts. Joseph knew the clock was ticking, and he continued to make himself available to Detective Stone for any help of any kind that he might need to aid in the investigation. Joseph knew of the ransom note, but at this time Detective Stone decided that it was in the best interest of the investigation not to mention the existence of the note or its details. Joseph thought to himself that he was unsure as to why this had been decided in this way, but he trusted Detective Stone implicitly.

Joseph still had a few things left to do to get ready, including ensuring that the commercial loading docks were being shut down tight and made storm-ready. Joseph planned to leave the office in just a few minutes to go over to the loading docks himself to double-check and ensure that all containers, both full and empty, were adequately secured. These containers were less tightly moored, which could result in them becoming loose and then being blown apart, causing massive property damage and potentially loss of life. Joseph would meet one of his staff at the loading dock that was there on-site and already anticipating his arrival shortly.

Joseph's site visit to the docks went smoothly with his staff member having explicitly followed the detailed hurricane procedures exactly. As Joseph was driving back to the office, he picked up his cell and dialed Detective Stone, who answered on the first ring. Joseph said, "Hello, it's me Joseph. I know you have your hands full with both the storm and with Mary missing, but I want you to know that I am here and I support and believe in you no matter what. I will do absolutely anything that you need."

Detective Stone was in his office still focusing his one-hundred-percent effort on the investigation and its continuance, in spite of the storm. Detective Stone knew that he only had eighty hours left before the ransom note's one-hundred-hour deadline lapsed. Accordingly, Detective Stone was diligently working with all of his staff members and detectives to give enough directives and resources so as to ensure that their efforts could continue even during the height of the storm. Although no one would actually be assigned to be out in the storm itself, there would be substantive man-hours of research and investigative analysis that could be done while inside during the storm. Most of Detective Stone's task force would ride out the storm there at the office, where there would be more than enough desks, computers and telephones. The offices were manned with emergency backup power that had been tested recently and had proved sufficiently reliable.

As Joseph spoke to Detective Stone, he listened intently to Joseph's reiterations to do anything he could to assist in the investigation. Thinking aloud, Detective Stone acknowledged that to Joseph, "I really could use your help, especially after the storm passes. I'll need every boat I can get out into the harbor, along the Atlantic shoreline and up into the rivers to see what can be seen and to stay on alert on our waterways. As you know, several of the missing were found out in the water and I feel that he either lives along the water or is often out at sea. I'll have one of my staff call you with details of how you might be able to assist. I greatly appreciate your help. I know how much Mary means to you. I want to bring her home safely too."

It had been several hours since her captor had led Mary out of her room. Mary could hear muted wind noises as the tip of the hurricane was now upon the Charleston area and where she was being hidden. Initially, Mary could scantly hear the rain that plummeted the building that she was in and the hurricane-force winds whipping about, but as the eye of the storm approached, the intensity of the rain and the wind dramatically increased. Mary could tell it was a massive storm but being unsure of where she was and how deeply secured in the bowels of the building she was in, it was difficult to accurately estimate just how big the storm was or might be.

Mary continued to read on in the Bible that had been left there, finding more red markings with tense wording that appeared to be threats to those who might threaten the world that God had intended. Beside the verses in Matthew 5:5 where Jesus promised, "Blessed are the meek, for they will inherit the earth," were notations made that said "Woe be to those who do not protect our world."

Mary wondered if her captor might be an avid environmentalist or perhaps a "tree hugger" or maybe even a zealot from Greenpeace who might do anything to stand in the way of progress. Mary, herself, was a fervent believer of protecting the environment and maintaining the beauty of God's creation. Yet Mary also believed that it was possible for property to be developed both commercially and residentially while still maintaining the beauty of older trees, especially the old oaks that graced the city of Charleston and her surrounding areas and marshes. Mary said aloud to herself, though she was the only one there, "I fight to save history and to keep it alive, and now it looks as though I am doomed to die at the hands of someone who believes more like I do than not. Who would have thought the irony of it all."

Mary could now begin to feel the whole of the structure of the building that she was in begin to shudder and shake from the hurricane-force winds that blew about outside. Though she had no windows in her room, she could hear the wind howling through them as well as what had to be debris that was being blown against the building where she was being held. Initially, the debris being thrown by the wind seemed to be smaller pieces of debris and perhaps mid-size sticks and twigs. Now, however, with the rain's reaching full force, large thuds, which she imagined to be trees or large logs, tore against the building. Also, there were large clankings and groanings of debris and material she believed were perhaps pieces of sheet metal signage that had been loosened and were now being thrown against the structure.

Mary had stopped reading for some time now and listened intently as the rain continued to plummet the roof so fast and so furious that Mary imagined the water to literally be falling in continuous sheets against everything in its way. Mary remembered riding out Hurricane Hugo in a storm shelter, but even in the deepest part of the storm, she never heard howlings and tree cracklings as often and as severe as now. Mary had not heard any noise of any type from her captor for some time and well before since the storm had reached its zenith. Mary imagined that he must have left shortly after he had returned her to her room. Mary knew that the room she was in was solid but hoped that the exterior of the structure was just as solid. Mary sat reflectively thinking and hoping that her captor had left her in a secure facility and had not left because he knew that it was unsafe. Mary could not help but muse about the irony of wondering if the serial killer had left her alone in a building that was unsafe. Mary almost smirked, thinking that she hoped he had not left there for safer quarters during the storm, almost like she would have wanted him there to help ensure her safety.

Joseph arrived back at his office just an hour before the storm's true intensity began to be felt at his office along the docks. Joseph and several other key harbor personnel had holed up in one of the inner offices of the building on the second floor. Their cars were protected from the hurricane-force winds as Janet roared with ferocity against the sea and everything within miles of it. Joseph knew that his car and those of his key personnel were at risk from flooding as they were at or slightly below street level. With the volume of rain, as well as the predicted storm surge, there were bound to be areas of localized and widespread flooding.

Joseph had opted, and in accordance with his prescribed procedures, to send all but essential and critical staff home to join their families in the evacuation of the city. Joseph had never himself been through a hurricane before but had heard the frightening tales of others who had. Already, the whole of the building moved and squawked with each microburst of wind that buffeted about the building. Joseph knew that his location was still perhaps thirty minutes away from the worst of the storm. Upon its arrival, forecasters were anticipating that the worst of the storm would be over his area for about three to four hours. The storm was moving at approximately twenty-four knots and the swirling winds around the eye of the storm were almost one hundred miles in circumference. Then torrential downpours and widespread tornadoes were predicted over the whole of the area for another eight hours. The storm surge itself was anticipated to begin arriving near its zenith in approximately an hour, but with it, the waves were expected to pound the coastline and everything near it for over three hours. The surge itself was now already at six feet and was estimated to soon be approximately fifteen feet. Joseph knew that anything near the coast could well be soon under water. Remembering Detective Stone's words, Joseph now feared for Mary even more, as Detective Stone believed the killer to live near or on the water. Trying as hard as he might to focus on his tasks and required job responsibilities, his mind never swayed far from her.

Detective Stone sat at his desk and for the first time in weeks, allowed himself but a moment to relax. Hurricane Janet had hit the city of Charleston as predicted, dead center and with hurricane-force and sustained winds of one hundred forty miles an hour and a storm surge ranging from fourteen to eighteen feet depending on location. Several of the smaller inlets and creeks had the higher storm surges as the waters just had nowhere else to go, while some of the larger tributaries and marshes had many square miles for the water to spread over.

Now in the zenith of the storm not even emergency personnel were allowed out and into the streets, as the risk to their own personal safety was too grave. Emergency calls poured in, with police personnel trying to do their best to help each and every one over the phone. Only one ambulance was allowed to venture out as a mother was giving birth while talking to emergency personnel via phone and it appeared as if the baby might be breach. The husband had followed the steps diligently but when it became a matter of life and death for both the mother and the child, an ambulance was dispatched. As luck would have it, their residence was only a few blocks from the police station.

Detective Stone's task force and personnel had direct orders from Mayor White that none of his men were to be pulled off the case for any reason. Although Detective Stone had his full complement of personnel that were assigned to him, they were all but useless as phone lines were down, people had evacuated, and only emergency power was left on in the station. The usual staff was reduced to try to focus, during the worst hurricane in recorded history, to hit the city of Charleston, while having only at their disposal, notes, pictures, and brainstorming with each other. On the hour, Detective Stone rotated around to each and every one of this people to intently encourage and to challenge them to focus and to move forward. Detective Stone knew that it might be even tougher after the storm as a result of downed power lines, trees, debris, and swarms of emergency personnel. The National Guard had already been readied and was on standby to enter Charleston as soon as the storm cleared the area. Detective Stone was betting on a hunch that the killer had not left the area during the throes of the storm. Detective Stone was planning, as soon as possible, to get his people out on the streets looking for any sign at all that might lead him to Mary. Rather than viewing the storm as a curse, as he did initially, he now believed that indeed it might be an opportunity to assist him as only a few wayward souls and emergency personnel would be left in the city. Detective Stone knew that he only needed to find one of them, the one that held Mary captive.

Chapter 13

Hurricane Janet bore down in its intensity upon the entire city of Charleston. It was an hour into the storm now and the winds and rain continued to pelt the dwelling where she lay captive. As the storm's eye neared, Hurricane Janet raged in fury against all that she encountered. Water began seeping into the room where Mary sat motionless. It began ever so slowly and then the drops of water started pouring in more rapidly. Trying to slow down the flow of water into the room, she removed the sheet from the bed and patted it tight against the wall. It seemed to work at first, but soon the sheet became drenched and the water came over the top. Within a few minutes, water covered the entire floor of the room. The electricity to this point had still remained on, but soon, a microburst of wind sheared off most of the tree from the ground just outside. The tree fell in a loud crack, severing the electrical supply to the dwelling, and Mary's sole light was immediately doused and she was plunged into total darkness.

As the winds continued to howl and swirl, numerous tornadoes were spawned, especially on the northeast side of the hurricane, where winds were at their highest speeds and most tightly wound. Unbeknownst to Mary, a tornado was bearing down on her. Mary sat back down on the bed, her feet now ankle deep in water. Not knowing where she was in the dwelling, she hoped that she was not in the basement and that she might avoid drowning when the storm surge arrived. No sooner had the thought passed her mind than she heard a rush of water against the building, slamming debris with it as it came. Immediately, water rushed into her room, raising the water level to just below her knees. As the water continued to rise, she climbed up on top of the bed and then, pushing the lamp off the nightstand, she chose to sit on the night stand leaving her feet on the bed.

Right when Mary thought it could not get any worse, it got much more so. The tornado that bore down on her was now within a hundred yards of her location. Mary had previously thought the howling of the hurricane to be severe but now she found the raw, directed and specific power of the tornado bearing down on her tormenting. As it neared, it shattered every tree in its path in an awesome array of damage. The tornado now was within a hundred feet of where she was held hostage. Here, tied up, with nowhere to go to protect herself, she feared as it drew closer. The tornado's roar now resounded hauntingly as it sounded like a diesel locomotive bearing down on her. Fearing the worst, Mary huddled in the corner of the room with the water now about her knees, waiting and not knowing.

Grandpa Billy and Grandma were huddled along with Mary's son, David, and with hundreds of others in a city storm shelter. Beneath a blanket, more for comfort than for warmth, Grandpa Billy help Grandma tight and close. "Grandma, you know we've been through a lot. We'll get through this too. I just know they are going to find her. They will bring our baby home."

As he spoke, Grandpa Billy gained confidence in his own words and in their truth. Relishing in this power, for the first time since Mary's disappearance, Grandpa Billy knew Mary would come home and they would all be together again soon. Holding Grandma tight, she sensed his words were confident and Grandma knew Grandpa Billy believed each and every one of them to be true. As the storm raged on, Grandma sat in his quiet embrace as safe as the day they met. Grandma loved Grandpa Billy, she always trusted and always believed in him. As the storm raged on outside, Grandma leaned deeply into his arms, comforted by his words and clinging deeply to their truth.

Hurricane Janet now drove head-on into the glory of the city of Charleston. Janet buffeted the city with heavy seas, 140-mile-an-hour winds, and relentless rain. The heavy seas, combined with the sustained winds, created a storm surge that destroyed everything in its path. Beachfront homes just north of Charleston, in the Isle of Palms, were decimated. Fifteen-foot storm surges roared over the beachfront, both moving entire homes from their foundations and washing away the entire contents of others. The storm surge washed homeowners' cars away and dumped boats in the front yards of others.

The Battery was awash in waves beating both on and over it, causing massive flooding for up to one half a mile deep into the rows of old homes and the historic district of Charleston. The main levels of the homes both along the Battery and several blocks inland were awash with over five feet of water. Most of the homeowners in these homes and within several blocks had moved all of their furniture and keepsakes to upper levels of their homes in order to protect them. All electrical power in the city was off to both homes and businesses, and only those with generators or emergency backup power had any at all. Trees and debris fell against homes, shattering windows and roofs alike. Many of Charleston's oldest and grandest oak trees fell as if they were toothpicks, creating huge gashes in everything they hit and holes in the ground where the roots were uplifted.

Joseph was at the office electronically looking on as the hurricane ravaged the coast and the harbor. As harbormaster, Joseph had three separate weather and water analysis buoys that were still operational. Being self-contained with their own battery source, they continued to transmit data recording wave action, water temperature, and speed of the current and tidal action. The buoys were being hammered by the storm but so far, they had held fast and dutifully reported their data. The storm surge at the varying weather buoys ranged from twelve to sixteen feet based upon where in the harbor they were located. Joseph knew that the harbor and the navigable rivers leading into her could be one of the first modes of transportation that would be viable after the storm. The debris thrown into Charleston's rivers and harbor either quickly sank or would be gently moved out, and water currents after the storm would be much higher than normal after the storm's passage as the driving forces of the hurricane would be gone and the water would soon settle back out to where nature and her gravity pulled it.

Joseph's office continued on using emergency backup power as the storm roared on. One of his staff, using the inner stairwell, had ventured downstairs and opened an inner door just enough and verified that as of yet, their cars had not been flooded. Perhaps there might be a saving grace or two here yet.

Mary continued to huddle in the corner of her darkened room with her feet bound in knee-deep water. Now Mary could hear more and more debris being thrown about outside as the tornado that was headed her way moved ever so closely. Each time a large piece of debris hit the building, she shuddered as she felt the walls do the same as she leaned against them. The pounding of debris became a roar and she imagined the outside of the building had been heavily damaged. Incessant lightning streaked the sky and the thunder resounded and echoed against the sky and the ground. One of the streaks hit so close, Mary shuddered as the ground reverberated and shook against the power of the strike. Mary strained against the darkness to see, but the room seemed to capture and remove all the light. All of Mary's visual senses were gone, leaving her surrounded in darkness, huddled even closer still to the corner of the room saying aloud to herself, "It will be all over soon. I do not want to die! Not now and definitely not this way." Mary knew she was speaking aloud, but the pounding winds, flying debris, and thunder made it impossible to hear herself speak.

Mary braced herself as best she could with her arms and legs still bound. Mary's knuckles, though she could not see, were white from clenching them tightly, but with nothing to hold on to but her other hand, she clenched them even tighter all the same.

Detective Stone watched the news releases reporting on the intensity of the hurricane as it battered the city. Although his staff had been given specific directives not to lose their focus on continuing the investigative leads of the case, he worried about their doing so all the same. Detective Stone listened as forecasters expected the worst of the storm to continue for approximately an hour more. Although the basic center of the storm itself would be gone within the hour, the remaining swirling winds would still be in excess of a hundred miles an hour. These winds would still be capable of spawning tornadoes and causing substantial damage. Roads were expected to be largely impassable as downed trees, limbs and power lines blocked virtually every street in the city. Luckily, immediately before the storm hit, Detective Stone's staff had been fortunate enough to procure chain saws and work gloves in order for his people to both get around and through the debris. Several of the detectives and investigators also had jeeps, which would prove greatly useful immediately after the storm. The clearance of these vehicles alone would be useful in going over and around the rubbish that would be strewn everywhere.

Detective Stone's staff was poised and ready to hit the streets looking especially for those who had stayed during the storm. Detective Stone believed even more that the killer had not left town, nor had he moved Mary, resulting in a very small population of people who would be left for this staff to focus on. He hoped that Mary was being held in a secure location so that she would not be a storm casualty. Believing that the killer lived on or near the water, Detective Stone knew that there was great potential for her to be in harm's way. Detective Stone knew that it would be tough going immediately after the storm but believed that it would indeed be a target-rich environment to search for the killer and for Mary.

Mary huddled, cowering as the tornado came even closer. The swirling winds continued to throw debris in every direction. The fierce winds continued to throw loose items of every type in all directions. Mary grimaced, waiting for the tornado's full impact, leaning into the walls of the building so she could feel it vibrating wildly from the ferocity of the tornado's winds. Closing her eyes tightly, Mary prepared for the worst, which she knew would soon be upon her, shredding the structure and everything within it. Holding on to herself as she waited, she grasped her own ankles holding tight.

Continuing to wait for the impact that never came, Mary kept her eyes shut. Suddenly, the tornado made a large whooshing sound as it was pulled back into the skies from which it came. Initially, Mary did not even know what it was or what happened as the tornado continued to pull back up towards and into the sky. The tornado hardly grazed the building in which she was held, only slightly touching as its swirling winds retreated. The tornado, as it withdrew, dropped its debris on the roof of the building. Most of the debris hitting the roof was of moderate size, while the larger debris held within its winds fell as the retreating tornado had cleared the structure.

Mary allowed herself to open her eyes, though still seeing nothing in its darkness; she now knew that the tornado had blown over the building. Letting go of the grip that she had on her own ankles, blood flowed back into her knuckles, hands and face. Mary knew she had dodged a bullet and that she had one more to dodge.

The hurricane raged on outside, but Mary knew that she would survive and live, at least until the storm had run its course, but she knew little else.

Joseph's office, staff and equipment had suffered little damage so far during the storm. They had been very fortunate indeed. It looked as if the hurricane's westerly end would be taking her winds inland within the hour. The harbormaster's hurricane procedures required that no one venture outside until sustained winds were less than sixty miles an hour and had been so for over an hour so as to preclude one of the swirling bands circling back around and raising havoc when least suspected. It was now two in the afternoon and based upon current forecasts, Joseph's people might be able to get out in the next three hours. Perhaps if they were able to get out soon, they would at least be able to perform a cursory review of the docks and review the harbor's waters using electronic equipment, radars, and visual inspection. The seas and winds would be too high until tomorrow when the higher winds would have moved even further inland. By late tomorrow afternoon, winds were expected to be gusting slightly higher than normal ocean breezes that occurred this time of year and skies were anticipated to be partly cloudy with all of the heavy rains having moved out.

Joseph's first concern after they were cleared was to personally check on the harbormaster's harbor ship. As he planned to personally be on board when it set sail touring the harbor, its inland waterways and just outside the Charleston harbor up and down the Atlantic.

The harbor ship had been moored in a deep-water channel and was slightly sheltered from the wind by a small outcropping of marshland and trees. Also, its moorings were located such that no direct waves would be received. Yet, as with all things anywhere near the water, the vessel would be impacted by the storm surge. Before the hurricane arrived, the moorings were adjusted so as to strive to allow enough flexibility for the vessel to rise and fall with the waves and the storm surge but secure enough so as to not cause damage to the vessel.

Joseph's first responsibility would be to clear the harbor after the hurricane. Initially only small vessels would be cleared, and it would be several days to perhaps a week before all of the channel's depths could be verified to be clear of shifting debris and silt, thus setting the way for the large cargo and container commercial ships to enter the harbor. Joseph had already planned for extra personnel to be assigned to the vessel so that they could complete the assigned tasks as harbormaster and then he could dedicate as much of his time while on board to the search for Mary.

Joseph counted the hours in his head since the ransom note detailing the hundred hours. It was now forty hours into the hundred-hour period and it would be approximately another eighteen before it would be safe to venture out into the harbor. Joseph quickly calculated; this would only leave fifty-two hours to look for Mary with only a few late afternoon hours tomorrow in which to look. Gritting his teeth and lowering his head and placing his hands over the top of his head, he said aloud, "I've got to find her. I'm going to do it if it's the last thing I do."

Hurricane Janet raged on through the night and on toward three in the morning. Janet had been downgraded to a Category 1 hurricane. The rains continued to plummet the city, with flooding now rampant on Charleston's streets and byways. Already twelve to fourteen inches had fallen with several more expected as the tail of the storm moved out of the area. The storm surge was now starting to retreat back into the vastness of the Atlantic Ocean. The storm surge had arrived just as feared, at high tide, causing extensive damage up and down the coast and throughout the entire area of Charleston. As the waters retreated, they revealed a wake of damage and destruction that had been the path of Hurricane Janet. Low-lying areas and marshland remained in several feet of water and it would yet be several days until the water evaporated or soaked into the already saturated ground. As Janet moved further inland, it continued to weaken as its supply source of energy, the open seas, had been taken away. Forecasters were expecting Hurricane Janet to be out of the Charleston area by noon and to be downgraded even further to a tropical storm.

Although power was out in much of the city, Mayor White was to go on regional television and radio to address the city and region. Joseph listened intently as he spoke: "My fellow Charlestonians, Hurricane Janet has almost fully left our city and we should see the remaining remnants leave our city soon. Reports are still coming in, but the storm has caused damage even exceeding what was expected. Our president has committed to doing whatever is necessary including declaring the city a disaster area. National Guard troops have already been readied and are set to start arriving within twenty-four hours and will be here as long as it takes. Emergency ice, water, food and medical supplies are even now being logistically organized for immediate arrival. Hurricane Janet caused widespread damage from high winds, heavy rains and flooding, and the storm surge wreaked havoc for all those near the coast. Charleston is a strong city, filled with fervent and great people. Charleston has consistently overcome each and every obstacle in the past and will do so yet again."

Joseph appreciated Mayor White's words of encouragement to the people of Charleston and to himself. Mayor White's stock went up even further as he addressed his city and his people. However, at the present moment, Joseph had more on his mind than rebuilding a city, more than recovering from a hurricane; his mind was on finding Mary and finding her now.

———

Mary continued sleeping. After the tornado had passed overhead, Mary allowed herself to relax. She found that she was so exhausted that she had lain out on the bed and had soon found herself fast asleep. Luckily the water in the room was only deep enough so that it touched the bottom of the box springs but had left the mattress substantially dry. When the water had first started seeping and then openly flowing into the room, Mary had taken care to place the ends of the sheets up on top of the bed so that they would not become soaked.

Although still bound, Mary had slept soundly through most of the second half of the hurricane. Mary awoke briefly only once when a lightning strike had hit a nearby oak tree, causing it to splinter at its base and fall. She had pulled the sheets up and over her body, being sure to tuck them around her so as to ensure that they stayed safe and dry. After the first and only time she had awakened and then fallen back asleep, Mary dreamed. She dreamt that she was back at home and she was safe. As she slowly awoke, she could tell that the hurricane had greatly subsided and was beginning to leave the area. Mary groggily moved about; although the foot of water had drained from the room's floor, it was still wet and had a few remaining puddles scattered about.

Mary's throat was parched dry and she realized how hungry she had become. She guessed it had been approximately eighteen hours since she had last eaten. Mary rubbed her eyes, trying to rid them and herself of the sleepiness that she felt. Rubbing her eyes as she might, she could never seem to feel awake as the total blackness of the room served to keep her disoriented. Mary reached for the lamp and pressed the button a few times but she found, exactly as she had expected, that the power remained out. Mary resigned herself to the pitch-black darkness and lay back on the bed. As Mary began to recall her dream, she thought of a time when she might make it safely home and be reunited with her loved ones. To be able to see Joseph and David again brought joy to her face, and through the darkness, her eyes twinkled. Mary lay there hoping and believing that all might yet be all right. She had come this far through the ordeal and believed that maybe, just maybe, Jesus could see her through.

Mary knew that her kidnapper would more than likely return soon. Due to the size of the storm and the tornado that had befallen the property, Mary knew that it would be perhaps several hours before he returned. Mary believed that this was the serial killer that had already killed several and that he would kill again. She resolved herself to do the best that she could to be steady and to strive to not be afraid. Mary shuddered as she thought to herself of his returning and what would come next. Gritting her teeth, Mary clenched them tight, hoping, praying, and knowing that it all had already been decided. Mary believed in the sovereignty of God and that all things had already been decided but that yet she had a part to play; to exercise her free will and to live in accordance with His precepts. Mary knew that God never caused unjust people to do wrongly but that He always used everything good and bad to accomplish His purposes. Mary, with darkness all about her, felt like she was being held hostage almost like Jonah in the belly of the fish. Mary determined to do everything she could forevermore, no matter how long or short, to serve Him and His Kingdom.

Detective Stone's people were beginning to venture out. The skies were beginning to have open patches of blue between the steel-gray clouds.

Detective Stone had dispatched his investigators and detectives to various locations throughout the city. He had lots of office time during the storm to strategically locate his people to have the most exposure, especially to those who had remained in the city. Detective Stone remained confident that the killer still was here in the city and that this might be the best chance to catch him. He knew it was necessary to act fast as the end of the hundred-hour deadline was rapidly approaching.

As the detectives and investigators spread out and into the city, they found the chain saws to be invaluable in removing debris just enough in order to pass. Almost every hundred yards the trees were so badly strewn about that they would have to get out of the car periodically to clear a path. Occasionally one of the larger oak trees would totally block a thoroughfare and force them to turn around and to choose another route. When possible, if the sides of the roadways were open, they would simply drive through a yard or over a sidewalk in order to avoid the unnecessary delay of removing the debris from the roads. Most of the roads they traveled had not been traveled yet even by emergency personnel as Detective Stone wanted his people to be on the scene before anyone else.

Joseph's staff had checked the harbormaster's boat and found it had weathered the storm quite well. There was storm debris tossed on board by the waves and then wind blown as well on board which was quickly cleared. Heavy rains and the storm surge each contributed to water that had partly filled several of the ship's bulkheads. With the ship's pumps running at full throttle, they were able to quickly clear the vessel of all standing water. Joseph was well pleased to find the ship in such good condition, and they made arrangements to ready her for tomorrow as they would be on board for the whole day. Stores were inventoried and the captain's log checked to be sure that all would be ripe for an early start.

The sun was beginning to set through the remaining clouds and it shone brilliantly through the clouds, promising a new day of hope. A rainbow appeared alongside and parallel to the Cooper River Bridge. The rainbow shone bright red, yellow, green, blue and violet. The size of the rainbow was like nothing ever seen before. The sunlight danced across the sky. Locals and emergency personnel alike were drawn out of their homes to admire its radiance. The rainbow spanned from the Charleston Bridge all the way to the other side of the Cooper River Bridge over and into Mt. Pleasant. Many who saw it simply gasped at the height and depth of the rainbow and its beauty. Many just stood silently and fell deep in prayer and thankfulness of what God had just brought them through. Townspeople prayed both silently and out loud but as all one people relying on His promises, not of ever flooding the earth again, but of

His eternal love and grace. Some fell to their knees awash in the Holy Spirit and His cleansing and preserving love. Several, for the first time ever, accepted Christ as their Savior, letting Him indwell in their hearts completely. Though the city was awash in the debris of Hurricane Janet, Jesus showed up in a big and powerful way, calling and beckoning His people while filling them totally.

Joseph looked up in awe as the rainbow soared over the harbor and dwarfed the city. Joseph knew it was He that had sent it and that He had sent it for each and every one of them there. For all who saw it, God promised everyone who believed and met each believer exactly where they were. As a rainbow reflects light to the one seeing it, only that person sees the rainbow from the perspective. As such, no perspective or life is identical; Jesus used the rainbow and then the Holy Spirit to speak to everyone just where they were. No one received the same message as God knows that all of His children are unique and they all need love, understanding and guidance. Miraculously, Jesus spoke to all, each to their need and each to their heart's desires. Joseph was reminded of Jesus' promise to give to us the desires of our heart and Joseph knew and believed the words to be true. Each believer heard, each in his own way, Jesus saying, "I am here. I will never leave nor forsake you. You are mine and I am yours. I raised you up to be with me, to be my bridegroom, to share in my Father's Kingdom. One day at a fast, I will celebrate your arrival to be with me. Please note that I am your God, you are my people, and I will always love you, well beyond the end of time. Come to me, my child, let me hold and comfort you. Draw to me and I will draw near to you. I love you and I want you to live with me forever."

Joseph fell to his knees weeping, full of Jesus' peace and His love, thankful for all he had been given and the love of God so graciously and overwhelmingly given. Joseph wept deeply, praying between the tears, thanking God for His love so deep that no one be lost, no not one!

God spoke to Mary though she was not able to see the rainbow in her captivity, God sought out all believers wherever they were. Speaking to Mary, God whispered quietly yet words of strength into her heart and soul, "I am here. I did not forget the Jews when they were in captivity as in Egypt, and I will not forget you. I brought them out from under the Pharaoh and I also will deliver you. I will never leave nor forsake you. I will be here until the end of time. I am the great I AM and I am your Father. Abide in me and I will abide in you. Apart from me, you can do nothing, but with me you can do great things. If you have the faith of even a mustard seed, you will do great things in my name. You are my child and a sheep in my pasture. I will always be there to watch over you."

Mary wept deeply as she knew it was only He, the great I AM, that spoke and she leaned into, believed and depended on every word.

Chapter 14

JOSEPH AND HIS staff arrived early at the harbormaster's boat complete with an extra complement of staff and a full day's stores. Arriving at 6:00 a.m. just as the sun was coming up, they began boarding, bringing on board the needed supplies and within a little over a half hour, they were ready to set off. The engines were warm and ready as they had been idling since the time they had arrived. All systems had been checked to ensure that they were fully functional and operational. Joseph planned to spend the first part of the day close to where they had stored the ship during the storm. They would first cruise out from their berth along Shem Creek and then into the harbor itself and then turning westward up the Cooper River and past Patriot's Point on the right and where the mighty aircraft carrier, the USS *Yorktown*, aka The Fighting Lady, of World War II was kept as testament to those brave men and women that served. They would start there and then cruise up the Ashley River. Joseph had spoken to Detective Stone the day before and obtained a briefing on what to look for and to be inquisitive about. Joseph, like Detective Stone, believed the killer and Mary were still in the area and that this would be their best chance to catch him.

Though almost forty hours remained on the hundred-hour ransom note and deadline, Joseph believed today would be their best chance for returning Mary alive. He believed that the killer would do his fateful work should the hour strike.

Although Joseph had never used it in the past, he did have a permit to carry a handgun. Today Joseph decided was the day that he needed to carry it. Yesterday he had taken it out to both clean it and check the firing mechanism, ensuring that it was ready. Though Joseph had been a seaman in the Navy, he received substantial amounts of training and instruction on the use of handguns. When not out at sea, they would train three times a week with both an M-1 and a handgun. Several years ago, Joseph had purchased for himself a nine-millimeter handgun that was silver clad and had an ivory handle. Though he usually practiced with his other more practical handgun, today he opted to bring the most precise handgun that he had. Joseph had always been a fine marksman and routinely exercised those skills to keep them sharp.

Joseph trusted Detective Stone's instincts, knowing that his record of success spoke volumes. Grandpa Billy and Grandma had made arrangements to move the requested $200,000 ransom at a moment's notice. Joseph knew that the future had already been written and that the rest was in God's hands. To date, Detective Stone had not decided on what to do regarding paying the required ransom but the critical point for that decision had not yet come.

Joseph decided to wear a shoulder holster so that he might keep it under a light jacket that he had decided to wear. Mentally, Joseph was ready and he set himself on the day ahead, silently praying and trusting God to bring Mary safely home.

As they motored under the Cooper River Bridge, Joseph already had his people in place. Five people were assigned to running the ship, including steering and managing the electronic equipment, especially the sonar and radar. These instruments would allow them to learn if the harbor was clear of significant debris. Soundings would be used to see if the channels remained deep enough so the draft, the distance from the waterline of the boat to the deepest part of its keel, of the large commercial ships could still utilize the channel. So far, only minor debris had been noted but the crew stayed on vigilant alert, for any failure to find a larger piece of debris might result in the grounding of a ship, or worse yet, even its sinking. Joseph had calculated that a speed of seven knots would give them just enough time by the end of the day to cover the whole harbor and the Ashley, Cooper, and Wando. Then they would head out into the Atlantic Ocean several miles north along the most densely populated areas and then just a few miles south where there were not quite as many people.

Joseph also believed that seven knots, which was roughly eight miles an hour, would afford him the chance to scour the coastline with his trained eyes as well as with his field glasses. Counting himself, Joseph had three people assigned to help him in this task. Joseph shared with all in detail the briefing that he had received the day earlier from Detective Stone so they could keep their eyes sharp. Joseph stationed himself in the middle of the ship so that he might be available to the bridge if needed and then stationed one man at the foreword of the boat and one man toward the rear.

———

Mary sat up on the bed and tried to look about but the darkness and the black encompassed every part of her vision. The darkness seemed to envelop even her inner being as there was not one single shred of light in the room. Mary thought by now she might be used to the darkness that she saw and felt, but it continued to engulf her more and more every hour. Mary wondered if perhaps this might be the way it would feel is she were blind. Mary's hands and feet were still bound tight and the ropes were now rubbing deeply into her skin. The knots were still held tight and no matter how often she pulled on them, she could not get them to budge nor unravel. The ropes, which were a tightly wound nylon, were causing several abrasions on Mary's skin where the blood had been raised to the surface of the skin. The ropes now greatly irritated her arms and hands from every movement. Mary longed to be able to stretch out her hands and arms and to freely move about.

Mary estimated she had been asleep for about eight hours. Though the walls that held her were very thick, she could tell that all but perhaps some of the remaining remnants of the storm had left. Mary had not heard any rustling about outside and wondered when her captor would be returning. She was sure the roads would be at least initially difficult to pass but Mary expected that he would arrive soon. It had been almost twenty hours since Mary had had any water, and now she was even looking forward to her next peanut butter and jelly sandwich that he might bring.

Unbeknownst to Mary, there were only thirty-five hours left on the ransom note for her life. Mary, however, had already decided to take each and every minute from God as a gift, no matter whether it was forty minutes for forty years. Resigned now to be always who she was in Christ first and then to use her time for the betterment of the Kingdom, saying, "Dear God, I know I've been building up my riches here on earth and I want to start building them in your house in heaven. I do not know what today will bring or even if there will be a tomorrow, but I want to live them all for and with you. Guide me in the way you would have me go and I will follow all the days of my life. I know you are here. You have promised to always be with me and in that faith I will rest. Thank you for dying for my sins and all the wonderful things that you have given me. Into your hands alone, I commit my spirit. Please be with my parents, take care of my son and be with my beloved Joseph and his daughter, Sara. Please put a protective shield over them and if it is your will, please reunite us soon. In Jesus' name I pray. Amen."

Mary knew God heard her words and she resolved to never be without his guiding hand on her again. Through toil or sorrow, joy or pain, she had finally been brought home. Mary knew that her captor would be more than likely returning soon to check on her status and perhaps worse. In her heart and in her mind, she decided to steadfastly hold tightly to the one true God as her deliverer and Savior.

———

Detective Stone's detectives and investigators were under strict orders to remain focused on the task at hand. He knew his people would be asked several times during the day to assist people with downed trees, where to put emergency supplies like water, ice, food and medical needs. Only an exception of an emergency life-or-death medical need was allowed to slow or derail them from their assigned task even temporarily.

Detective Stone had time during the storm to contemplate and carefully plan and lay out the current day's search efforts. All of his people had set out early in the day to their assigned locations with specific tasks at each. Other emergency personnel and the National Guard who would also be present this day had been briefed on what to look out for, especially at roadblocks. Roadblocks after a hurricane were set up to keep even locals out so that National Guard and emergency personnel could be moved in to stabilize an area prior to letting others in. This served as a bonus to Detective Stone as he was able to have roadblocks as well without having to reassign detectives and investigators from other assigned tasks. It was almost as if his staff had doubled overnight. Each detective was to call in as soon as they arrived at their assigned location. All but two teams reached their destinations by the required time mainly because the major arteries had been cleared just enough to pass. The other two teams were late, with one being twenty minutes late and the other an hour. The latter team had to retrace their steps several times and chose alternate routes because of several large, downed, one-hundred-year-old oak trees that blocked their path. But soon, they arrived and called in ready. Detective Stone knew that on all the back roads and side streets they would not be quite so lucky unless perhaps, homeowners had cleared their own streets as emergency personnel did not have time to clear them.

Joseph and his crew were finishing up what amounted to be the first third of their planned itinerary. So far they had seen that the dolphin population had done quite well during the storm and that not much else had. Joseph could not help but feel sorrowful for the people whose homes were severely damaged and for the owners of all the boats that were just strewn awry almost as if a child had come into a room and kicked them about. Joseph continued to perform dual duties from midship, serving to direct his crew as harbormaster and to continue on today with what he knew was his greatest mission, finding and rescuing Mary. They had been out now for almost four hours and they expected to be on mission for another eight. Initially they had cruised up the Wando River and past Foster Creek, where the body of the first real estate agent in Charleston had been discovered. Joseph winced as he passed the spot, causing him to briefly lose the resoluteness that he determined that he would need the whole of the day. Joseph bore down once again knowing that he needed to stay sharp and on task.

Joseph's preparation of the morning reminded him of the diligence that he had exemplified when he was in the Navy. He was meticulous in his planning of both the itinerary of the ship and the specific crew he wanted and assigned to where. Joseph assigned his two best overall thinkers to help him in the observation tasks, as he wanted generalists and people who could think outside the box to help him there. Freethinkers always seemed to be able to see both the forests and the trees at the same time, and Joseph needed people who could see what others did not. They had just finished up their planned route on the Ashley River and would soon be heading up the Cooper River.

So far most of the docks appeared not to have suffered much damage. As they drew closer they discovered that any container that had not been tightly secured had been tossed about and most were found to be either on their sides or upside down. Care had been taken to secure the dock's cranes and to lower the boom on all of them so as to shelter them from the wind as much as possible. It appeared that they too had only incurred minimal damage. Joseph knew that regardless of how things looked no chances would be taken, especially with the loading docks and the heavy machinery that moved the cargo about. Engineers would be brought in to perform visual, mechanical, and instrument checking to ensure that everything was ready before the docks would be reopened. Engineers would carefully check for any hairline cracks or latent defects. Often this would be the longest part of readying the equipment, as it seemed to take forever to clear any machinery to ensure there was no doubt as to its usability.

Going up the Cooper River with Daniel Island on their right and the large loading docks on their left, the current was just slightly more than normal as a result from all the additional water that was finally starting to drain back into the rivers and basins from where Hurricane Janet's high winds had pushed it. Occasionally they saw some smaller pieces of debris in the river but it seemed as if most of what had remained in the water had already been carried on further out into the harbor and the vastness of the Atlantic Ocean by the current. Daniel Island is a large island that is accessible only by bridge that has been developed and has almost two thousand homes. It is mixed-use residential and commercial property that has been built out over the last several years. Egrets and other local birds predominantly had used the area, until several years ago when the property began being developed. Now it was complete with its own schools, firehouse, and even a hotel. Although newer homes seemed to have fared better in Hurricane Janet than the older homes, there was still widespread and extensive damage. Joseph knew that it would take several years to totally rebuild that which had been destroyed in just a few hours by nature's fury. Many of the older one-hundred-year-old oak trees had also been felled by the storm. Joseph often thought of what all these fine old oaks had seen over the years and hated that they had been felled like a toothpick in the hurricane's high winds. Some things Joseph knew would never be the same and others he knew would be rebuilt better than before. In his naval career, Joseph had seen what the ravages of war could do and knew that people seemed to have an insatiable spirit to persevere. Joseph knew that he too would continue on past this storm and through no matter what might lie ahead, but he committed to God that he would do all that he did from now on in the name of Jesus no matter what lay ahead.

Detective Stone continued to work the plan that he had set before him on that day. On staggered intervals Detective Stone had all of his teams calling in every forty minutes to both keep him abreast on their current activities as well as to give them additional instructions as situations warranted. This kept him almost exclusively on the phone non-stop, but Detective Stone knew that today he had to be a leader only, and not a doer, in order to ensure that the whole of his team remained effective. Several of the teams were working their assigned grids and, in spite of the damage, had made good progress. Other teams were to stay on guard at heavily traveled intersections and byways and were advised to be on constant alert. Detective Stone had already received one call that initially seemed to be a positive lead but upon further review was just a homeowner who had not left their home during the storm. Detective Stone knew that with all the storm damage, emergency personnel, National Guard, and cleanup and rescue teams that there would be an inexhaustible supply of abnormal events occurring during the day. Accordingly, during the storm, Detective Stone had spent several hours detailing what his people would be seeing and strived to give each and every team as much wisdom as he might in order that they indeed might be his eyes and ears on the street.

Detective Stone had already had a successful career and he knew that finding and returning Mary alive would certainly be another feather in his cap. But to be honest, the only thing on his mind today was not what it might do for him and his career, but what it would mean to Mary and her family and especially to Joseph. Detective Stone had a very finely trained and well-tuned eye for character and he deeply respected and even revered Joseph. He admired Joseph for his openness and resoluteness in his search for Mary, and he personally wanted to ensure that he helped them reunite. Undeniably, the killer to date had played him, but Detective Stone simply lowered his brow and marched on, firmly setting in his mind to find the killer and return Mary to Joseph and he to her.

Grandpa Billy and Grandma, with Mary's son, David, in tow, had just returned from the storm shelter to their home. As with all of Charleston's Historical District all of the power to their home was out and theirs was no different. Both Joseph and Detective Stone had checked in with them several times during the storm and this morning to ensure that they were all right and ask if they had heard anything at all. Grandpa Billy remained ready and willing if he were needed to pay the $200,000 ransom via a wire transfer to the Swiss bank account listed. Care had been taken to gain access and to move needed funds to a bank that was not in the hurricane's path before it hit so that Grandpa Billy might be able to perform the transfer without pause or hesitation if the need arose.

Though Grandpa Billy and Grandma had substantive damage at their home, they weren't focused on that at all. Their thoughts were on Mary and her well-being and bringing her safely home. Grandpa sat down in his chair there in the study and in the dark reflecting on the joy that had been brought into his life by Mary and hers. As he sat there observing all the cleanup and the repairs they would have to do all he could focus on was finding Mary alive. His eyes heavy, his heart deeply hurting, he lowered his head into the palms of his hands and first shed one tear and then another. Grandpa Billy had always been a man's man and nothing to date had moved him like this. Although he was deeply afraid for Mary, for the first time ever, his own pain forced him to get in touch with his own fears and self-doubt and his true inner self. Grandpa Billy had always been a people person but he had always kept his own guard up. He had always let people get to know him at least on the surface and to let others in, yet Grandpa Billy always felt that he had to be strong for those around him and to never show any fear. Today though, Grandpa Billy and God both really opened up, with Grandpa speaking first, "I know that you are here. I know that you love me and that you will have your will done. Dear God, Mary is so very special to Grandma, David, Joseph, and me. We have both so much to share with her and yet to learn from her as well. Dear God, please bring Mary home; please let her know wherever she is that she is deeply loved. Dear God, you know that I love you and that I look forward to one day, to be with you as Mary will be also, but please do not take her from us now but let us be rejoined with her now and let us all live together in your peace. Speak to me, oh Lord."

No sooner did Grandpa Billy get the last word out of his mouth than did the King of the Universe answer, "My son, my son, I am here. I have and will always be here."

Grandpa Billy removed his hands from his face and again felt God calling him to look out the window. It had been mostly cloudy all day but as God spoke, the sun had broken through the clouds and now its stream of light beamed brightly through the window.

As the sun shone brightly in God continued, "One day you will join me here but there is much for you yet to do. You have honored me with your life. Your family is a testament to your faithfulness. I have blessed you and all your years and yet I will continue to bless you. Seek me in all your ways and you will find me. I will always be here when you cry out, when you arise, and as you live the day that has been set out before you. Know that I am your God and that you are my son! I died for you so that you might live with me forever. When you first believed I forgave you and washed your sins as white as snow. I forgave them completely, I remember them not, and I washed them with my own blood so that one day you might join me in paradise. Apart from me you can do nothing, but in me you will still yet do great things. I am the vinedresser and you are the branches of my vine, come to me, my son, so that I might yet guide and direct you. I will never forsake you. I am your Most High Priest and your Father and you are my son! Dwell in me as I dwell in you. Go forth in faith, knowing and trusting. Always seek me and I forever will be here. One day we will be together forever but now your family needs you, your strength, and your wisdom. Go to them as I have come to you with a deep and abiding spirit. Give to them openly and freely as you have so often done. You are my son and in you I am most proud!"

As God spoke Grandpa Billy felt the very hands of God on his shoulders. Grandpa Billy continued to sit in the study for a few moments thanking God for the gift that he had been given and how God's words moved him and touched his heart. Grandpa Billy had never endearingly been called son before and it had never been said to him by his own earthly father that he was proud of him. Grandpa Billy's earthly father, albeit a very successful businessman and well respected among his peers, was a hard man at home and was unwilling to share any of his own true feelings. Grandpa Billy knew that his dad loved him because of all the things that his father had done for him in his life, but never once had he heard those words of deep affection and his acknowledgment that his father was proud of him. All the missed opportunities and longings to hear those words from his earthly father immediately passed as God himself had accepted him completely and praised him as His own son. Speaking these words of love and praise, God had filled the void of self-doubt that had plagued Grandpa Billy the whole of his life. God filled him completely as only the words of a father can do and as only love's true words can cure.

As the sun continued to beam in, it reached the prism paperweight that had been on his desk, reflecting the light into the colors of the rainbow that had shone so brightly the day before. Grandpa Billy and Grandma too had seen the grand rainbow over the Charleston Harbor and had heard God's voice the day before. Grandpa Billy knew that this rainbow was specifically for him and that His words had filled his own heart to overflowing. Speaking back to God, he replied, "Use me, I am here, I want to do your bidding. Guide my steps so that I might always look to your will in my life. I love you and I thank you for all that you have given and all that you are yet to give. I will praise you all the days of the rest of my life."

It had been since his early childhood when Grandpa Billy last wept. But in praise and thankfulness, he wept openly and deeply, continuing to praise God for His majesty and His Grace. As the tears poured down his face they erased year after year of his own self-doubt as he now knew that the one true God would always be his father and would love and care for him. As he cried he felt the fears simply fall away and the strength of God began to rise up in him. Grandpa Billy looked up into the sun beaming into the room and at the rainbow reflection from the prism on his desk and he knew that this rainbow and that this promise was especially for him. Beaming and confident Grandpa Billy responded to the Most High God, "I hear and I will obey. Thank you so very much. I will never forsake you. I will go take care of my family now that you alone have so graciously given. I know that you are here and that you are with me. I will always need you and your guidance, especially now. Lead me and I will follow. I am so very proud to be your son and to have you as my Father! In Jesus' name I pray. Amen."

Mary suddenly sat straight up on the bed and she felt the hairs on the back of her neck stand on end. Shuddering in spite of her desire to remain calm, Mary listened intently as she thought she heard someone operating a chain saw just outside the structure. She knew that from the hurricane and the tornado both that there had to be an abundance of downed trees. Anyone who approached would have a substantial amount of obstacles to overcome, especially if they were to try to get a car to wherever she was. Mary's heart leapt for joy in the hope and the anticipation that she might finally be free. Mary immediately began praying that it was a rescuer and not her captor. It sounded as if the chain saw might still be a ways off, perhaps as much as a hundred yards away. As the saw droned on seemingly cutting log after log it seemed to be approximately the same distance away for quite some time. Mary imagined that perhaps several of the larger oak trees had been felled, blocking whatever walkway or driveway there was to where she has being held. Mary continued praying that it was someone coming to her rescue and not just someone doing work to clear their own property. As Mary had been drugged and then brought here while unconscious, she still knew nothing about the surroundings of where she might be. Mary continued on with her optimism of her impending freedom as the saw continued on against the downed trees.

The Coast Guard was just getting its first helicopter crew up in the air over the Charleston area to survey the damage and to be on the alert for any emergency needs. Like before, the Coast Guard would be available to Detective Stone if needed for a specific task if needed, but their main responsibility of the day was to assist in damage assessments and emergency rescue needs. Coast Guard flight personnel had been well briefed by Detective Stone's office and were ready to assist in any way they might either by directing visually or by intervening themselves, if needed. The helicopter was usually kept locally, but when forecasters announced that Hurricane Janet had turned and was headed straight toward Charleston, they had immediately moved it several hundred miles inland and to the south and out of harm's way.

It had taken a while to clear the normal landing area of debris so the helicopter could be moved back to Charleston and then readied for today's flights. There were to be three 2-plus-hour flights so that information that had been obtained from each flight could be shared and so that routine maintenance of the helicopter might be done. The initial flights were approximately the same geographically as those that Joseph would travel but he would be evaluating everything from the water, while the Coast Guard observed from the air, and Detective Stone's people would be busy on the streets. All emergency personnel had direct accessibility to Detective Stone and he to them in order to ensure that a quick response could be directed to any need. Clearing through the final checklist, the pilot set the throttle to full power and headed off for their assigned routes and duties.

Once airborne they gained witness to the massiveness of the destruction and the havoc that Hurricane Janet had played on the city. As they flew over the historic district of Charleston they quickly realized that the wrath of Mother Nature had been complete. From the air it seemed as if no structure was unharmed by the fury that had just besieged the city. Street after street that was once nicely arrayed homes seemed now to be in total disarray. Most roofs had missing tiles, chimneys, and for some of the more unfortunate ones, the roofs were totally gone as if just plucked up by the sky. Decks and porches alike were both torn from homes or simply shattered, leaving debris strewn about and boards and wires droopily hanging from sides of homes. It seemed to the crewmen so surreal or perhaps a bad dream but unfortunately it was all too real for all. They continued on in their picture taking and recording and would do so for another two hours. Every thirty minutes they were to check in, reporting their progress and to report immediately any emergencies.

Joseph and his crew were now coming back down the Cooper River and would soon be passing under the Cooper River Bridge. As they did so, just over to their right the commercial portion of the Historic District of Charleston came into view. They passed by the Charleston Aquarium and soon they would be coming alongside the Battery at what just a few days ago had been the grandeur of the beautiful old and restored homes. Home after home had been battered by the storm and had suffered greatly. This is one area on their journey that Joseph did not expect to see anything suspicious but he kept a keen eye out nevertheless. Yelling out to his crew, "Keep an eye out, men," he reminded them to stay sharp.

Joseph's naval training had taught him many things over the years and one of the most valuable was to consistently stay diligent and to always do the next right thing. As an naval officer, he had learned how to lead men and how to always be thinking several steps ahead of where he and his men were while always contemplating their next move. Many times in his duties in the Navy and as a harbormaster, he had learned that thinking ahead had often been the only difference between success and failure while on a mission or on an assigned task. Joseph kept his eyes sharp. From his viewpoint standing midship, Joseph could see the whole of the ship and off and along the Battery. Many of the homes had lost entire verandas and porches alike. Joseph knew the city would recover from the hurricane's damage and that Charleston once again would be rebuilt. Her people were of the finest ilk in the land and were proud of who they were both as citizens of Charleston and as Americans.

As they rounded the point of the Battery, they would soon be entering and heading up the Ashley River. As they passed alongside one of the marinas on the Ashley, Joseph noticed several boats that through the pounding of Hurricane Janet's high winds and waves had been severely battered against the docks and their moorings. Many of them had been beaten so badly that Joseph was sure that they would never be functional again. Some had been blown up onto the shore, which in normal conditions was about eight feet higher than what the water level was now and before the storm. As they cruised on and under the Ashley River Bridge, Joseph kept his eyes sharp, always searching and looking both back and forward constantly scanning the horizon as they went.

Mary was listening intently and it suddenly seemed as the roar of the chain saw was now just outside. Hoping against hope she continued to pray that it might be someone coming to free her, but with every moment lapsing her belief in this waned as Mary imagined that a rescuer would simply go around the obstacles to see who was there and if anyone needed help, rather than worrying initially about moving the debris. As the saw continued to rev, Mary resolved herself that it was probably not a rescuer at all but her captor. Mary began to prepare herself for what she now feared was the inevitable and that soon she would be near him once again. Mary prayed aloud to encourage herself, "God, you know that I am yours. You and you alone are in charge of my destiny. In you alone I place my life and my trust. Ready me, Lord. Guide me. Help me to be strong. No matter what befalls me now or ever, let me live in the peace and the confidence of your love. In your hands I stand. In you, I will live all the time that you have set out. I love you, Lord. You know that I love my family and that I love Joseph more than anything here on earth. But Lord, I want what you want. Lead me to see your total will for my life and if today I pass, let me do it in some way that edifies and brings glory to you. In Jesus' name I pray. Amen."

As Mary finished up her prayer, she heard the chain saw being turned off and she began to hear what seemed to be the front door of the building squeaking as it opened. Though Mary was still hesitant and now fearful of what might befall her next, she knew that Jesus was there and that God Himself would stand along by her side. As the door slowly opened she knew that next she would hear the muted sounds of steps as he came down the hall toward her room. Listening intently as he came, Mary backed into the corner of the still pitch-black room as if looking for someplace to hide. Of course finding none, she mentally prepared herself as she heard the door's unlocking and then the sounds of the large boards braced over the door sliding over the top of the outside of the door as they were moved aside. Slowly the door opened. Keeping an eye open in the pitch darkness and the other closed as if to hide, Mary looked intently towards the door.

Detective Stone checked his watch, noting that it was now a little past twelve in the afternoon and that there were now just twenty-two hours left on the ransom note's one-hundred-hour deadline. It had now been three days and six hours since the time on the e-mail that had been received and they still did not have anything substantive to go on. In a little over seven hours it would be getting dark again as evening would be approaching, leaving only then maybe an hour or so of daylight of the next day before the deadline's final hour. Calculating quickly, he realized that only about half of the remaining hours would be daylight. His detectives and investigators to date had done everything asked of them and done it well, but he knew that time was not on his side. His people had stayed on schedule today and were continuing to check in and report and to get further guidance as directed, but time was running out. He knew that the killer had so far been ahead of him every step of the way but Detective Stone believed that Hurricane Janet might just be the thing that broke the case wide open. Though only twenty-two hours away from the deadline, he continued to trust his instincts and that the killer was still here and that he had stayed in the Charleston area. Detective Stone believed that today or this evening would still prove to be his best chance of seeing justice done and Mary returned safely. Detective Stone refortified his resolve with this belief and knowledge that if he just stayed on task and did not waver that his instincts would be finally rewarded.

This investigation, more than any other, had greatly tried Detective Stone's will and wits. Earlier in the investigation the killer had played him by having him track down the cell phone that he knew was Mary's only to find the killer's message still laughing and toying with him. Every time he thought of it resulted in him being greatly infuriated all over again. Indeed since then, the investigation had become deeply personal. Also Detective Stone's deep affection and admiration of Joseph made him want more than ever before to bring Mary safely home to be reunited with Joseph and her family. Though today he was more personally intense than he had ever been before in any investigation, he steadied himself to remember the basics and to always follow his instincts. He knew that relying on past achievements meant nothing in the circumstance and that the killer especially did not care about what he had accomplished in the past. Detective Stone continued on in the day as he had set out, resolute in his determination to succeed.

As Detective Stone continued to receive calls, he also monitored police and fire emergency channels, listening for anything at all that might warrant further investigation, as he knew that this moment was indeed his best chance of success. It had to be now, it had to be certain, and he could not afford to overlook anything that might require his immediate attention and further analysis. Mary's life hung in the balance and he knew whatever was to happen would depend upon it.

Mary cringed as the door slowly opened. At first she could not see at all as her eyes had been so accustomed to the darkness that the light at first slightly blinded and blurred her vision. As her eyes began to clear her worst dreams came true. There he was just like before in the same baggy clothes and the mask as he had worn before. Mary, for a moment, felt like she was dreaming and that she was almost outside herself as she looked on, but she knew that the situation was much too real. Mary knew that it would be of no use to fight, as he was obviously bigger and with her hands and legs being tied tightly together the potential element of surprise was certainly not an option available to her. Mary continued to huddle on the far side of the room as he knelt and placed water and a sandwich—no doubt a peanut butter and jelly, Mary thought to herself—just inside the room. He also placed a battery-operated lantern just inside the room evidently for her comfort so that she might see as the electricity that had been lost during the storm was still down. The lantern emanated a soft glow that made it easy to see about the room and her eyes quickly adjusted to its light. It had been almost a day and a half since she had taken any nourishment of any type, and the prospect of something to eat and drink soon made her mouth water. As he began to back out of the room, still disguising his voice, he gruffly stated, "We will be leaving soon. Eat; I am sure that you are hungry."

As he closed the door and began to lock the doors back tight, Mary then heard the boards being slid over the front of the door, further locking her into place. As he slid the final board over, she began to pick up the sandwich and water. Peanut butter and jelly, what a surprise, she thought to herself. Mary forced herself to slow down and to drink the water in small sips so that she might savor each and every mouthful. She was so hungry, never before had peanut butter and jelly tasted so good. She could not help but think that this might be her last meal as he had always been known to kill his captives and to her knowledge none of them had ever escaped. Mary thanked God as she ate for the blessings of her food, her family, and for Joseph, a man she knew that she could always respect. Her mind, over the last several days, had never strayed far from thinking about Joseph and what might be. Savoring the last sip for all she was worth, she prayed whimsically, "God, if it is your will, I will be all that you would have me to be. If given the chance I promise to edify and to love Joseph and I pray that I will always be there to support, encourage, and respect the man you have made him to be. In Jesus' name I pray. Amen."

The Coast Guard crew had just come back from its first mission. The roar of the blades overhead loudly reverberated off the buildings and the ground alike as it gently placed one of its landing gear down and then the other. With each turn of the blade anyone nearby could feel the whole of their body vibrate with each rotation. As soon as all of the helicopter's systems had been checked and then rechecked, the flight crew stepped off and joined the maintenance crew nearby. Briefly catching up, as there was much work left to do, the maintenance crew quickly got to work readying the craft for the second mission of the three scheduled for today. The flight crew refreshed themselves with the food and water that had been provided for them to partake while the helicopter was readied for flight. As soon as they had finished eating, the pilot and flight engineer went over to the craft and removed the flight recorder, which had been recording by video the whole of their flight. The courier just arrived to speed the video to headquarters for review and dissemination. As soon as the video arrived at Coast Guard headquarters, it was to be copied again and that copy was to be made available to Detective Stone's office. There his people would have a chance to review the tape in detail, looking for anything unusual. Detective Stone's man was set to meet the courier at the Coast Guard headquarters as soon as he arrived to enable getting the video copy back to the task force's headquarters as soon as possible so that the review might begin.

Within moments of the maintenance crew clearing the helicopter's required procedures and its refueling, the flight crew quickly boarded and readied the craft for takeoff. As they went through the checklist procedures with methodical accuracy they turned the engine on to ready it for takeoff. The flight crew was made up of highly disciplined and well-trained aviators and was among the best the Coast Guard had stationed anywhere. The helicopter being flown today was just under a year old and had all the latest technology on board for both day- and night-time observation. The craft was also armed with an eighty-caliber machine gun, which was able to pierce through just about anything other than a heavily armored tank. To date the crew had not had occasion to use the weapon in a live circumstance but nevertheless were well trained and able to do so when needed. Just having the weapons available had often been more than enough in the past to slow down and stop anyone who might have otherwise wanted to challenge their authority. Each flight crew member also carried a side arm in case any circumstance occurred that might require their use.

Joseph looked on as they headed out of the Ashley River and towards the westward part of the harbor near Fort Sumter and the whole of the Atlantic Ocean. As they cleared James Island and then Morris Island, both on their right, they entered where the Charleston Harbor intersected with the Atlantic. Tides in this area were often severe, as the three rivers that formed the harbor then spilled out into the Atlantic Ocean and the rising and the falling of its tide. Waters would often ebb and flow at the same time as waters of the different bodies of water collided in a relatively small restricted area. The area has always been unsafe for swimming of any type, as often the colliding waters would create a substantive downdraft, making it difficult for even the most powerful of swimmers to stay afloat.

Joseph and his crew were still on task and on schedule. The plan was to head north and up the coast for several miles while staying just offshore and as close as possible to the land that they were examining. During the earlier part of their day on the more inland waters they had to use their binoculars only sparingly, while now, being farther way from the landmass, they had to use them almost exclusively. Keeping his eyes sharp, they headed up the Atlantic and towards the northeast edge of the harbor and while going northward they passed Sullivan Island on their left. Sullivan Island was approximately four plus miles long and then they would cruise along the Isle of Palms, which was approximately the same length and width as that of Sullivan Island. Motoring at about seven knots they headed northwards and up the coast. Seven knots continued to seem an ideal speed for observation although the seas were a bit rougher out in the Atlantic than they had been in the safety of the harbor and the guarded rivers of its waterways.

Joseph braced himself as the waves picked up. Being a seaman of many years he was used to standing amidst the pounding of the surf. He had many years of training out at sea and often had found himself feeling slightly landlocked by predominantly serving in the harbor itself. Joseph caught himself being distracted by the thoughts of Mary, he and the kids being out at sea cruising as they often had done on the late summer and early fall days. Those days seemed idyllic then and even more so now. Catching himself, he refocused his efforts on the task at hand and finding Mary alive. Joseph knew they were winding up towards mid-afternoon now and that they would be finishing up their journey within three hours or so. Undeterred Joseph resumed his search with renewed vigor, determined to bring the love of his life home.

~ ~

They would soon be heading up to the northernmost tip of the Isle of Palms, where the old lighthouse was located. The lighthouse was on the very northern tip of the island and been originally commissioned in 1830 for the burgeoning maritime trade. The lighthouse itself was a brick-built structure that was completed in 1832 and was used to guide ships traveling southward around the tip of the island and along the coastline to the Charleston Harbor. Trading had been the leading commercial activity since the formation of the city of Charleston itself, and shipping had always been its primary medium. Ships frequently traveled both up and down America's eastern coastline and to Europe, exchanging their wares for predominantly agrarian products grown there. The lighthouse had taken a little over two years to build and was initially operated by a Theodore Brown, who was a local whose family had always been active in the shipping industry and still owned and operated docks along the Charleston Harbor. Standing at over a hundred feet high, the lighthouse sat on a rise of land just along the coast that was twenty feet higher than sea level. The light itself was magnified for both power and direction and used the Fresnal lens, which was able to substantially help stream the light's power. The lighthouse had attached to it a home that had been built for the operator to both live in and work at while he performed his duties, keeping the coastline well marked and its beam brightly burning. Complete with the rise of the land and the sheer height of the lighthouse itself, it was able to cast its beam that could be seen from over twenty miles out into the Atlantic. Commercial fisherman and maritimers alike benefited from the navigational aids the lighthouse offered.

During the Civil War, the Southern states of the Confederacy had taken the lighthouse from Northern Union control the week after the initial firing on Fort Sumter that began the war. It had been quickly wrestled away without firing a shot, as Union forces had not been able to adequately mobilize and fortify the position with troops. Within six months, however, the Union forces were able to retake it from Confederate forces with a small battery of troops. By shutting the lighthouse down and others like it the Union was able to complete their blockade of the Southern states and the Confederacy, taking away the source of much-needed military and food supplies that were supplied by sea during the war.

Chapter 15

MARY CONTINUED to hear her captor rustling about outside and shortly thereafter she heard the chainsaw rev up again and resume its cutting of the downed trees. Mary assumed that her captor was trying to clear a path for his vehicle to enter and then to leave. She believed that if she was led out alive she most assuredly would be blindfolded like before and maybe even gagged. Looking down at the ropes that bound her, Mary knew that her time was running out. Thinking that perhaps he was getting ready to take her to another location, or worse yet to take her body elsewhere, all of the options and scenarios that went through her mind caused her pain and reflection, as she could not come up with any option that involved her being released alive. As he was out cutting, Mary heard off in the distance the roar and reverberation of a helicopter heading her way. Her pulse raced wondering what they would see. Would they see a homeowner simply clearing his lot of debris, would he still be wearing his mask, or would they see something entirely different? "Lord, if it is your will, I want to go free. I am yours no matter what comes."

The helicopter almost immediately appeared overhead the Isle of Palms lighthouse on the very northern end of the island. Upon seeing it, her captor immediately turned the chain saw off, put it down, and looked up. With all the downed trees about, he knew that he did not have time to run inside and if they saw him doing so they would most certainly be alarmed. Not wanting to bring any additional attention to himself, he put down the chain saw and waved with his arms back and forth and then raised both of his hands and formed a thumbs-up sign indicating his well-being. The helicopter was so close that it picked up debris and spread it in all directions about him. Looking up he could see the whites of the eyes of both the pilot and the flight engineer. Looking into their eyes, he could see them return his gaze and then they gave the thumbs-up sign in return and smiled. The pilot slowly eased the craft away and they headed about their business. After a huge sigh of relief, he resumed clearing away the trees that blocked his vehicle.

Mary's heart raced as the helicopter neared and then paused overhead. Though the sound of the pounding of the helicopter's blades as they cut through the air was deafening, Mary cried out for all she was worth. Screaming at the top of her lungs with all the strength she could muster, Mary cried out over and over. At first the helicopter seemed to pause, as it seemed to be hovering right above, and then just as quickly, she heard it soon speed away. Feeling defeated she sat down on the edge of the bed as if trying to look off into the distance. Mary now resigned herself to her fate and steadied her heart.

The Coast Guard flight crew immediately called into headquarters and then were quickly patched over to Detective Stone, "I don't know if we have something here or not, but we just left the old abandoned lighthouse on the north end of the Isle of Psalms and there was someone out cutting trees. Two years ago, I heard an individual who was looking to restore it had purchased the place several years back. I can't imagine why in the world anyone would be out here now, but I think you might want to check this out."

Detective Stone immediately summoned cars to the scene and called for the police helicopter to meet him at the helipad. His instincts told him that this was his serial killer. He could not think of any logical reason why anyone would be immediately clearing trees at an old and abandoned lighthouse just after the hurricane. On the way over he briefed the detectives on how to proceed if they arrived there first. Although he had two cars and four detectives in the area, he knew it would take them extra time to get there with all the felled trees about. Telling them, "I think this is it, men, the real McCoy. This time I think we got him. Everyone be on your P's and Q's. Let's look lively."

Finishing up his briefing with the detectives, he then called Joseph, who answered on the first ring. "I think we have something. It's the old abandoned lighthouse on the north end of the Isle of Psalms. I have two cars on the way now and I am heading to the helipad now."

Joseph responded, "I am just south of there now, I can be there in just under ten minutes. I know the area well. We'll be there in no time at all. I will give you a call as I get closer."

"Go to full power, men!" Joseph bellowed. "There's something going on up at the lighthouse and we need to go take a look. Everyone be on full alert now."

The engines roared as they came to life. Hesitating for a second and then quickly surging to full speed ahead, the boat accelerated rapidly towards her destination.

Nearing the helipad Detective Stone jumped out of the passenger side of the car even before it had stopped moving. The helicopter was already being warmed up and was quickly set to full power even as he was closing the door and locking it. "Let's go!" he yelled over the engine's roar.

In no time at all, they were in the air and headed northward. The Coast Guard helicopter and her crew had moved about three miles away and were lying back so as to not arouse any suspicion until they could get people and assets into the area.

Joseph could not yet see the lighthouse but he knew that they would be there within five minutes. Though he had checked it already several times during the day, he pulled out his nine-millimeter, checking its gun clip one more time and ensuring that there was indeed a bullet in the chamber. Easing the safety off, he looked forward and then re-holstered his side arm. Still too far away to see anyone about on the ground, especially with the downed trees, he pulled out his binoculars and studied intently. Although dashing off in the harbor boat seemed all too much like the last time he had done so, he somehow knew and said to himself as no one could heard him over the roar of the engines, " I think this is it."

Mary heard her captor rapidly unlocking the doors and quickly sliding away the boards that bound her door tightly shut. Quickly he moved towards her with a white cloth being held out in his right hand speaking as he neared while still disguising his voice, "Come here, now!"

"No!" Mary retorted, moving backwards until she was backed up against the wall. Still facing him she continued, "No, leave me alone." Still shuffling her bound feet backwards but there was nowhere else to go. As he neared closer, Mary's attention moved away from his masked face and focused her attention on the cloth that was in his hands. Noticing he was holding it outwards and away from his own face and self, Mary feared what it might be laced with. Worried that perhaps it was something to make her groggy, unconscious, or worse, she raised her bound hands to defend herself. As he reached out his hand, Mary was able to continue to raise her own arms and hands and knocked the cloth out of his hands and onto the ground.

As he watched it fall, Mary readied herself and then kicked for all she was worth, hitting him sharply in the shin causing him to yell out in pain. Her kick had the desired result as he retreated. However, as she had kicked it caused her to lose balance as both of her bound feet continued forward, throwing her legs forwards and out from underneath her. Her defense caused her to fall backwards and up against the wall. Trying to break her own fall, Mary bowed backwards instinctively trying to avoid her head striking the wall as she fell. Falling hard and in a heap, she hit the wall with her back first, and then with a hard but glancing blow her head ganged back and against the wall. As soon as she hit the ground, she immediately pulled her bound feet up and towards her torso binding up in a ball to try to protect herself. Mary's head pounded from the pain as she lay there recovering from the blow.

Gathering himself from the blow of the kick, he did not bother to pick up the cloth that had been knocked from his hand, thereby letting it drop harmlessly to the ground. Not bothering to pick it up, he moved toward her again as she lay there in a fetal position on the cold and still wet floor. Grabbing her by her left arm, he pulled her up and as he did so, he spoke, "I guess it really doesn't matter. You are going either way."

As soon as Mary got to her feet, he began to lead her towards the door and down the hall. Stopping to cover her eyes with one blindfold and then another, Mary once again was thrust into darkness. Pulling even more intentionally and tightly than before, she struggled against his grasp only to have him squeeze her arm even more tightly causing her to grimace from the pain. Leading her on and disguising his voice, he spoke, "There's a step down here." While Mary tried to gingerly step down, he pulled on her quickly, causing her to stumble on the steps and lose her balance. He continued to firmly hold her while still easing her forward, allowing her to regain herself and not fall. No sooner did she take another few steps than she heard what she knew had to be the sound of keys as he fumbled in his pocket retrieving them and quickly unlocking the trunk. Picking her up from the back he pushed and prodded her into the trunk of the car. She thumped down hard as her weight shifted from the side of the trunk and to its bottom. As soon as she was fully in, he slammed the lid shut, cloaking her even further into darkness. Mary then heard the garage door being manually opened and then the car door and then as he slammed it shut, she heard the starting of the engine. Slowly he began to back the car out of the garage and onto the driveway as he then turned the car around.

As Mary's hands were out and in front of her, she was able to pull her hands up and in front of her face and then pulling on the back of both of her blindfolds, she pulled them both up and over the top of her head. Mary, now unmasked, could not see much more than before as just a small amount of indirect light emanated from around the black rubber molding that rimmed the trunk lid. Bumpily they moved along, seemingly hitting every pothole and limb that made up and lined the road.

Once again Mary could initially hear and then feel the reverberating blades of the helicopter as it neared. The helicopter's pounding blades cut through the air, though much more quietly than before, causing Mary to believe that it was a different helicopter. Her heart sank, as she believed that the initial helicopter had left and that the occurrence of the second was a coincidence rather than someone coming to rescue her.

Mary quietly prayed, as they suddenly increased speed and moved bumpily forward, "Dear Lord, I am here. I am your child and into your hands I commit my spirit. Be with those that I love and allow me to be your witness even now as I ready myself to meet you. Still my heart, ready my spirit, and help me to be strong for your name's sake and honor. In Jesus' name I pray. Amen."

From his vantage point several hundred feet high, Detective Stone was able to look out and see the lighthouse on the northern end of Isle of Palms. In only a little over a minute Detective Stone's helicopter flew the entire distance to the northern end of the island. Flying at approximately one hundred and thirty miles and hour and with no fallen trees to block their path in the air, they were quickly over the scene. Detective Stone was the first to see the garage door being opened and the blue sedan backing out. Yelling out over the noise of the engines, "There it is! I want you to get me overhead. I need to get a better look."

As they hovered overhead at about one hundred yards high, the helicopter spread the debris of the storm and the sand in all directions, some hitting the car and making a pinging noise as they did so. Watching the car as it began wildly racing down the driveway, Detective Stone immediately grabbed the radio to his detectives. "Suspect is on the move and will soon be headed in your direction. I want to know the location of all cars within five miles of the Isle of Palms lighthouse now! He's in a blue four-door headed south from the lighthouse. He's not going to get away this time. "

Seeing the second helicopter overhead he knew that he had been discovered and that he had to move quickly. The car was sliding on the loose gravel as he sped along the driveway back towards the main road and the path that he had just cut through the fallen trees. As soon as he had left the safety of the garage, he had removed his mask so as to not unduly draw attention to himself, but that seemed to be of no use now. The tires squealed loudly as the car slid sideways as it hit the blacktop asphalt heading south. Quickly turning the wheels into the direction of the spin, he regained control of the car and sped down the road. For the first half mile, he passed nothing but downed trees and soon entered a residential area. Traveling at excessive speeds he moved on rapidly, moving the car back and forth dodging the fallen trees that littered the roadway. At one point he left the road and traversed through a ditch, while only slightly slowing, to avoid a large oak that blocked his path.

Watching the car swerve wildly onto the road, Detective Stone put in a call to Joseph, "It's our guy. He's headed south towards the Isle of Palms Connector. If you can head that way now, you can meet me there. I will call ahead and have my guys set up a roadblock on the Mt. Pleasant side. We have him cornered now."

"We'll be there," Joseph responded, hanging up the phone and yelling out to the wheelhouse, "Get me over to the west side of the Isle of Palms Connector, and I mean now!"

He braced himself as the craft sharply turned left between the northern end of Sullivan's Island and the Isle of Palms and towards the Isle of Palms Connector. They would be there in just a couple of minutes. With all the downed trees and the lighthouse being located on the north end of the island, Joseph calculated that they would arrive there at about the same time as the killer. Looking back and to his right, Joseph saw the police helicopter that was following safely behind yet never far from sight distance of the killer's vehicle. Joseph knew this had to be the helicopter Detective Stone was in, as it had turned and continued to echo the path of the killer's vehicle.

Mary could still hear the helicopter overhead but it appeared to be further off than before. Although he had cleared the driveway and out onto the main road the force of the turn threw her head against the side of the trunk. Grabbing her head with her hands, she held tightly as the car swerved back and forth on the road. As he left the road to avoid the downed oak, she felt herself become airborne even while in the confines of the trunk, hitting its lid and then slamming her back downward. The car continued to careen back and forth across the roadway while traveling at over sixty miles an hour on the tree-littered road. Soon they entered the beach area of the island and then took a right while heading towards the Isle of Palms Connector.

Detective Stone continued to follow prescribed procedures. He had the helicopter lie back and behind the killer's car as he fled. This had the advantage of keeping a firm view of the landscape both out in front and below, while not creating any more panic than necessary in the car's driver. Detective Stone continued to focus his eyes and attention on the car while continuing to direct the movements of the detectives' cars up ahead. Placing a call in to the Coast Guard helicopter, "I need you to stay on the scene for as long as you can. I'll want you to back me up."

As they neared within a mile of the Isle of Palms Connector, Detective Stone could make out over the waterway the detectives' dark cars setting up a roadblock with their vehicles as several more squad cars raced up and behind to reinforce them. Detective Stone had called in and asked the Isle of Palms police, "Let him safely pass out and onto the bridge, then follow up behind him so he can't get back on the island. I have cars set up on the other side. We have him cornered now; he'll have nowhere to go."

Normally there would be several spots for Detective Stone to safely put his helicopter down, but with all he debris strew about from Hurricane Janet there was a great risk from having debris sucked up and into the rotors. This ran the risk of potentially causing trash to be sucked up onto the blades causing them to be damaged and then to spin wildly out of control. Detective Stone knew they would put down if they had to, but that they would be much safer in the air. He thought briefly of setting the helicopter down on the bridge if need be, but decided to think of this as a last resort. If the blades were to move even slightly to one side or the other during landing, they might hit the bridge's side, causing severe damage to the helicopter, bridge, the pilot and he as well. He did not want to unnecessarily add another casualty to the investigation and decided that this would only be done if there were no other options.

Joseph's vessel was just clearing the west end of the Isle of Palms and was turned immediately to the right and headed northward up the inner coastal waterway and towards the Isle of Palms Connector.

191

He could see the police cars already setting up their roadblock on the west side of the bridge. Joseph pointed ahead and had the ship's pilot bring the ship about and towards the most western side of the bridge. As he sped towards the cars on the bridge, he saw the blue sedan begin to head out over the bridge and towards the western side, at this point, still oblivious to the trap that lay for him ahead. Joseph's craft was about halfway across and several hundred yards south of the waterway when the killer turned onto the bridge.

The killer's car headed across the bridge at speeds of over ninety miles an hour as it rapidly headed towards the roadblock and other side. The car rapidly closed the distance to the other side and arrived there just ahead of Joseph and his crew. Joseph had assumed a position at the forward part of the boat and readied himself for what may come.

As the killer's car careened and turned onto the bridge he quickly accelerated forward and was soon speeding across the bridge towards the other side. As the bridge's height peaked in the middle, he was yet unaware of what lay before him and the volume of attention that would soon be right in his face. As he topped the hill, he gained speed and was soon over one hundred and ten miles an hour. As he leveled out at the bottom of the bridge, soon came into view the plethora of vehicles that awaited him on the other side. Slowing as he observed, he saw that there were more than seven vehicles aligned across the road blocking his way off the island and to freedom. Trying to gain time to think, he slowed the vehicle to a little over forty miles an hour and then slowed to a stop about two tenths of a mile away from the bevy of detectives, officers, and police cars that awaited. Looking back into his rearview mirror, he noticed the four Isle of Palms police cars and the island's fire truck that had approached from his rear, sealing off where he had just come from and his entryway back onto the island. Not knowing what to do next, he sat there with the engine idling while he contemplated his next move. With all of his attention on the officers and vehicles in front of him, as well as the noise of the helicopter behind, he just sat.

Joseph continued to approach by water unbeknownst to the killer and slowly eased up alongside the bridge while his crew tied up just underneath. Looking off just slightly to the right Joseph noticed a set of stairs that had been built into the side of the bridge. Leaving the engine on low idle they eased the boat over so that Joseph might grab hold and hoist himself up to the first step.

From his vantage point high in the sky and on the same side of the bridge that Joseph had approached from, Detective Stone watched as Joseph swung out and grabbed a hold on the first rung and started up. Knowing that he might potentially alarm the killer to Joseph's presence if he called on Joseph's cell phone, he simply looked upward crying out, "It's up to you, Lord. Be with them all."

Leaning over and grabbing the pistol that was on the seat beside him, the killer then tucked it in the front of his pants. After popping the trunk-release button, he slowly opened the door and began to walk to the back of the car. He reasoned that as of yet they had not definitely identified him as the killer and as such they would not take a chance on shooting an unarmed civilian. The afternoon sun shone brightly in his eyes and off the water as he strode to the back of the car and its trunk as if walking through the park on a Saturday afternoon. As he slowly opened the trunk he grabbed Mary with both hands and helped her out of the trunk, placing her in between him toward the police at the front of the vehicle. Retrieving his gun, he pulled back the trigger and cocked it, bringing it forward to her head just alongside her temple. As the police out in front were almost two tenths of a mile away he knew that they could not adequately see his actions with the naked eye but that they would be able to with binoculars.

From his perch high above in the helicopter Detective Stone's worst fears and best hopes came true all at once. It was the killer and Mary was indeed alive. It was finally her. Radioing ahead and behind to all, "It's him, he's got a gun to her head. I want our best marksmen out there now and if a shot presents itself without putting Mary in harm's way, I want him put down hard! Joseph is climbing up the side of the bridge just behind where they are; the killer doesn't seem to know that he's there. I think we need to wait a bit to see what happens."

Joseph finally reached the next to the top rung and ever so slowly eased his head up just enough to have a look. The killer had Mary on his right and was facing the array of police cars and detectives that faced him. It was the first time that Joseph had seen Mary in five days and this time he knew that it was really her. Joseph knew that the police would send out their best marksmen but he knew that at least for now, he alone was Mary's best option. Steadying himself against the side of the bridge, he lowered his head and pulled his own pistol out of its holster.

Mary stood though weak and exhausted from the scant nourishment and water she had received during the ordeal. Looking ahead and then back, Mary could tell that they were surrounded by police cars both out in front and behind as well as a police helicopter overhead. There she was so close to safety but yet still so far away, still in the clutches of a serial killer who had killed so many before her and would most certainly kill again. Although feeling tired and helpless, Mary tried to think clearly to see if there was anything she might be able to do to help her own cause.

The killer continued to hold Mary tight as he knew that at this point she alone was his best insurance. Deciding to drive forward and to use Mary as a bargaining tool, he would use her life to gain his own freedom. Walking back to the driver's door, which remained open, he slid her in the door quickly and then followed.

Joseph knew that he would only get one shot and that it had to be right on in order to stop the killer and to set Mary free. Joseph eased his head back up over the bridge, slowly pulling his right arm up and over along with his pistol. Joseph closed his left eye and then quickly aimed. Steadying himself again, he breathed in and held it so as to not let even his own breath interfere with his aim and pulled the trigger. Slowly the force of his finger caused the pin to strike the bullet in the chamber, speeding it exactly as intended. The nine-millimeter bullet found its mark, instantly dropping the killer to his knees beside the car's door. Joseph's second shot also found exactly where it had been aimed, felling him forward. He was dead even before he hit the concrete of the bridge.

Jumping up and over the side of the bridge, Joseph ran towards Mary. Detective Stone radioed out, "It's Joseph, he got him. Don't shoot. She's safe. Get over here now!'

Turning away as the shots had been fired, Mary moved back and away from the killer and towards the passenger-side door. After the gun's blast, Mary watched as he fell to his knees. She watched as he lost his grip and slowly let go of the gun and it fell from his right hand and to the ground. The gun had already fallen from his hands by the time the second bullet was sent speeding toward its intended mark felling her captor's face straight down and onto the ground.

Seeing the second bullet bring him down, Joseph sprinted the some fifty feet to the passenger side of the car, where Mary was leaning against the door and crying out. Slowing as he neared the car so as not to startle her, Mary looked up and saw Joseph's eyes and then pulled back and away from the door so that he might open it. Helping her gently out of the car by first pulling her feet around and then placing his arms around her holding her firmly, Joseph helped her to her feet. Crying now, Mary sobbed deeply, feeling awash and safe in the arms of the man that God had placed right in front of her.

Joseph held her closely but carefully as to not squeeze Mary too hard. Placing both of his hands on her cheeks, he slowly led her eyes up to his. Mary never looked more beautiful to Joseph than she did that day. Slowly Joseph held his right hand up to her blonde bangs that still fell over her eyes. Placing his right index finger on the middle of her forehead and just above her eyes, he slowly moved her hair to one side and then another. Then even more tenderly Joseph moved his hand up and under her chin and slowly inclined her head upwards and towards his own. Mary's deep blue eyes returned his gaze, meeting that of his own with Joseph speaking first, "I will never let you from my side again. I didn't know if I would ever see you again. I love you so very much. I am so glad you're home."

"Me too, Joseph, me too." Piercing through to her own soul, she knew that the man that God had placed in her life was for her to keep and to hold in sickness and in health, for richer and for poorer, and until death did they part, was standing right in front of her. "You are so very special to me, I love you with all my heart."

Chapter 16

JOSEPH WITHDREW a knife from his pocket and ever so carefully freed Mary from the ropes that bound her arms and hands first and then freed the bindings from her legs and ankles. The bindings had cut into her skin, leaving them deeply reddened from the blood that had been drawn to the skin's surface. Gently rubbing her hands where the ropes had been, she reveled in the exhilarating feel of freedom.

Putting the helicopter down nearby, Detective Stone quickly joined Mary and Joseph on the bridge. He knew there would be plenty of time later to ask any needed questions but for now, the best thing was to get Mary back home.

Mary, using Joseph's phone, called Grandpa Billy. He immediately picked up the phone on the first ring, "Have you heard anything yet?" he asked.

"Daddy, it's me, Mary. I'm safe. Joseph is with me. It's all over. We will be over in a few minutes. I cannot wait to see you. I love you all so very much. Tell David his mommy is okay. God has so very deeply blessed me. I'm alive."

Joseph continued to hold Mary as the squad car headed directly over to her parents' home. Although there were still downed trees throughout the city, it had been cleared enough so they could just pass. Most of the limbs had been sheared off at the street's side, allowing just enough room to get by. When they arrived at the house, Grandpa Billy, Grandma, and David were all outside to greet them, and David was the first to reach the car yelling, "Mommy, Mommy!" with her parents close behind.

They all embraced together tightly in one big group hug and love fest, giggling and giddy from the sheer joy of their reunion. Grandpa Billy spoke first, "Thank God you're home. We all love you so very much. Thank you, God. Thank you."

Mary's clothes were still at the house from before her abduction and she was able to get a cold shower, as the electricity was still out. Mary reveled in getting cleaned up and being able to change clothes. It felt awesome to be able to rub away some of the memories of the ordeal. Afterwards Grandpa Billy cooked a small meal of steaks and potatoes out on the outdoor grill. The main course was not the meal but all the hugs and celebration of what God had done for them all, not just today but in all the days past. They had a lot to be thankful for and they praised Him greatly. Praying before they ate, Grandpa Billy cried as he spoke humbly to the Most High God, who had brought him here and given him fifty-three years of marriage with the bride of his youth, a beautiful daughter who was now home safely, a handsome grandson, and if he had anything to do with it, a wonderful future son-in-law.

During the course of the evening, Mary decided to stay in her own home that night. Joseph, not wanting her out of his sight, opted to spend the evening downstairs on her couch. Not afraid any longer, Mary just wanted Joseph to be nearby. Electricity was being restored in a few small pockets of homes in the city and Mary's was restored just after midnight. She and Joseph decided to stay up late talking by candlelight. Though exhausted Mary didn't want the day to end or her reunion with Joseph, but finally about one in the morning she fell hard asleep on the couch. Turning off the lamp, Joseph just sat and watched her sleep, listening intently to every breath she took. The moonlight shone brightly in her living room window and where she lay, the light dancing softly on her face. Quietly, but audibly to only himself and to who he prayed to, placing his hand on her arm. "I know that you alone made all of this possible. I deeply love and appreciate the gift that you gave me when you placed this woman in front of me. I knew it the fist day. You are the God of second chances and I thank you for the chance you have given me. I am your son to do as you will. Guide me in the steps I should take so that I might lead her, as you alone would have me do. I dedicate this family and myself to you and to your service. In the matchless name of Christ I pray. Amen."

After watching her for a few more moments, Joseph gently picked Mary up and carried her upstairs and placed her gently in bed. After covering her, Joseph headed back downstairs for the evening, thanking God for the great gift of life that He alone had bestowed.

It had been over a week now and Detective Stone was still putting the finishing touches on his final report. The day of Mary's rescue, Detective Stone started going home again in the evening and was relieved to find that he could once again sleep through the night and in his own bed. The task force was mostly disbanded and now all that was left was a skeletal crew whose predominant responsibility was to wrap things up and get back to their regular duties and schedule. All the other task force members had already been reassigned and were back to work. Most of them were assigned to emergency personnel that had arrived from all over the Southeast and the nation to assist in the cleanup after Hurricane Janet.

Immediately after the killer had been shot and killed, it was determined that he was none other than Tim Tuttle, who had initially discovered the historical home being restored by the Charleston Historical and Preservation Society. From searching Tuttle's home, it was determined that he was a zealot preservationist whose motive for good deeds had gone awry. In his house, he had an entire room dedicated to newspaper clippings which hung from every corner of the room, detailing environmental disasters, the possible extinction of certain animals, and what local preservationists were doing to protect the environment. Just like in the Bible in the lighthouse where Mary had been held captive, there were notes written on the articles with a red marker documenting his anger.

Detective Stone himself had researched further and discovered that Tuttle's wife, who had passed several years ago, had died from leukemia. Since her death years ago, he apparently still harbored a deep resentment for all those who, in his mind, would unduly damage the environment where he lived. Unfortunately in his quest, Tuttle had lost sense of the difference between right and wrong. He had fought a bitter and long legal battle with the chemical company that he blamed for his wife's leukemia. The battle of legal affairs spanned over four years, only to result in him losing at every turn and every appeal. Apparently he was never able to let it go and eventually turned his hatred towards others who would, in his opinion, develop the environment unnecessarily and thereby harm the environment. Somehow Tuttle had decided to focus his ire at residential real estate agents while having chosen to prey on women. Detectives also discovered in his home several personal items of those Tuttle had killed in Wilmington, North Carolina, where he had moved from just over six months ago, as well as prints at the lighthouse of his two latest victims while he lived here in Charleston.

It was Tuttle himself who had purchased the lighthouse where he held Mary. It was his intent to restore it and turn it over to the National Park Service as a national monument. Apparently he planned to use the ransom monies to further fund his misguided intentions.

Detective Stone thought that he would have a greater sense of personal achievement as a result of the crime's resolution and to be frank, he felt none of that at all. Though his reputation grew even larger still, he contemplated what might lie ahead in his career path and if he would even stay on the force at all. Certainly the drain of the case and its endless weeks of pressure had worn heavily on him, but he did not feel the same sense of satisfaction as he had at the end of big cases in the past. However, this time was different, as now he saw something special in those with whom he worked and served, about those lives that had been inextricably drawn into his. His concerns now rested with the victims and their surviving family members, and most of all about Joseph and Mary. Never before had he seen such dedication and fervor as he witnessed Joseph's resolve to return Mary safely home. Detective Stone's key skill that he relied upon most was his ability to read people and their true intentions. Watching Joseph these past several weeks, Detective Stone knew that Joseph was the real deal and that something special was happening in Joseph's life and he wanted to find some of it for himself. Always having been a career man over the years, he had plowed all of his energy, time, and talents into furthering his work life and had always proved a success in doing so. Now, however, he sensed that there was something more for him to do and he set out to truly find this God that Joseph talked to and walked so closely with. Tomorrow was Sunday and he had already looked into what time church services would be starting and had made plans to attend.

Masses of volunteers continued to flood the Charleston area, bringing with them foodstuffs, water, ice, and medicine from all over the country. Neighbors helped neighbors as the walls that normally separated and divided them from each other were all broken down. The whole of the city pulled together to rebuild Charleston and to place her once again as a proud and beautiful city. Through the devastation of Hurricane Janet, a people became one again, raising up the love of the South for each other once again. Mayor James White spoke to the city on both television and radio, sharing words of encouragement and commitment to do everything he could to return Charleston to her original splendor and to far greater heights, exhorting all those around him as he spoke, "We have been down before and we will be knocked about again. But we, the people of Charleston, are what America is all about. It is about a land filled with people, a people with a fierce pride, and a citizenry who are always at their best when things are at their worst. We are a people who will pull together and we will rebuild. No, the effort will not be easy. It will take great sweat and toil, but in the end we will find peace, a peace that surpasses all understanding. We will find each other and we will find that God will always be faithful. Through the devastation we will build back even finer and better than ever before. We will always believe, always persevere, and always survive. I believe Charleston's destiny is to be a shining city on a hill for the whole of a nation to see, to see how we live, and how we carry on. Be strong, be courageous and know that He alone is God and in that in He alone will we trust. I will be here each and every step of the way helping and guiding along the way. We will rebuild, we will overcome, and we will be the city that raises itself up from the ashes."

Mayor James White spoke openly and freely from his heart. His speechwriters had carefully drafted words that he might say, but as soon as the camera came on, he put aside his notes and spoke with the love and affection that he had for the city of Charleston and her people. It was the furthest thing from his mind that day as he spoke, but he won his upcoming re-election that day. Speaking words of encouragement from his heart and not his mind alone, Mayor White reminded the citizenry of Charleston of their strength, their dignity, and their proud heritage. Mayor White shared with the people of

Charleston the zeal he had to rebuild her to be once more the most welcoming city in the United States of America. He exhorted her citizenry so that people from all over the world might see the greatest city in this the greatest country the world has ever known. One who fought for rights and freedom of those throughout the world while defending those who could not fend for themselves and giving to others what had been so freely been given to themselves, their freedom.

Electricity was slowly restored to the whole of the Charleston area over a span of three weeks. For most of the more densely suburban areas power was resumed within two weeks, but it took an extra week to reach the more urban and less populated areas. The city's populace was asked to continue to boil their drinking water for an extra week to ensure that it was potable. Gradually much of the local activity was beginning to return to Charleston, as its citizenry were no longer afraid to be out on the streets and as they recovered from the hurricane's damage. It would be months before the hundreds of thousands that visited the city each year began returning and that enough of the repairs to hotels and restaurants alike would be completed.

Almost all of the debris had now been removed from Charleston's streets and most businesses were operating at least at partial capacity, especially the smaller ones where the owners' very livelihood depended on it. The city continued on in its rebuilding and began reshaping an even newer and better historical version of the Charleston of old. The Charleston Historical and Preservation Society continued to work alongside the people of Charleston, ensuring that its proud history and heritage continued to be preserved for future generations.

— —

Joseph's mind would never stray far from his God ever again. He continued in deep appreciation and thankfulness for the blessing of Mary and what she meant to him in his life and to that of his daughter Alison. The four of them picked up right where they left off, spending most evenings together and all of the weekends. Joseph had a lot on his mind and he knew that it had to be right and it had to be in God's timing and not that of his own. Joseph continued in deep prayer endlessly seeking what God would lead him to do in their relationship. It did not take God long to answer Joseph as He alone knew the purity that was in both of their hearts. By now all but the most severely damaged of the restaurants had reopened and all of Joseph's favorites along Shem Creek in Mt. Pleasant were ready and open for business. Joseph decided to take Mary back to where they had enjoyed the magic and the ambiance of their first date.

Calling ahead, Joseph again reserved his favorite table seeking one overlooking Shem Creek and the shrimp trawlers as they brought their wares in from a day out at sea. As the sun set Joseph began, "You know that I love you. You are all that I aspire to be. You are the most incredible woman that I have ever known. I knew it from the time that we met and through the time that I thought I had lost you. When God reunited us once again, I believed that it was for good. I know we have only known each other for five months but I also know that in you, I find Him our Creator. I know that with you I can accomplish so much more for the Kingdom than I can ever do apart from you. I think the two of us are the best that He ever made, and I have deeply prayed and sensed what I now know; we should be one, Mary," he said, getting down from his chair and down on his knees. "Will you marry me?"

Returning his gaze with the same intensity, she looked deeply into his eyes, seeing through to and from where the question had arisen. It was from the one true God. "Joseph, my dearest Joseph. From nowhere you showed up in my life and you have changed everything in my life for the better. I have intently prayed that this day would come. I will definitely marry you. Absolutely the answer is yes!"

Joseph continuing on his knees, "I have to admit I have already asked your parents for their consent which they have so willingly given. Today you have made me the happiest man on the face of the earth. I promise that I will look after you always and I can't wait to begin our lives together. When you are ready, and only then, I will be ready."

"Joseph," Mary responded, "I do not need any time to think, I have had thirty-eight years to do so. When we first met I knew that there was something special, something that I could rely upon and build my life on. I am yours whenever you want me."

Smiling, Joseph slid his hands up to middle of her forehead and just above her eyes and ever so slowly moved her wispy bangs that danced over her face first to the right side and then to her left. "I just want to see you, to see your face, to see the beauty that God Himself has placed so well and perfectly right in front of me. You are absolutely beautiful. You are my child, my bride, and in you I am most proud. I will love you all the days of the rest of my life. "

Looking down at him, she heard God speaking, not as He had spoken to her from above but speaking to her as a sister and a fellow heir to the throne. Joseph spoke volumes of love through those words and his face so full of love and compassion for her. Using Joseph as his chosen vessel, God spoke into Mary's heart and soul, filling her completely with His love and peace. Releasing herself from her sitting position and kneeling beside him facing him eye to eye, she said, "Me too, Joseph, me too! Tomorrow like today is not promised but I know that I want to spend each and every day with you. I love you. I cannot wait to start to spend the whole of the rest of my life with you. I am so thankful that God brought us together. I will always abide, always believe, and will always look after and trust you. I love you so very much."

Joseph looked intently into her eyes. "I think I have something for you." Reaching into his vest pocket, he pulled out a box and slowly opened it to reveal its contents. Mary gasped as the diamonds sparkled as she got a glimpse of a symbol of his deep and abiding love for her. Holding the box in his left hand and then pulling the ring out of the box with his right, he very gently placed the ring on her finger. Placing it securely on her finger and against her hand, he spoke softly yet with a strength that surpasses all understanding, "Mary, I am yours and you are mine. Your people will be my people and in you I find great peace and joy. You are so deeply a part of who I am and who I will yet be. I do not know where this world will lead us but I can't wait to be your husband." Holding her tightly in his arms, not bothering to rise, Joseph wept openly with awe, abiding in her deeply and in sincere appreciation of the One Most High God!

The days were starting to get longer again and the morning chill in the air was now all but gone and had been replaced with a warm breeze off the Atlantic. The amazing peace and tranquility offered by Charleston and her charms were once again obvious to all. All of the debris was now gone and most of the construction resulting from Hurricane Janet was either completed or substantially underway. It had been six months since the storm and life was back to normal in the city. There was a spiritual awakening surging amongst Charleston's citizenry. Many attributed it to Hurricane Janet and others to the serial killer who had previously stalked her streets. Most Christians, however, would tell you of the promise of the rainbow that graced the city the day after Hurricane Janet had left and the promises that God alone had spoken into each of their hearts. Many of Charleston's citizenry had started afresh in the city, rebuilding their homes and their lives from the ground up. Many a better foundation was laid up under the homes and the families of believers now knowing deep in their heart that God Himself was in total control of their lives. Many had believed before, but most have given only intellectual assent to what their heart told them. Many had begun to take seriously the question WWJD (What Would Jesus Do?) in making it the most critical factor in making all of their business and life decisions alike. Many began to step out in faith by turning over their lives to full-time Christian service while others felt God's calling to involve Him in making decisions involving all facets of their lives.

Sam Evans, the publisher of the area's newspaper, *The Charlestons Sentinel*, felt the calling of God on his heart and on all the affairs of his business. Although it was a very difficult decision for him to implement, he felt God's calling for him to close the paper on Sunday. Sunday had always proven by far to be the largest dollar amount of advertising they received for a day's issue but he felt God calling him to keep the Sabbath holy. Sam Evans also felt the calling of God on his life to cover stories that kept God at its center and brought glory to His name. At first all of his writers were greatly flustered, as now all of their stories were kept clear of gossip and innuendo. Articles now emphasized only on the good in people and stories began to come in from all over of the volumes of good deeds done daily to help and to assist those in need. For the first few months, the paper struggled financially as it strained to re-brand itself, but as of late its economic outlook had begun to turn for the better.

Dave Sims, the owner of the Charleston's largest chain of local liquor stores, felt God calling and beckoning his name to step out of the industry and to devote his life to full-time ministry. At first he resisted but the more he did so, the more God had continued to pursue. Soon it became blatantly obvious to him what he was supposed to do and immediately set out on that course. Dave Sims was able to locate a local business broker to sell the business and soon afterwards a purchaser surfaced and offered him the price that he had asked. God instructed Dave to use the proceeds from the business's sale to carry he and his family financially while he studied and readied for what he believed would be a staff position at a local church. In order to ready himself for whatever God led him to, he enrolled at a local seminary so when God called him to action that he might be ready.

From all over the city stories were told over and over again of individual after individual that put it all on the line for God and to live all of their lives as God would have them do. Churches were soon filled to overflowing and new ones were being formed all over the city. For the first time anyone could ever remember, there was more than moderate traffic on the way to and from church on Sundays. People were no longer hurrying to and fro on His day but were seeking others out to revel in God's goodness and to bring His peace to the brokenhearted. Thousands were being saved each month as the Word became alive and the Word was with them. People rededicated their lives, husbands and wives renewed their marriage vows, children were led to know the One who loved them and knew them yet before they were even born. God's name was spoken boldly as Christians became beacons of His name. Though many prospered, there were also those who were put out or held down because of their faith by the multitudes that yet still did not believe. Even though all had witnessed the rainbow and its promise there were those who still would not accept the gift of His love. However, believers knew of His promise and that He would always be there and that their God would always take care of them. A spiritual awakening and renewal not seen since the Civil War rocked the city with God's love.

⁓

It was now mid-April and it was one of those Saturdays that you dream about. The seas were calm and the breezes were filled with the warm air blowing in from the ocean. The moss hung heavy on the oak trees, gently blowing to and for as if slowly dancing in the wind. The sun was starting to set with its light dancing in an endless array of lights as it shimmered off the harbor's gentle waves. The ceremony was humble but lovingly delicate in its flower arrangements and their presentation. Joseph and Mary decided that they would marry where they had their first walk out on the Battery. Both of them remembered the magic that occurred in their lives that evening and how miracle after miracle was occurring all about them every day. Joseph didn't know where God would lead them, but he knew that together he and Mary could accomplish all that God had set out for them. The pastor was from Joseph's church, where they still attended and planned to make their church home.

Joseph, dressed in a handsome black tuxedo, stood intently looking at Mary as he waited beside the pastor for his bride. Mary was radiantly aglow, her flowing white wedding dress blowing and swaying gently in the breeze. Joseph's heart was completely filled admiring Mary's beauty and her heart emanating love and peace as never before. Grandpa Billy beamed as he walked alongside Mary slowly walking her to Joseph's side. When asked by the pastor who presented her to be given to this man, Grandpa Billy lifted up her veil while placing a kiss on her right cheek exhorting, "It has never been more right. You and Joseph have your mother's and my blessing, and I know that God is greatly pleased."

As Mary turned to face Joseph, he could not restrain himself and whispered so that only she could hear, "You are so beautiful. I love you with all my heart."

As Pastor Louis read from the Bible about how love always perseveres, always believes, always cherishes, and always conquers, Joseph and Mary looked deeply into each other's eyes and souls and promised to always be there, in sickness and in health, for better for worse, for all the days of their lives. Joseph first repeated his vows, clearly speaking each and every word, wanting and knowing that Mary could dwell and rely on each word as he spoke. Mary softly and gently, through the Spirit of Christ, spoke words of commitment, continuing and abiding respect as long as the two of them might live.

Pastor Louis then prayed and after doing so looked to Joseph and then to Mary, announcing to all present, "What God put together, let not man put asunder. I now pronounce you husband and wife. Joseph, you may now kiss your bride."

Looking deep into Mary's eyes he saw truth, a committed bride and he saw himself. Joseph knew that he had indeed found home and a safe place to fall when life's trials came their way. Through thick and thin, Joseph knew that Mary would always be right by his side. As he looked deep into her eyes of blue, he held her softly with his left arm around her waist and with his right hand reached just above her eyes and gently brushed her hair first to one side and then the other. Joseph's right hand then slid through the front of her hair and along to the back of her neck. Ever so gently pulling her towards him, he slowly moved his head towards her while tilting his slightly to the right while she turned hers to the left. Just inches away from her lips, he stopped and led her to look up at him with his eyes.

Joseph went on, "Mary, I am the luckiest man on the face of the earth. You are my wife, my bride, and I am so grateful that we are one in His eyes! I promise I will love you all the days of my life."

Joseph now again eased his lips again toward hers, kissing her gently yet passionately, each knowing that the love being both given and received by them was His will and that they would be together forever.

Turning now to face the small assemblage of friends and family, Joseph and Mary looked out to those who shared this moment with them. Smiling faces were seen all about as Pastor Louis pronounced, "I would like to now introduce to you Joseph and Mary King." Holding her tightly, Joseph again turned towards Mary and looked deeply into the eyes and into the love of his bride, and in her did he abide and dwell deeply!

The Charleston Trilogy Series

by

John Dillard

You have just read the first installment of *The Charleston Trilogy Series*. This Christian fiction romance series is set in the ambiance of Charleston, South Carolina, and combines everything from historical homes to lighthouses, chase scenes both in the air and on the ground, an F-18 Super Hornet flying and downed in Iraq with its occupants striving to evade capture and certain death. And taking a turn further into the heart of Charleston, a criminal attorney struggles with his oath to protect and serve versus his own moral compass. *The Charleston Trilogy Series* keeps the reader on the edge of their seat as the reader turns each page.

Learn about the unique city of Charleston, its enchanting past and the story's characters' faith in God abounding despite and amidst life's trials and difficulties. *The Charleston Trilogy Series* combines ambiance, action and comes full circle with a spiritually uplifting revival offered by God's grace at each story's end.

The Charleston Trilogy Series includes a murder mystery, action-packed flying in an F-18, one man's calling to being a full-time pastor, and an attorney who makes a difference for the kingdom of God. Come along and see how its characters find God amidst real-life issues. *The Charleston Trilogy Series* speaks boldly about the Christian life and how God wants us to live.

For more information, visit www.CharlestonDawn.com.

COMING SOON...

Low Country Calling

Low Country Calling, a Christian fiction action romance, is second in the trilogy. David Jones has dreamed of being a fighter pilot since he was a child. Born into a Christian home in Charleston, SC, David joins the Marines and ultimately meets his bride-to-be as their romance develops while he goes through training. After graduation David is assigned to fly his F-18 Super Hornet off the aircraft carrier *The Roosevelt*, stationed in the Mediterranean Sea.

Ride in the cockpit as David completes feats never before done in an F-18, but he is ultimately downed and forced to ditch his plane in the Iraqi desert. While running from terrorists who would claim his life, David hears God's call to be a full-time pastor. Come along as David answers God's call back to the low county of Charleston. *Low Country Calling* is sure to keep you wanting more.

COMING SOON...

South Carolina Justice

A renowned criminal lawyer enjoys unparalleled success and is at the very pinnacle of his career. *South Carolina Justice* takes the reader to the sanctity of the inner rooms of the courthouse where deals and not justice are meted out. Sworn to protect the law of the land, Allen Bowen struggles to maintain his moral compass as each time the law is bent he comes closer to the very face of God and its truth.

South Carolina Justice is page-turner as things are not always as they seem. As Allen discovers the truth he also discovers God and who he really is in Christ. The last of a trilogy, *South Carolina Justice* brings *The Charleston Trilogy Series* full circle as God and morality prevail.

ALSO BY JOHN DILLARD:

The Inspiration Series

John Dillard's *The Inspiration Series* is for those looking to become more like Christ. By studying the Bible and applying it to our lives we are able to live the full life that God always intended. Come along as *The Inspiration Series* leads you to a deeper understanding of God's precepts for your life and how to live a life full of Him!

You alone are uniquely positioned to achieve God's vision for your life. A God who knows the number of the very hairs on your head has a great purpose only you can accomplish. Learn how one man, Nehemiah, made a difference in the lives of many. Seeking God's will each and every step of the way, Nehemiah prayerfully seeks to rebuild the walls that protect the city of Jerusalem.

Come alongside one man's journey to fulfill God's best for his life. An all-knowing God has placed before you a unique opportunity to accomplish something of lasting value. Perhaps in the life of only one or of many you can perform great and miraculous things to reach others in the name of God. Whether serving in your family, your work, or globally, God has a task for you.

By faith as small as that of a mustard seed, you can step out of the relative safety of your present position, and watch God guide and measure your steps. Dare to dream, dare to achieve, and most of all dare to accomplish something so great that it is doomed to failure lest Christ be in it!

Nehemiah's Prayer

ACCOMPLISHING GOD'S SPECIAL MISSION FOR YOUR LIFE

Nestled deep in the Bible's Old Testament lived an ordinary man who stepped out to accomplish great things in God's name. Leaving the safety of his position as the cupbearer to the king of Babylon, Nehemiah put himself into harm's way, exposing himself to enemies who intended and purposed to see him fail. Overcoming each and every obstacle, Nehemiah was to rebuild Jerusalem's city walls that were essential for the nation's very survival. *Nehemiah's Prayer* will assist you in accomplishing God's Special Mission for your Life.

The remnant of Israel had been in exile and was returning to the Promised Land only to find the land of their forefathers in disarray. Jerusalem's city walls lay in ruin, exposing her to enemies who would threaten the nation's very existence. Following the burden God laid on his heart, Nehemiah rebuilt the city's walls in just fifty-two days. Leading the way, Nehemiah asked for assistance from those who could help him the most and prayerfully developed a team and unified them to accomplish a miraculous feat.

Prayerfully, Nehemiah set out and quietly brought together the whole of the Jewish nation. Finding doomsayers at every turn, Nehemiah overcame each and every obstacle and built brick by brick the ramparts that would protect the city from her foes. Never deterred in his vision, Nehemiah continued on and united a people by giving them a clear vision and leadership and ultimately rededicated the city and its people to God.

Nehemiah never faltered and never swayed from his mission. Against all odds Nehemiah, an ordinary layman, stepped out in faith to accomplish great things in God's name. God has a special plan for your life and a reward at its end. We serve a God who wants the best for you and your life. Ask and act boldly to serve and to do great things in God's name.

Printed in the United States
67497LVS00006B/133-150

9 781413 799927